SWIMMING

IN THE RAINBOW

REBECCA LOCHLANN

ERINYES PRESS

BOOK NINE

THE CHILD OF THE ERINYES SERIES

THE LOST YEARS

Praise for Swimming in the Rainbow

"The writing here is dreamily beautiful; I am reminded of Patricia A McKillip's marvelous book *The Forgotten Beasts of Eld.*"

"Rebecca Lochlann's *Swimming in the Rainbow* is among the most beautifully written novels I've ever encountered. The content lives up to the magic of the name."

"The lively imagination and intelligence of the girl with a backdrop to the darker events around her reminded me of the deliciously dark tale of Pan's Labyrinth."

"Reminds me of Cornelia Funke, but darker and more mature. Unconventional, sure, but organically unusual, not contrived to impress or shock. I can't pick out anything to praise in particular, because it's all praiseworthy. Truly original ideas, beautifully executed. Some readers might not get it, but those who do will treasure the experience."

"What appears to be an effortless flow of detail, imagery, and pathos captivated me from the start. Engaged by the author's romantic writing, lyrical flow, and emotionally-packed action, I was brought in close and primed for the tragic loss, which I felt intensely. Bravo!"

The Story so Far

Two brothers topple a society that flourished for thousands of years.
Goddess Athene resurrects them, along with the Cretan princess both
men love but betray, forcing all three to live seven distinctly different
incarnations.
In *When the Moon Whispers*, Aridela and her followers open a path to
new possibilities.
So, what has happened, eighteen years on?
Here is the rest of the story.

Swimming in the Rainbow

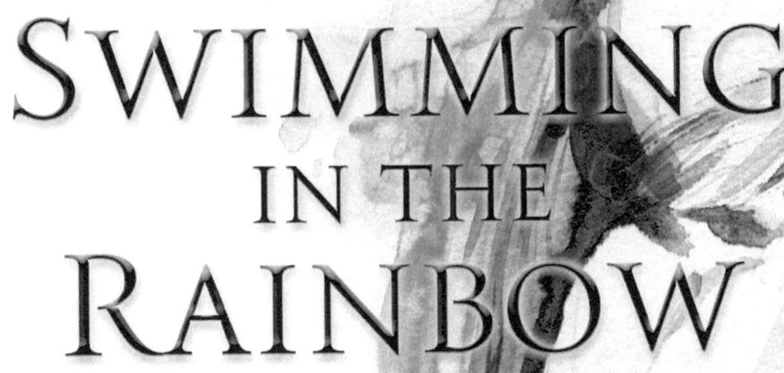

Rebecca Lochlann

ERINYES PRESS

To my kids
And all kids balanced on the teetering precipice of life

"We are standing at the summit, looking out at infinite paths. Some paths will lead to a destination. Some are loops that will trap us into repeating the past, over and over and over again, eternally. Some destinations will lead to our extinction and some to joy."
~~~Adamantinus

"I tried to steal women's magic and give it to men. And here we are. Staring into extinction."
~~~Raphael Konstantinou

"It is no fabrication, my mother, when a man willingly dies for a woman. You see it before you."
~~~Adamantinus
~~~

THE COMPANION

October, 2090

Chapter 1

"TEÓFILO, MUST YOUR THIGH BE SO HARD? ONE CAN NEVER GET comfortable."

"I apologize," he replied in his soothing manner. "Why don't you bring a pillow next time?"

"It would be noticed. Someone would tell Mama and she'd have hysterics. Papa would forbid me to come just to shut her up. I'd have to be even more sneaky."

"Blow the bubbles." Teófilo's expression grew mournful. "I feel I can move when I see them—break my bonds and fly. Try, do, Mistress, so I can carry you into our rainbows, where you will be forever happy. That is the promise they shared with me."

He'd described the enchanted world inside a rainbow thousands of times, and I never tired of listening.

It is an endless ocean. You will swim, breathe, and drink color. Colors will burst on your tongue and in your throat, purple like grapes, brown like earth, white like salt, blue like twilight. You will become color, freed of human limitations.

The thrill of that fluid fantasy never relinquished its hold even when I grew old enough to realize it was no more than a fairy tale, fashioned to entertain a lonely child.

True, we both saw rainbows out of the corners of our eyes, rainbows nobody else appeared to detect, but he couldn't take me anywhere, no matter how many promises he concocted.

His shoulder blades quivered. The ridge of black hair along his spine rose like the crest of a tropical parrot.

"Blow the bubbles," he whispered. "One of these days, one will—"

"Yes, yes, wrap round you without breaking. I've heard this before."

"Transform me into the one who can grant your every desire."

"I like you as you are."

"But one day, I will not be enough. And on that day my heart will break. I fear the pain of it…"

"Little Miss, are you there? Your dinner is ready."

I got up, wiping my hands on my flannel trousers.

"Kiss me?" He gave me that look he knew would melt my resolve. I pressed my palms against his hard narrow cheeks.

"Close your eyes, Teófilo," I said, as sternly as I could beneath that burning, fire-jewel gaze.

He did.

I kissed his lids, one by one, and went down to dinner, my bare feet making no sound on the stones. His sigh followed me like a shadow.

I CAN'T REMEMBER HOW OLD I WAS WHEN I FIRST CLIMBED TO OUR rooftop, alone. I have only vague memories of Teófilo wrapping one of his clawed hands around my forearm so I wouldn't fall to my death. I do remember that conversation, though. I remember leaving him, trailing down the dim, winding stone steps and through quiet cold corridors, following faint scents of food—onion, garlic, rosemary, and some sort of meat. Probably pork, maybe chicken. The corridor gradually warmed as I neared the areas more frequently traveled by those in the household. Bare wood floors gave way to carpet—a wide runner of Turkish design, held in place on the last four steps with gleaming brass rods.

I heard my mother speaking in a low drone as she always did, without the need for another's input. Bending, I peeked through the keyhole in the door and saw her, one hand fingering the string of pearls around her neck, the other plucking at her left eyebrow as if searching for hair, but she'd long ago yanked them all out. A servant constructed a fake brow out of paint each morning, but by dinnertime constant rubbing and pulling usually erased it or turned it into a messy smudge.

Having no brow didn't look quite so bad as it could have, since her hair, I'd overheard one of the servants say, was prematurely white. The whiteness of old ashes. Contrarily, Mama's eyes were dark, intense blue, almost black. As a child, I often compared her eye color to the blue of night when our moons were in crescent.

Stately pines blanketed the mountains around our estate, standing out like skinny giants when the moons rose behind them, highlighting the summit of Alecto, tallest of the peaks west of the Schloss. Megaera and Tisiphone skulked on either side, lower and shadowy.

How shyly our heavenly orbs moved, like two bright and wonderful girls chasing each other, believing themselves hidden, but, drifting behind the trees as they did, they merely accentuated their presence.

We haven't always had two moons. The second, smaller and blue-tinted, appeared thirty years or so before I was born. It follows our old moon around like a baby sister. A vertical scar runs through it. I know now what happened, but back then, I was told it was damage from an asteroid.

My mother's pale skin and hair was, I suspected, what had drawn my swarthy father to her.

I opened the door, a venerable thing carved with an intricate design of ivy and pinecones—the knob itself was a brass pinecone—and entered the dining room.

My mother stared, as she often did, her expression puzzled. *Who are you?* I fancied her thinking. *Should I know?* My father turned his head, which reminded me of a snowy mountaintop robed in clouds because of the perpetual smoke from his cigar or pipe—on this day a cigar.

"Well, well," he said. "We've been waiting, you know. The food's congealing." He frowned as he noticed my bare feet. "Is that how you come to dinner, girl?"

"Sorry."

A black-coated servant bowed as he lifted my chair to prevent it from squealing against the floor and set it down again, leaving just enough room for me to squeeze in, my solar plexus pressed against the ivory tablecloth and rigid edge of the table.

"Dreadful waste." My mother's gaze leaped over the shining silver dishes, following the steam that curled like ringlets of hair from the green beans. One white-gloved hand, the one that had been kneading her pearls, waved irritably, destroying the patterns. "Poetry and prose, *those people.* Can't smile, lock them up. Did you find out if the gallery has that painting—the white boat taking the star to the castle in the sea? *Those people* mustn't get their hands on it. It's a secret, you know. Will you promise me…promise—"

"Of course." My father tamped his cigar in a crystal ashtray. I'd watched him do this many times. It always seemed the smoke fought its inevitable demise. It burgeoned in an aromatic swirling grey-white tornado then wavered across the table like a live thing—and I really could sometimes see white, pupilless eyes for the slightest instant, and toothy, open mouths. But not this time. This time it simply made me cough.

"You're giving the child weak lungs." My mother glanced at me then away, nodding to the servant who offered whipped potatoes.

I BARELY SAW TEÓFILO. HE WAS HIGH ABOVE, TOUCHING THE CLOUDS. I LAY on my back in the late autumn grass, watching him, yes, but also observing the clouds and the swaying top branches of the nearest *Betula pubescens*, the downy birch. It was a love dance, a *pas de deux* between wind, branch, and leaves, the shape of which reminded me of the fancy onion domes on old Russian churches. Back and forth, flitter and flirt. Fingers, beckoning. *Come up and play little miss.*

Dance with me.

That same lecherous wind skimmed my face—fickle beast, to go with the first one who invites it in—as I did, inhaling deeply.

Run fingers over brows. Ghost-touch. Kiss of wind. Am I here or not? I can see through my fingers. Cloud wisps. Blue sky. Teófilo.

Sometimes I forget I am speaking of the past. I get so immersed in my memories. I am not there, on that grassy steep hillside, wind stroking me like a wishful lover, Teófilo leaning over the rooftop's edge, seeming to soar because of the swift progression of clouds behind him. I have often wondered how it would feel to be a cloud, to follow the wind, to majestically traverse that dazzling ever-changing upside-down bowl. The ceiling of our fancies.

Yet, if the universe is never-ending as my *Viewing the Night Sky* book claims, there is no ceiling. Our fancies spire without epilogue. Beyond our control.

It was Teófilo's most ardent wish—to move, to fly, to soar. To shatter his bonds. But I would not allow it. I wanted him to remain my constant, and, for me, he consented. Not that he had any choice. Not even his promise to take me into the center of a rainbow, tucked on his back between his wings, would make me relent. In those days I was selfish, with the unconscious selfishness of a child who never questions the turning of the planets but assumes with tessellated arrogance that they spin simply for her amusement.

Chapter 4

Little Indian, Sioux or Crow,
Little Frosty Eskimo,
Little Turk or Japanee,
O! don't you wish that you were me?
When I was very young, this was my favorite poem. I liked to read it to Teófilo. He liked it too. He would sing the first verse and stick out his blue forked tongue.
You have seen the scarlet trees.
And the lions over seas;
You have eaten ostrich eggs,
And turned the turtles off their legs.
It seemed exotic, eating ostrich eggs and seeing lions. I had only seen lions in pictures, and just the thought of an ostrich egg, lightly boiled, coated with butter, salt, and pepper, made my mouth water. I loved eggs. An ostrich egg must be much finer than a chicken's if for no other reason than sheer size. I didn't know what scarlet tree the author meant. *Sorbus aucuparia*, the rowan, perhaps? Or *Acer japonicum*, the Fullmoon Maple with the gigantic leaves? *Rhododendron arboreum*, maybe, or *Nyssa Sinensis*, its tapered leaves slim as fingers?
Such a life is very fine,
But it's not so nice as mine;
You must often, as you trod,

Have wearied not to be abroad.

This matched our feelings exactly. Teófilo and I had the perfect situation. Other than the time I spent being educated, we were left to ourselves. I sometimes wondered if anyone would notice if I walked away and didn't return. Of course, I would never abandon Teófilo. He kept me locked in one place every bit as much as I did him.

You have curious things to eat,
I am fed on proper meat;
You must dwell beyond the foam,
But I am safe and live at home.

Well, I must admit…much as I loved that poem, part of me…a tiny part, sometimes wondered what the rest of the world was like, and thought it might be exciting to explore. The poem inspired visions of Indians in America, clutching their dappled stallions between strong thighs, red-cheeked Eskimo toddlers tucked into sealskin coats, Turkish men, scimitars gleaming at their waists, and Japanese women in colorful kimonos.

I had read that the author of this poem, Robert Louis Stevenson, was chronically ill as a child and confined to his bed for long periods. In solitude, he invented wondrous realms of adventure. He summoned characters out of dust motes—molded castles, dragons, and heroes from folds of blanket and cubes of sugar.

The poem had a wistful air, as though Robert Louis was trying to persuade himself that he was lucky and satisfied. Perhaps, when he wrote it, he was remembering days of loneliness and how he secretly wished he could be healthy and widely traveled.

That's what I thought, because he did travel as an adult.

I loved Robert Louis Stevenson. I adored him.

If there were some way to manage it, I would don chains and become his slave just to be near him, to hear his voice, to bring him cups of water.

Even before I learned how to read and write, I'd been captured by the magic of his words as I heard them on the old gramophone, translated into German. I loved them so much I wanted to hear them in English. I wanted to read them in Stevenson's native tongue and not have to listen through scratches and static.

I asked politely to be taught the English language. My father conferred with my tutor and my request was granted, probably because my tutor's mother was English, so no one special had to be hired. I grew up speaking two languages and became fluent in both.

Ensconced in my bed, watching the fire in the fireplace glimmer and spark, I'd wind my arms behind my head and fancy Robert Louis squatting in the shadows. My long-dead perfect friend. I had a picture of him. It was on the front of a book. His gaze was fixed on whomever was taking the photograph. He wore a dark coat over a white shirt and knotted tie. His stance was casual yet wholly alert, thoughtful, serious, and observant. *I am my own man*, the nuances suggested. *No one shall order my life but me.*

His face I could examine happily for long stretches of time; I don't think it was handsome or beautiful, though I am not one to judge. It was handsome and beautiful to me. His brown eyes spoke to me, tenderly at night, when I was alone and a dream had frightened and the world was cold and gloomy. They hinted of lust, though I was still young enough that such emotions were jumbled and confused. Those eyes followed, weeping, laughing, or simply gazing, always longing. They hid nothing from me. They were mine.

He was incomplete, my lover…the artist worshipped by emulsion, lens angle, light, and shadow. Incomplete because he could not escape his bonds and touch me.

Chapter 5

My tutor was an impatient, irritable man. He came five days a week, spent six hours with me, then retired to my father's study where he switched immediately to a laughing, garrulous creature smoking fat cigars and drinking vast amounts of a dark brown liquid poured into chilled green glasses so small they had to be constantly refilled. He drank so gratifyingly, throwing his head backward and swallowing in one thirsty gulp, that I thought the stuff must be delicious even though he gasped sometimes and his eyes watered. I wanted to try it. But my father kept the study locked in his absence.

I know these things because I peeked through keyholes. If a servant happened along and caught me, I was shooed away. I was like a mouse —there but hardly noticed, a minor nuisance, is all.

"You know what he said this evening?" I tucked myself into the crenellation that seemed molded for my convenience. I enjoyed gazing over my tempestuous, craggy world, swinging my legs, high as a bird with nothing to stifle or hold me prisoner. My bare heels butted rhythmically against the immovable wall, and I felt as safe as a kangaroo baby in its mother's pouch, protected on both sides by the strong loving flanks of the granite merlons.

"What, dearest Mistress?"

Teófilo licked his shoulder. He often complained of chilblains caused from constant exposure to the weather—and we had severe winters. I'd told him that licking the sore spot would make it worse, but he did it anyway.

Far below, a coachman brought his master's carriage around and stopped at the front steps. The conveyance was a black flat-roofed box. Two axles stuck out on each side, front and back, turning down to support the wheels. The entire thing resembled, rather uncomfortably, a thin, long-legged spider.

My tutor stumbled down the front steps as he did every night, weaving crookedly to his vehicle and falling in, making the horses snort and shy. He waved to my father, who stood in the doorway, framed in yellow light. Did they ever suspect they were being watched? Probably not. My father no doubt believed me asleep in my bedroom.

"He called me a—" Lifting one hand, I ticked off each name on my fingers. "Shrew, ogre, bitch, drab, and doxy. Oh—and skinny." The last one required the thumb of my other hand.

Beside and above me, the eternally gathered muscles in Teófilo's foreleg twitched. His whole body seemed to hum as he struggled with his limitations. "And your father?" he asked, hoarse and jagged. "What did he do?"

"Nothing. He laughed. Oh, he did say 'That skinny doxy is what provides all the jäger and vodka we can drink.'"

"If I could—if I could free myself—"

"What's wrong?" I swiveled, pressing knees to chest and wrapping my arms around them. There was barely enough room for me to do this between the merlons. The stone grated against the knobs of my spine. Truth be told, I was pretty skinny. "You're going to break something."

"I want to break something. Your father's head!"

"Mind your tongue." I mimicked one of the servants who often said that to me. "Show respect. He's the one paying the bills, you know."

"He should defend you. He's your father."

Not understanding why Teófilo was in such a stew, I shrugged. "Let's read from *Travels with a Donkey*." As I grew older and my reading tastes expanded, I'd put away Stevenson's poetry for children and embraced his love of exploration. He wrote visually, making me feel I hiked with him across the Cévennes. I sensed his grief. Every step he took was heavy and sorrowful, for he'd been separated from his

Fanny—the jad. Had I been his lover, I would not have left him for gold nor Paradise. Had I been his lover, I would have hiked by his side into Hades and never looked back.

"'For my part, I travel not to go anywhere, but to go,'" Teófilo quoted, his voice falling into softness as it did when we shared our mutual love of RLS. "'The great affair is to move; to feel the needs and hitches of our life more nearly; to come down off this feather-bed of civilisation, and find the globe granite underfoot and strewn with cutting flints.'"

Teófilo's grey snout was black in silhouette with the sun gone behind the mountains, leaving the sky a shivering purple. "That was lovely," I said. "Exactly what I wanted to hear."

"Promise you'll never leave me." His voice was now anxious and fluttery. "I smell it in your words, how much you want to go. I'm afraid, Mistress. Something is happening out there in the world of men. Won't you please, please blow the bubbles so I can come to life and protect you?"

"What do you mean, 'something is happening?' What?"

"I don't know. That is what frightens me. Things are changing…out there. Something is coming."

"Oh, stop it. You're trying to frighten me into doing what you want. And I won't, do you hear? I won't. Nothing would be the same. You'd get bored and leave me. Don't think I don't know. Yes, I know very well how much loyalty and affection I inspire."

"You're wrong. You are all that matters. I would give my life for you. If only I could prove myself."

"Yes, well, you won't have to. Because you're going to stay right there and I'm going to stay right here and we'll both grow old and die on this roof."

"Mistress…"

His voice was almost inaudible, for I'd jumped off the battlement and was running for the trapdoor. I flung it open and climbed down.

"There," I whispered furiously. "What can you do now? Nothing. Nothing, because *I won't let you*—you—you ugly ogre!"

Chapter 6

TEÓFILO OFTEN APPEARED IN MY DREAMS. THE NIGHT THE SOLDIERS CAME I dreamed of him. I was still angry about him wanting to change things. In the dream, his body gained life against my will, even though I shouted and screamed and clenched my fists. The dynamic force started at the tip of his thick rodent-like tail in a gold-rose-coral glow that spread like a sunrise as I watched. His tail flicked in the manner of an annoyed cat. His rear haunches trembled and the muscles, so carefully carved by his maker, whoever that was, bunched and loosed. When life arrived at his back feet one immediately lifted; a long claw dug into his side in a paroxysm of luscious scratching.

The glow continued along his spine and ribs and where it traveled movement followed—shivering skin, lifting hair, shakes and shudders. Forelegs straightened from their perpetual squat. One hand, with four long fingers and a thumb so like a human's, lifted and clenched. Wings, trapped in an eternal curl, unfolded and flapped, sending out the pungent scent of warm flesh and hair—the smell of a wild beast.

Life at last reached his head. His pointed ears perked, flattened, and turned from side to side. Nostrils quivered and widened. Baring long wicked canines, he gave a huge, luxurious yawn. He leveled a baleful yellow stare on me as he shook and straightened and stretched.

Why did you keep me bound in there for so long? All I wanted to do was love you, defend you, be yours.

I had a good answer—*Because I was afraid I would lose you*—

Before I could make this reasonable explanation, a gigantic crash reverberated, waking me and bringing me out of bed. A second crash rattled the windowpanes with such fury I feared they would shatter.

Someone somewhere screamed. Probably my mother. The sound was high, piercing, and somehow identifiable as female, and she was the only female in our household besides myself.

A third crash echoed. The floor shuddered. An earthquake? Volcano? Holocaust? One of the bookends fell off the shelf and behind it came books, clattering like dominoes. A print, *My Shadow*, it was called, tilted on its wall hanger. My bedroom appeared to be in imminent danger of foundering, taking me in a tangled glut of granite, wood, and glass, four stories to the ground. I wouldn't survive such a collapse—that much I knew.

Men raced past my door, their boot soles clattering. "Garth! Cannons!" someone shouted.

The answering reply sounded like, "Are the doors barred?"

I heard no more of that frantic dialogue.

Running into the corridor, I stared both directions. Odd bursts of light flashed against the walls. There were faraway shouts and a low keening sob—again, probably my mother. A series of sharp staccatos drowned that out. I'd heard the fire of guns before—my father hunted deer on the estate—and recognized the rapid detonations, though I'd never heard so many rounds so close together. There must be several rifles firing at once.

If I was going to die, I wanted to die with Teófilo.

I raced into my bedroom, grabbed my beloved biography of Robert Louis Stevenson, then set off for the roof.

Chapter 7

"Teófilo," I wheezed, my lungs protesting this mad race up steep stairs, through endless corridors, and a shimmy up the ladder to the trapdoor. "Teófilo—are you there?"

He didn't answer, for he was busy hissing his impotent rage as he stared at our front lawn.

I crossed to his side. What I saw as I stared through the crenellation made me forget the struggle to catch my breath.

Figures darted across the grass, dimly lit by a grey-washed dawn. They were hard to see but for the flicker of a fire somewhere below. One shadow stopped, aimed, and fired a long-barreled rifle, white light flashing at his shoulder area.

There was return fire from within the house. Two shadowy figures fell and lay motionless.

I heard shouts and strained to see. There was a brief, dull gleam, and again the Schloss rattled. I grabbed the solid merlon.

"Teófilo!" I screamed.

Finally, he looked at me. "Mistress, what is happening? Who are those humans? What do they want?"

"I don't know. Make it stop."

He glanced at the activity below then back to me. "Only you can make it stop. You must blow the bubbles. Then I can fly down and burn them into oblivion. Please, Mistress. Hurry!"

My hands were shaking. I could hardly open the iron casket I kept hidden in one of the niches. I fumbled with the catch three times and nearly dropped the bottle of soap and the ceramic bubble wand.

I blew so frantically through the serrated ring at the end of the wand that the liquid dispersed, dripping uselessly.

"Careful, Mistress. Calmly. Yes, now you've got it."

I pursed my lips and released my breath, aiming for the glistening ring.

A large bubble formed, wavered, snapped free, and floated towards Teófilo. Another followed. A third. Each one was bigger than the last, rainbow-tinted, fragile. The first two popped the instant they landed on his stone collarbone. The third played about his head, touched his eye, and backed away as though teasing. Teófilo inched his snout forward, painfully, I'm sure, his mouth opening, tongue extending. He wanted that bubble. It disappeared down his gullet.

The fourth and fifth followed, into his hungry throat. He appeared to expand, though the nebulous light no doubt caused the illusion.

"I feel it." His mouth strained as bubbles blew over him, disintegrating against his face, bouncing off his ears, drifting onto his tongue. "Oh, Mistress, you and I...we will soon be together..."

Another cannonball chose that instant to impact my home. This one didn't strike somewhere below. It hit the very battlement where we stood. The merlon beside me exploded.

Sharp splinters slashed my face and chest. I flew backwards. Air expelled from my lungs as I struck something hard, then dropped.

Dust and smoke clouded the air. I was dizzy. I couldn't feel my legs.

Surely Teófilo had swallowed enough bubbles. He would roar, soar, and destroy. Those men—or whatever they were—were going to be sorry.

I must get up. I had to protect Teófilo. I forced open my eyelids and squinted through drifting, swirling smoke.

The scream burst out of my mouth like vomit.

Teófilo.

A thousand slivers, shards, and chunks. Indistinguishable from the crushed remnants of the once-stately battlement.

A few feet away, one cracked, dead eyeball stared at me, still attached to half his head.

Chapter 8

I don't remember how I survived those next minutes. What I felt on our rooftop in the crisp, chilled, autumn dawn…dawn of the first day without Teófilo…well, I can think of no words to adequately describe it.

After some time, I crawled to the remains of his head. My muscles ached. My legs shivered, and were too weak to support me. I picked up the broken bit of stone and pressed it to my throat.

My friend. The only one on earth who loved or even noticed me.

"I would have given you life," I whispered. "You know that, don't you? I was trying."

I ran my fingertips over the eyeball, so recently imbued with tenderness and trust. Yes. He'd trusted me. That's what made this unendurable. Now the poor eye would never be anything but rock. It would never again level its yellow gleam upon me, laughingly, pityingly, or with understanding. The skull I'd so often stroked, or given a good scratch behind the ears, was blown away on one side, leaving a gaping cavern. Desperately I crawled across the rooftop, scraping my knees bloody, filling my hands with sharp shattered granite. Perhaps… if I could put him back together—

It was useless. There was nothing of substance. The cannonball must have hit him directly.

I curled up near the fractured battlement, holding tightly onto

Teófilo's head and gripping the shards so tenaciously that my palms ran with blood. There was no warmth in him any longer. Only the damp chill of lifeless stone.

Distantly, I heard the grove of *Populus tremula* set up a cacophony. I felt that Teófilo himself caused the wind to flutter those yellow leaves in farewell.

The sky turned pale, frosty blue.

Slowly, creeping through black despair, came the memory of what caused this ruin. Armed men on the lawn shooting—trying to kill us, I supposed. I wiped what I assumed were tears from my left eye but my hand came away streaked with fresh wet scarlet.

The splintered pieces I held could have been bits of Teófilo or just as easily rubble from the shattered merlon. My fingers grew stiff from cold and sticky with mingled blood and granite dust, but I would not release anything except Teófilo's head, which I could hardly bear to look at. Laying it beside me, I gazed over the edge of the roof.

I sobbed once as I saw parts of him on the ledge below, and more yet on the ground. I recognized a bit of wing and one of his forelegs—the hand still attached—open and splay-fingered, as though he'd tried to ward off the coming blast.

Beloved Teófilo had at last achieved his desire to leave the rooftop, but he would never know. Saltwater tears and blood dripped onto the ledge beneath me, onto his stiff, human-like hand. It was my life-juice flowing out, and I felt my soul drain with it.

Gradually it occurred to me that the shooting had stopped. Still clutching the precious fragments, I wiped the back of one hand across my eyes and looked down as the sun broke free of the ridge of mountains in the east. Crimson rays shot across the heavens, lighting the Schloss and property in a wash of red-gold.

I could hardly take it all in.

Bodies. Smoke misting from the open-barreled end of the now abandoned cannon. Prisoners standing in a knot, docile and cowed with guns pointed at them. All were dressed in black, their masks, caps, gloves, and clothing.

As I stared at the destruction, my attention swerved towards movement. Three men, on foot, the rising sun behind them, were striding over the east knoll and beginning the descent onto our estate. The one in the middle walked ahead of the others, forming the point of a triangle.

A shout pulled my gaze back. My father, waving madly, called something I couldn't catch. He ran across the lawn, avoiding the dead and wounded.

I squinted again at the approaching men, holding up one clenched fist to block the sunlight from glaring into my eyes.

Again…more shock. I almost started laughing, and bit my lip hard. Though I had never experienced hysteria, I recognized it, and knew if I gave in, I might well fling myself over the ledge.

Teófilo wouldn't want that. At least, I didn't think he would.

I extended my other hand to further shade my eyes.

I wasn't mistaken.

Two of the men marching on the road were unfamiliar and unimportant.

The third, the point of the triangle, was Robert Louis Balfour Stevenson.

THE ODYSSEY

October, 2090 - April, 2091

THE ODYSSEY

Chapter 1

Teófilo, dead. Robert Louis Stevenson, striding with assurance towards the Schloss.

It was impossible. This must be a dream. Half dream, half nightmare.

I set down one handful of granite fragments so I could rub my eyes. Perhaps I was hallucinating. But rubbing my eyes with my filthy hands was a mistake. They burned and watered. The left one throbbed and continued filling with blood.

Robert Louis Stevenson, writer, poet, and perfection incarnate, wandered through the field of slaughter. His closely-tailored dark grey coat fell to mid-calf. He wore black trousers, black boots, and a black tie over a white shirt. His straight dark hair was tucked behind his ears. There was the familiar mustache and aristocratic nose. The eyes remained a mystery because he had yet to look up. Every now and then, he turned over a body and spoke to one of the men walking behind him, which prompted the man to jot something in a book or ledger.

I'd never seen my father act the way I saw him acting now. Maybe the fright of the last hours caused it, but the only word I know to describe his actions was groveling. I couldn't hear him, but he gestured wildly and once clutched at RLS's sleeve, but was swiftly shoved away by one of the assistants. He covered his face with his hands and fell to his knees.

Robert Louis continued walking.

They were almost beneath me. I leaned farther out so I wouldn't lose sight of them, but in a few more steps the ledge would hide them from view.

Perhaps my injuries affected my judgment that day, I don't know. I lost my balance. To keep from plummeting, I clutched at the edge of the battlement, inadvertently releasing the stones from my right hand. Some struck the ledge, making noise like a miniature avalanche. Some bounced off and landed right in front of the men.

All four looked up.

I saw his eyes then. They were *his* eyes. Even as I struggled to scramble backward to the safety of the rooftop, I recognized them. Large, brown, utterly calm. The eyes of a seer.

My heart nearly exploded with fright. What if they started shooting again, thinking one of their enemies was on the roof?

I waited, holding my breath. I heard indecipherable shouting.

After a length of time the trapdoor opened. Two servants and my father climbed onto the roof.

"What are you doing up here," my father cried. "He is angry—so angry. Do you know what you have done?"

"Sir," one of the servants said. "You aren't helping the situation by screaming at her. Let's take her down and see how badly she's hurt."

I cringed and tried to crawl beneath one of the niches. The servant squatted and looked at me kindly. "Come along, little miss." He extended a hand. "I think you need a bandage or two."

I didn't trust him—not with my father scowling and clenching his fists. But when the other servant drew my father away, I took the first man's hand and allowed him to pull me out, snatching up Teófilo's head as I came.

Scooping me into his strong arms, the servant crossed to the trapdoor and carried me down to my bedroom as if I weighed nothing at all.

Chapter 2

STREAMS OF WATER RINSED THE DIRT AND BLOOD FROM MY LEFT EYE, AND A thick round bandage kept it closed. Layers of gauze wrapped around my head held the patch in place. My palms were washed, painted with disinfectant, and swaddled in gauze. My legs caused more concern. For a while there were whispered conjectures that I might be paralyzed, and this seemed to worry everyone quite a lot—especially my father, who turned pale and trembled. But the doctor said my spine was merely bruised and swollen. Given time, I would heal.

He shook two pills out of a container and watched while I swallowed them. "To help you rest," he said.

While he packed up his bag, my father's servant replaced the books and bookend on the shelf, straightened the picture, and lit a fire in the fireplace.

At last, I was left alone.

The servant had placed Teófilo's head on the table where I usually ate breakfast. I stared at it. Teófilo's eye stared back.

If it weren't for that unblinking eye, I could convince myself that I'd had a bad dream.

I couldn't read, write, or even drink the tea someone had left on the nightstand. My hands were bandaged into complete helplessness.

For the first time I wondered about my mother. Maybe she was injured, too. Otherwise, wouldn't she have come to see how her daughter fared?

It was too much. I turned onto my side and fell asleep.

THE ONLY LIGHT CAME FROM THE FIREPLACE, AND THAT HAD DIED TO little more than embers, so the figure beside my bed remained indistinct. I wasn't certain I was awake anyway. My mind wouldn't put a logical sentence together and my eyes refused to focus. I may have imagined or dreamed the entire thing.

Yet later, when I did wake, because it was morning and the doctor had come to check on me, I couldn't dismiss the fancy.

It seemed that someone spent time sitting beside the bed. This person's hair wasn't as short as my father's nor as long as my mother's, but lay somewhere between his ears and his shoulders. His clothing was dark. One leg was crossed over the other and his hands rested quietly in his lap.

I knew, even before he spoke, that this shadowy figure was a man. I'm not sure how. Maybe because, in my whole life, I'd only ever seen two other women besides my mother, and that from a distance.

As I blinked, groggy and floundering, he leaned forward and said quietly, "Don't worry, little jo. I'm going to take care of you. You need never be afraid again." He rested the back of his hand briefly against my cheek.

That's all of the vision or dream or whatever it was that I could remember when I woke, but I will say this. As I suffered the doctor to examine me, I felt almost real. As though there might come a moment when I could once again laugh or play or enjoy a sunset.

The doctor pronounced the swelling improved. He unwrapped and inspected my injured eye and said it should remain bandaged a day or two longer. He didn't look at my hands.

Shortly after he left, my father came in. He approached the bed and stood there, his lips white and tense. "I hope you know things will be different now." There was a hushed, contained anger in his voice. "You've taken care of that, my girl."

"Where's Mama?"

His nostrils dilated, making two sharp white dents on either side of his nose. "Quite ill and in her bed. Due to you. Where will she go? Do you care? What will happen to her? You should have thought of that before you went off to the roof and ruined everything for all of us. 'Idiot,' he called me. 'Incompetent.'" He drew in a harsh breath. "Well, we'll see, won't we? We'll see if he can find anyone else willing to give up their lives—for this."

He left, banging the door.

———————

Chapter 3

———————

I FELT SO MUCH BETTER THE NEXT DAY THAT I ROSE FROM BED AGAINST THE doctor's orders and slipped into the corridor, determined to find out if Robert Louis was still in my home.

My usual habit was to slink down the staircase reserved for the servants, which led directly into the kitchens. They congregated there for coffee and gossip whenever they could. If I stopped on the second to last step I could eavesdrop and avoid the last step, which creaked. Usually, I could flee back up if someone came near, but I had been caught before, so I was extra careful this time. Crouching there, I smelled tobacco smoke, strong coffee, and the particular scent of cold mountain mist clinging to woolen hats and coats. The gathered men talked idly about the attack and fire damage.

A door opened and closed. Someone sniffed and sneezed. "Is the coffee fresh or has it been on the stove all morning?"

"No, not long."

"My hands are freezing. Oh, that's good. Thank you, Anders. I wish he would leave and we could get back to normal—but at least we're done burying the dead. The entry will have to be stripped to the timbers. Damn me, but fire leaves a stink."

"I heard he's staying because of them. Because of how they botched things."

"She won't set foot out of bed and he...well, he's aged twenty years overnight."

"They'll never be given another chance. He'll get rid of them. And did you hear that other rumor, about the marriage?"

"I heard it, but I don't believe—"

"—They can't be serious," a graveled voice broke in. It was the gardener. He sounded angry. "She's only a child."

This made my ears prickle. I was the sole person in the house who could be considered a child, unless you counted Teófilo. Then I remembered.

Teófilo.

What one of the other men said gave me something to think about besides my sorrow.

"Look." I recognized the voice of the man who carried me to my room day before yesterday. Jonas was his name. "It's clear this place is no longer safe. Those men we buried? They're Russians. More will find us too, tomorrow, next week, who knows when? Maybe next time we won't be able to hold them off till help arrives."

"But—marriage. Isn't there another way? It's—why, it's disgusting."

"What do you think he's going to do, anyway?"

"Well, I don't know...but still, she's twelve and he's—he's got to be—"

"—That doesn't matter." Jonas sounded impatient. "The important thing is her safety."

"That's where you're wrong," the one who'd asked for coffee said. "Sounds like you two are getting sentimental. You don't think anybody cares about *her*, do you? Especially him?"

Anders laughed coarsely. "It isn't like she has beauty. Those big damn teeth, that skinny boy's body, and no milk-jugs."

At that point I shut off my mind. It was a trick I'd developed whenever I heard gossip about me. There were always disparaging remarks, if not about my looks, then about my presence. Since I couldn't change either and it hurt to hear those things, I'd learned to shut it out. I'd think about what Teófilo and I would discuss when I went up to visit him...

But that would never happen again.

It hurt less to listen to the put-downs.

"You can be sure the old man will try to talk him out of it. You think he wants to lose this cushy job? He probably got drunk in town and let it slip about her, you know. It was either him or the tutor."

"Do you think he'll face the hangman?"

Silence.

"Bad business," Jonas muttered. "Shouldn't have happened."

A bell rang.

"That'll be him. Has he been asking you questions?"

"Yes, yes," the other men replied. I heard shuffling and the scooting of chairs.

"A million of them," Anders said. "I hope we don't all face the hangman."

They left the kitchen.

It sounded like—preposterous idea—I was going to be married, but to whom? Someone much, much older.

Into my mind came the memory of a horrid old man who had once visited my father. "Uncle," my father called him. He'd been in a wheelchair. His face was covered in red, hairy warts. A stink had remained in the air after he'd gone, like camphor.

Who else but someone very old and very ugly would want to marry me?

Why did I have to marry anybody? Why couldn't everything go back to the way it was?

Without Teófilo, of course.

My back hurt and my legs tingled. I returned to bed.

Chapter 4

THAT NIGHT, VERY LATE, THE SOUND OF CARRIAGE WHEELS AND THE
whinny of a horse woke me. I went to the window and swung open the beveled glass.

Voices carried farther at night than they did during the day, especially when the air was still. It was an odd scientific phenomenon. I wasn't surprised that I could overhear the coachman and one of our servants four floors below.

"Are you leaving, then?" That was our servant.

"All I know is I got the order to bring the carriage around."

I'd never seen this carriage or driver, which meant it wasn't my father's or my tutor's. Could it be Robert Louis's? If so, this might be my last chance to prove to myself he was not the man I thought I'd seen in the throes of sorrow and fear. Donning robe and slippers, I left my room and tiptoed to the first floor.

My father's study was about ten steps from the front entry. As I approached, I smelled burned wood, fabric, and smoke. The entire vestibule was charred. The gold leaf and velvet wallpaper hung in sooty ribbons, and the heavy oak door with its iron hinges and studs had been destroyed. Someone had mounted a barrier of plywood to keep out the weather.

Sure enough, light glimmered beneath the study door and I heard voices. Checking for servants, I crept right up and squinted with my good eye through the keyhole.

I could only see the back of the mysterious man's head and his black-clad shoulders, for he faced the desk.

My father sat behind the desk, facing me. His skin was florid, running with sweat. His hands kept moving, picking up things, putting them down, tapping. "But—" he said.

I didn't catch the other man's interruption. He spoke softly, yet whatever he said seemed to unravel my father. He mopped his perspiring forehead with a handkerchief. "But sir," he said, "everything is all right. Nothing happened other than some damage to the house. Please—"

The man bent and put his hand into a knapsack, withdrawing a package of cigarettes. He tapped the edge against the index finger of his left hand and drew out a cigarette. His fingers were long and slender.

My father shoved his chair back and rushed around the desk, scraping a match as he came. He held it out and the gentleman allowed him to light the cigarette.

I glimpsed the side of his face—lean, rather long, and when compared to my father's sweaty crimson cheeks, quite pale. A mustache grew above his lips—the kind that drooped on either side of the mouth. His hair was again combed behind his ears.

This was the same man I'd seen walking among the bodies on the lawn. The same one who gazed up at me when I dropped the granite pieces.

My father shook out the match and dropped it in an ashtray. He fell to his knees, cupping his hands around the fellow's forearm, and spoke into his coat sleeve.

"Please, please sir, you must believe I have always done my best. You mustn't blame me for this. I've been so very careful. I swear they didn't find this place through me. I swear it. Have your men questioned the servants? The delivery people?"

The gentleman blew a cloud of smoke then tamped the cigarette out in the ashtray and rose from his chair, bending to fetch his knapsack.

I backed into an alcove that used to house a marble statue.

The door opened. My father, still clinging to this man's arm, walked with knees bent. He reminded me of a wolf displaying subservience to the alpha.

"We'll be back in two days," the man said.

Of course, since I had never heard Robert Louis Stevenson's voice, I couldn't say whether he sounded like my idol. But I will say that his voice sounded exactly like what should be Robert Louis Stevenson's. Low, well-modulated, flowing, confident, and calm. *I am a man*, the voice suggested, *who will never lose control of a situation.*

"Sir, I'm begging you—I'm begging—"

"Have her ready."

My father nodded. "If you insist. But isn't there any way I can prevail—"

The visitor stopped at the front entry. "Release me."

Instantly my father obeyed and backed away a few steps. He stiffened, clicked his heels, and bowed from the waist. "Please remember me to your good mother," he said, not lifting his head.

"I will do that." The man withdrew a pair of black leather gloves from the inner pocket of his coat. "Two days."

My father bowed lower. I wondered if his nose would scrape the floor, but he straightened and moved the plywood out of the way.

The man pulled on his gloves and descended the steps.

My father wiped his brow with his shirtsleeve, muttering vile curses as he shoved the plywood back into place.

While he was occupied, I crept to the staircase and ran up, light as a firefly, to the second-floor landing and its big window with the diamond-shaped bevels.

Too late. I saw nothing more than a black-gloved hand reach out and rap once against the side of the carriage.

The driver flicked his reins. With a snort and an energetic shake of its head, the horse set out and the carriage vanished into the night.

Chapter 5

Our gardener sent a pretty bouquet of late-blooming yellow *Saxifrage aizoides* and red *Arctostaphylos alpina* with the servant who brought my breakfast. The older servants called these *gulsildre* and *rypebær*. It was the nicest thing I could remember happening in a long time, and that scared me. Such a gesture said more clearly than words that change was coming.

The doctor gave me permission to get out of bed as long as I didn't overtax myself. He removed the patch from my eye. Other than a bruise, a scabbed-over cut on my lid and several sensitive lacerations on my palms, I felt fine. My spine hardly ached. The doctor swabbed a bit of ointment on the eyelid and re-wrapped the wounds on my hands just around the palms, leaving my fingers free.

Wherever I went I was covertly stared at. Conversations abruptly halted when I came near. Heads shook dolefully.

Teófilo could make me feel better. He could have me laughing so hard my sides would ache.

I couldn't stand his head with the one eye staring at me. Late in the night the day after I'd eavesdropped on my father and the strange man in black—*Robert Louis Stevenson,* my mind insisted though it was impossible—I descended to the kitchens and found a hammer in one of the catch-all drawers.

On the way back, as I passed the second-floor corridor, I heard raised voices. Sharp, harsh words. A woman's wail. This hall contained my parents' bedroom.

My feet were cold and I meant to carry out a funeral of sorts. I didn't want to linger here, but the argument drew me.

I crept to their door. There was no keyhole, but I pressed my ear to the wood.

Unfortunately, the door was made of oak. Thick and unyielding, it guarded all but the loudest snatches.

"I won't be a party—" That was my mother.

"Shut up." My father. "You'll do as you're told."

A lower passage I couldn't decipher.

"Well-paid…loyalty…you signed…"

"He'll use—"

"None of our business."

"He'll *kill*—"

"Yes, that's right, damn you, it'll be the firing squad for you *and* me!" my father almost screamed.

"Well, well, Missy."

The voice came from right above me. I'd been so engrossed that I hadn't heard him approach. Jonas again, the big servant who could usually be found at my father's side or nearby.

The hair nearly sprang out of my scalp. I yelped.

"Shouldn't you be in bed?" he said mildly.

The door opened, crashing against the wall. Tears streaked my mother's face, runnels of water blackened by cosmetics. Her right brow stood out darkly painted on her pale face but the left was altogether missing. Her white hair hung lank and snarled to her chest. She wore a silky nightgown that didn't leave much to the imagination. My father, for the second time in two days, was sweating and scarlet, big wet patches making his shirt cling to his skin. He looked like a prime candidate for a heart attack or stroke.

"What are you doing?" he shouted. "Get her away, Jonas. I cannot stand the sight of her. Selfish damned—sneaking around like a cockroach—"

I didn't hear the rest because he slammed the door and Jonas pulled me away.

Chapter 6

I SPENT THE REST OF THE NIGHT REPLAYING WHAT I'D HEARD BETWEEN MY father and mother. The ticking of the wall clock took up a refrain.

He'll kill—

He'll kill—

It was clear the man I'd dubbed Robert Louis Stevenson held the power of life and death over people. More importantly, over my parents. He meant them to do something they didn't want to do, and if they defied him, they would die.

Did you hear that other rumor—

She's only a child.

But—marriage.

My father, though never demonstrative—usually smilingly dismissive—had not ever treated me with the cold impatient fury he'd shown since the attack. Obviously, I'd caused something terrible to happen. Something that put my parents' lives in danger.

If I understood correctly, I was the price for their lives. I was to be given in marriage to some old man. A man so old the only reaction the servants could muster was disgust and pity.

We'll be back in two days. Have her ready.

My mind locked on one word. *We'll.* Not *I'll.* He meant to return, and he was bringing someone with him.

It had to be that old fart in the wheelchair. As the night passed, he

40

grew larger in my imagination, like a barn rat feasting on spilled grain. Fat, wheezing, and warty. His wheelchair creaked and I heard his raspy breath. His nose elongated over bloodless lips and he stank—stank—stank. Rotted flesh, camphor, garlic.

He would want to do things I didn't understand. Things I'd seen my mother and father do through keyholes, things that left me frightened and queasy.

I'd questioned Teófilo and he'd gently explained how grownups made babies, how semen fertilized the egg. I was repelled.

The old man in the wheelchair would want to do those things to me. Picturing it almost made me puke.

About five o'clock in the morning I lit three candles, setting them on the floor in a triangle. I placed Teófilo's head in the center and the hammer to one side.

For an instant, I thought that lone eye blinked at me, but I knew it for what it was—wishful fantasy caused by flickering candlelight. He would never again blink, speak, reassure me, or laugh. He was forever gone, leaving my life in ruins. Sold to the old wheelchair man as a sex slave.

I knelt. "I'm sorry I let this happen," I whispered. "All I thought about was myself. If only I'd blown the bubbles before it was too late." My tears dripped onto his poor broken head.

"Give me again all that there was," I quoted.

"Give me the sun that shone.

Give me the eyes, give me the soul,

Give me the lad that's gone."

I picked up his head and kissed the eye. Placing it on the floor, I wrapped both hands around the hammer handle, ignoring the sting of the healing cuts, and brought it down as hard as I could. The eye splintered. Granite flaked. I hit it again, and again, and again.

"Billow and breeze, islands and seas,

Mountains of rain and sun,

All that was good, all that was fair,

All that was me is gone."

And so was Teófilo.

Chapter 7

My tutor arrived about nine o'clock, subdued in a way I'd never seen. There was no sarcasm, impatience, or the warning sound of a ruler slapping against his thigh. Instead, he spoke little, and that, softly.

He took me out of the house for a nature lesson. This was my field of excellence. I loved to learn, read, and study, so I was good in all subjects, but more than anything, except being with Teófilo, I loved wandering among the trees.

Trees have spirits. Dryads, they're called. They're invisible to most humans, but not to me. They resemble their homes. The oaks that live in the southern reaches hold big, bare-chested men, Viking warriors with long flowing hair, bushy beards, and rough skin. Willows shelter beautiful maidens with fluttery, wispy gowns. Skinny, like me, with fragile wrists, they walk almost on tiptoe like ballerinas. Birch dryads are tall and clipped—their speech short and of the necessary variety, never flowing in the way of the whispery mountain pines. Rowans contain soldiers with squared shoulders and a prickly sort of war-poetry.

My favorite trees, though I never told my tutor, were the aspens. They were the most willing to accept me, to talk to me, and I felt our conversations travel over vast spaces through their entangled roots. I remember how gentle their voices were, how they showed their affection by brushing their soft leaves across my cheeks. When I pressed my ear to the bark of an aspen, I would hear a deep, humming melody. I always believed they watched us through the eyes on their trunks.

Trees mostly communicate through their root systems, but wind provides another means. Teófilo and I used to try to understand what they were saying. Nearly every day, weather permitting, I would go out among them, drift between the trunks, sing, and run my fingers over their flesh. Their voices surged through the ground and into my feet. That was the main reason I never wore shoes, so I could feel the vibrations of our trees. Whenever a tree seemed particularly receptive, I would wrap my arms around it as far as I could, press my cheek against the hard bark, and listen.

As I think about it now, I believe this may be the secret humans lost somewhere along the way. We forgot how to listen to trees.

My tutor was distracted. He looked sharply behind us. Blinked at shadows. Muttered. He had me recite the botanical names of everything, which was stupid. I'd known those for untold years.

Suddenly, he asked, "What do you think of your education? Have I been a good teacher to you?"

I had nothing to compare him to, so I didn't know what to say. I stared at the ground and hoped he wouldn't slap me.

He grabbed my shoulders. "What are you going to tell him about our years together? I must know. I haven't been so bad now, have I, girl?"

Why could he never say my name? I wanted to shout it in his face.

Zoë! Zoë!

Chapter 8

Tomorrow, Robert Louis Stevenson would return...with someone. My husband-to-be. A much older man. A match some in the house considered repugnant.

I lay on my side spackled in dying firelight, one hand cupped around shards of Teófilo. I knew I should sleep, but knowing that made it impossible. My eyelid, the one cut on the day of the attack, throbbed.

Around midnight I heard padding footsteps along the corridor. They stopped outside my door. I stared, unable to see the latch but hearing it click.

A candle glimmered in the hand of a ghostly white figure.

I clenched the granite shavings. Then I discerned the white hair and knew it was my mother.

She stopped. The flame flickered as though she'd jumped, or breathed hard.

"Mama?" I sat up.

She came closer, placed the candle on the nightstand, and sat on the bed beside me.

"Men," she said, beginning one of her breathless choppy dialogues where she didn't seem to know or care if anyone listened. "It's their fault—and they know—but won't admit—they blame—when it's patently—but they can't stand to face the—"

Here she stopped and stared at me, her face registering surprise as though she realized for the first time I was there. Lifting one hand, she stroked my hair. "They poisoned—*poisoned*—they're evil—and you'll be the payment. Do you know? Do you?"

"Know what, Mama?" I tried to follow but it was hard, with such disjointed sentences. She started pulling at her absent left eyebrow, a sure sign she was disturbed.

"You're nothing but payment. An *experiment*. Wrong to use you—to use you—*wrong to use you!*"

I recoiled as her voice rose. She stopped pulling her brow and tore at her hair as though creatures were nibbling the inside of her skull.

Then my father was in the room, and Jonas, both of them wearing undignified striped nightshirts. They pulled her off the bed. She twisted, fighting to see me.

"Don't do what they—if you do, *they will never let you go!*"

"Shut up, you crazy old witch," my father shouted, and slapped her.

She slumped, sobbing. They dragged her out.

Mother, mother, speak low in my ear,
Some of the things are so great and near,
Some are so small and far away,
I have a fear that I cannot say.
What have I done, and what do I fear?
And why are you crying, Mother dear?

Chapter 9

I woke with a stomachache and couldn't get my fingers to stop trembling. As I sat at the table pushing oatmeal around with my spoon, someone knocked and the door opened.

My father and Jonas entered. With no more than a glance that somehow left me feeling guilty, my father crossed to the chipped old wardrobe and flung it open.

"This is what I was thinking of." He tugged on the hem of a pink frock.

"Too small," Jonas said.

"Oh, how could it be? It was only purchased last…well, who can remember. Last year or so."

"Little girls grow in a year."

Jonas sent me a brief smile. They both wore suits. My father's black hair was slicked down with oil. This helped cover his bald spot but emphasized the fleshy cheeks, the tracery of purple blood vessels and bulbous nose. Jonas's hair was thick and curly. It might need half a bottle of oil to make it obey. Maybe that was why he didn't bother.

My father had apparently drenched himself in cologne, too. The smell was formidable.

I rose, dropping a napkin into my bowl. "What are you doing, Papa?"

"Finish your breakfast." Resentment simmered in his glance.

I couldn't put a name to what I felt. Up to that point I had hoped my conjectures were wrong. Perhaps someone else was getting married. Maybe one of the servants' daughters, though I'd never seen any other children.

"Am I going somewhere?"

His fingers, round and swollen as pork sausages and overlaid with heavy gold rings, yanked another dress from the wardrobe. This one was blue. A man who'd come to the Schloss several months ago had brought it for me.

Jonas's gaze seemed pitying. Terror leaped through me like deer fleeing a forest fire.

If only Teófilo…

But I had to face this alone.

"What do you think, Jonas?"

"It might do. Would you try this on, please?"

"Why?" I asked.

"Just do it. Hurry." My father thrust out the garment. "We haven't much time." He fumbled for his pocket watch and flipped it open, frowning.

I stood there, clutching the stiff, still new-smelling frock against my chest. Protests rose and retreated. I wanted to demand answers, but I did nothing. The men turned their backs.

"What are you waiting for?" my father said. "Do you want to make up for the bad you've done? This is the way. Put the dress on and brush your hair."

It was too tight. I'd never worn it. Why wear fancy dresses when one never goes anywhere?

Where's Mama? I wanted to ask, but my father's brooding grimace stopped me.

I couldn't reach the buttons in the back. If I tried, the material would rip. Leaving them undone, I picked up my hairbrush. My hair has always been prone to tangles. I've learned that braiding it before bed helps.

But I shouldn't get ahead of myself.

Jonas turned around. "Ah," he said, giving me a meticulous once-over. "Well. Let me fix your buttons, Missy."

His fingertips touching my skin made me shiver.

"It's tight," Jonas said. My father stared critically. Wherever I was going, whatever their plans were, I recognized that everything about me would embarrass him.

The outfit was ridiculous. It wasn't anything I would ever choose to wear. I wasn't the lace, puffed-sleeve, powder-blue type.

"Where are her damn shoes?" My father rummaged through the wardrobe again. "Here." He pulled out a pair of shiny black shoes that buckled. I had never worn them. "Put these on."

They were too small. The moment I stood up my feet hurt.

"It'll have to do. Wipe that sulk off your face. This is an honor happening to you today, one you don't deserve." My father came close, his gaze threatening. "If I hear that you've complained—said anything about me or—" he shook his head. "I'll come after you. Don't think I won't." His hairy nostrils flared and I got the feeling he would enjoy it if I made him come after me.

I stepped backward.

He gave me a grim, pitiless smile, took my elbow, and led me out of the room.

Chapter 10

A pebbled road behind the Schloss led to a small chapel near a cliff that offered an exceptional view of the enormous scooped-out valley and on the far side of that, forbidding, ice-crowned mountains. This was where my parents and I worshipped every Sunday morning.

Mountains surrounded my childhood home, all of them high and snow-capped year-round. When winter brought winds shooting out of the passes, they made you believe they would crush everything in their path including the house, but it was made of granite, and even cannonballs didn't faze it much.

A carriage waited at the foot of the steps. My father motioned impatiently for me to get in. He sat across from me. Jonas sat next to me on the leather seat.

"Can't you do something about her hair?" my father said as the driver up top sent the horse cantering.

"It's all right," Jonas said, but he took the brush I'd forgotten I held and swiped through it a few times.

The carriage had a square back window that framed my house as we drove away. I watched it grow smaller then vanish as pines and spruce formed an impenetrable curtain of green.

I wondered if I would ever see it again.

"Let's get those bandages off." My father leaned forward and plucked at the knots, unwinding the strips from around my hands. "We don't need to give him any reminders of…that day."

My palms were pink and wrinkled, like the belly on a newborn puppy. I closed my hands into fists and ground them into my lap.

It took about five minutes to reach the chapel. Another carriage was already there. We got out. My father straightened his tie and touched his hair as we climbed the steps. His face was shiny with sweat. Jonas placed the palm of his hand lightly against my lower back, which made my flesh creep.

My father opened the door and stood aside for me to enter. As I passed, I smelled his sweat and fear beneath the heavy wash of cologne.

A sick lump putrefied in the pit of my stomach and I felt shaky, like my body was feeding off itself, ruthless as a hungry shark. I glanced back at the forest, entertaining a fancy to run as fast as I could, to hide until they gave up searching for me.

Then I was blinking in shadowed dimness, following where that hand, pressed so resolutely against my spine, guided.

Three men stood at the altar. One, the priest in a white robe, faced us. The other two kept their backs to us, but at least, I thought, relieved, they were both standing. No wheelchair in sight.

I ordered myself to take nothing at face value. The old man could be in another room, waiting to burst out like a rapacious spider.

As we walked up the center aisle, the two men turned.

Robert Louis Stevenson. Yes, I'd expected that. He'd said he was returning. So the other…the other must be—

He wore wire-rimmed glasses. His beard was cut close, coming to a point beneath his chin. He was slightly shorter than his companion.

RLS stepped forward, hands extended. He smiled.

"Hello," he said, in the gentlest voice I'd ever heard. He clasped my hands in his then knelt on one knee. "Zoë," he said, "I'm here to marry you, if you will have me."

In that instant, washed in his dark gaze, I thought, *Teófilo, what is there here for me now?*

And I said, *Yes*.

Chapter 11

I HARDLY REMEMBER THE CEREMONY, THOUGH I'VE TRIED, MANY TIMES. I remember my knees shaking. I've forgotten everything else except Robert Louis's grave brown eyes and that he never released my hand.

When it was over, he bent and kissed my cheek. His mustache tickled. He brushed his thumb across my other cheek and smiled. Everyone signed the bottom of a long, wordy document. We walked into dappled evergreen sunlight where the horses nickered and my father babbled, simultaneously mopping his forehead with a limp handkerchief.

"Congratulations," Jonas murmured.

I glanced up at him. I didn't know what to say. Had it really happened? Had my father given me, an immature twelve-year-old girl, in marriage to the most brilliant man who ever lived? A man who knelt and asked for my hand as though I were a desirable, beautiful, grown-up princess?

The man who stood at the altar with Robert Louis spoke in an undertone before entering the other carriage along with Jonas. The rest of us climbed into our carriage. I sat beside my father. Robert Louis sat opposite us. "You have grown up in a very pretty place," he said.

I nodded. I didn't have to think of a reply, because my father erupted into descriptions of the property, how big it was, what buildings it held, how many deer, etc. Robert Louis watched me with a sort of half-smile that curved only one side of his lips beneath the droopy mustache. I was too afraid to smile back.

They hadn't married me to the old man in the wheelchair, but to Robert Louis Stevenson, writer, adventurer, and poet.

I'd been certain my dictionary and encyclopedia had given the date of his death as December third, 1894.

Under the wide and starry sky,
Dig the grave and let me lie.
Glad did I live and gladly die,
And I laid me down with a will.

How could he be here, riding opposite me in a carriage, giving me that achingly beautiful half-smile, studying me from eyes as softly brown and limpid as a deer's? Yet unlike a deer's, Robert Louis's eyes held immeasurable intelligence and…sorrow.

Oh yes, I may have been only twelve at the time, but I recognized sorrow when I saw it.

Why hadn't I paid more attention during the service? The priest must have spoken his real name.

The driver returned us to the house. At the top of the steps by the doors sat a valise topped with two sturdy leather handles.

"Here are your clothes, all ready for you," my father said with a false note of cheer. "But, sir, you cannot leave yet. We've prepared a small party. Tea and cake and such. Would you like a sip or two of spirits to warm your cockles? The nights get very cold up here."

"We must go." Robert Louis's voice remained smooth, unruffled, lacking even the hint of hostility, yet instantly my father bowed.

I remembered my conviction that this man had threatened my father and mother, and that the price for their lives was me. I'd nearly forgotten that important fact because of his benign gaze and melodious voice. I'd nearly forgotten that this man, Robert Louis Stevenson, could order someone's death if he wished.

Do you think he'll face the hangman? someone had asked about my father, and another said, *I hope we don't all face the hangman.*

"Get your wife," Robert Louis said.

My father bowed again and vanished into the house. As he entered, I smelled again the stench of burned wood, cushions, and carpet. I doubted if the front vestibule would ever be returned to its former grandeur.

I looked up at my husband.

His head tilted slightly. "What is it, Zoë?"

"Will you let my parents live?" I asked, before losing my nerve.

He didn't answer immediately. Instead, one hand touched my temple then strayed to my hair. He picked up a few strands, letting them fall between his fingers. I was embarrassed. My hair wasn't what I imagined a lady's should be, like my mother's when she coifed it, winding it into fancy curves on the back of her head, tendrils brushing her neck.

"You have hair like a tree nymph's," he said.

My whole body stiffened in shock and delight. How did he—.

"Like copper beech leaves in autumn," he went on, his words making me reel and quake. "Bright and fluttery. Answering the slightest breeze, changing color with the light and wind. I've never seen anything change color like your hair, but it does remind me of those leaves." He smiled and his dark brown gaze met mine directly. "If color had substance, this would be it, Zoë."

I stared at him. I was only twelve. I had no sophistication. Remembering that moment, I know he must have seen every one of my emotions right there, bare naked, on my face.

His hands gripped my shoulders, not hurtfully but firmly, and he said, "They don't deserve—"

He stopped. He blinked and frowned.

My father and mother came out of the house.

My father led my mother by the elbow. She stared. Not at me. Her gaze never once rested on me, even at this time of goodbye. Her eyes were locked on the grove of aspen as though mesmerized by the quivering yellow leaves. Her hair was brushed and coiled and a brow had been painted over her left eye, but I saw that she wasn't really in her body today. She couldn't have done those things herself.

As I watched, her mouth opened and a glistening rope of saliva dribbled over her chin.

I wanted the earth to open and swallow me.

"Not one of her good days," my father blustered. I stared at my shoes and hunched my shoulders.

"Is this everything?" Robert Louis asked. "Zoë? Is there anything else you want to bring besides your clothes?"

His words made me think. For the first time since the attack on the house I recalled my book about Robert Louis Stevenson. "My—there's a book. And Te—I mean, yes, there are other things. I'll get them."

Chapter 12

I ran upstairs.

The bed was unmade. A lone hanger swung gently in the open wardrobe. My books were still on their shelf. Nobody had packed a single one for me.

Throwing aside my pillow, I scooped the remnants of Teófilo into a purple velvet bag I'd had for many years, pulled the drawstrings, and dropped it by the door. I searched for the biography, but it was not in any of its usual places, the shelf…the nightstand…or the floor.

Then I remembered. I'd taken it to the roof the day my home was attacked.

Clutching the bag, I raced to the trapdoor.

Broken granite lay everywhere. I wanted to stop, linger, and weep, but Robert Louis waited, and I feared making him angry. I ran across the rooftop to the edge where I'd been when the cannonball struck.

There lay the shattered bubble wand. The bottle of soap was nearby, on its side. All the liquid had evaporated.

The need for my book overwhelmed me. I had to have it so I could compare the picture on the front jacket with the man who had this day become my husband. Only then could I make sense of the events transforming my life. I bent and rummaged through the debris.

I found the book finally, clear on the other side of the roof.

It had rained.

The pages had begun to mold. The spine was broken.

Worse, the face on the jacket had torn. All that remained was the front of his coat and the knotted tie.

Everything—absolutely everything that meant anything to me was being snatched away. The trees I'd become friends with…my books… Teófilo…even the bed I'd slept in for as long as I could remember.

I looked down at my dress. Dirt smudged the bodice. The lace along the hem was torn and grimy.

Tears welled and spilled. My nose clogged.

"Goodbye," I whispered, touching the pedestal from which Teófilo used to guard our home.

I clutched my velvet bag and the book,

and I turned away.

"Is that all?" His dark gaze absorbed the grime, the book, the little bag.

I nodded. Wiped the back of my hand across my cheeks and sniffed.

He remained motionless but for a slight movement of his hair as the breeze toyed with it, and the nearly imperceptible lowering of his brows.

Then, with a nod, he escorted me down the steps and into the carriage.

Chapter 13

As Robert Louis and I left, I looked back for the last time.

The mountains behind the Schloss were high, remote, lacy blue—almost transparent. Clouds nestled in every crevice. They seemed no more substantial than gauze. The afterimage of a dream.

Suddenly I felt certain the last twelve years had been phantasm. Now that I was leaving, the world I created—perhaps inside one of Teófilo's fragile bubbles—would vanish like the magical isle of Avalon.

As we entered the forest, I pictured the entire estate rising into the heavens—the house, the merlons, the trees, Papa and Mama. The servants.

Sparkling briefly, then—pop!

Nothing but a scatter of iridescent mist.

Chapter 14

THE CARRIAGE CAREENED INTO AFTERNOON, EVENING, TWILIGHT, AND night. Its motion lulled me but as soon as I would drift off a pothole or bump would jerk me awake again, renewing my conjectures and bewilderment, trepidation about the future, and anxiety about our destination.

Robert Louis gazed out the side window, hands folded over the silver heron head on a cane propped before him. As the light faded, he turned into a silent, still shadow, and I couldn't help wondering if the sight of me, after my excursion to the roof, had made him regret what he'd done. Perhaps, seeing me dirty, snot-nosed, and weepy, he'd changed his mind about being chained through marriage to me and my ugly, uneventful life.

He showed no sign of weariness or any need to fidget. I didn't want to annoy him by speaking. Putting my book against the wall of the carriage, I rested my cheek against it and finally fell asleep.

A shout woke me.

The carriage made an abrupt turn and stopped. My book fell. I had to grab the swinging hand loop to keep from falling myself.

Flaring torchlight made me blink after so long in darkness.

Robert Louis stepped out and offered his hand to me. He smiled as I clasped his fingers and exited the carriage. The men holding the torches stared as though they'd never seen a girl before.

Maybe they'd never seen one so disheveled. I could imagine how tangled my hair was by now. I tried to surreptitiously wipe my face with one sleeve, but it's hard to be surreptitious with twenty torches and the eyes of countless men glaring at you.

Tucking my hand under his arm, Robert Louis gave me escort into a building—an inn, I guessed. He patted my hand. "Would you like a bath? Something to eat?"

My stomach growled and he smiled. "I apologize for taking such poor care of you. It was important that we make haste."

A bearded fellow, roughly dressed, came up and said, "It's ready, sir."

Robert Louis nodded. "A room has been prepared for you. I must stay here and speak with my men."

The idea of disagreeing with him never entered my head. I trailed up the creaky wooden stairs behind someone who could, if I let my imagination run wild, resemble a pirate or highwayman.

He led me down a corridor to a room well-lit with candles and oil lamps. A bed stood against the far wall. A big brass tub filled with steaming water sat in the center. I smelled something wonderful, like sun-warmed wildflowers in a meadow.

My escort laid towels, soap, and washcloths on a footstool beside the tub before taking his leave. The moment the door closed behind him, I removed my shoes and white stockings, drawn to the warmth, scent, and promise of a long, hot soak.

The tiny buttons still ran up the back of the marriage frock though, trapping me like a straitjacket. I craned, twisted, and bent to no avail without the acute danger of ripping out the underarms.

Perhaps it didn't matter. My traveling bag sat on the bed. Wadded inside were my comfortable loose trousers, high-necked sweaters, front-buttoning blouses, and the soft half-boots I wore when I couldn't go barefoot because of snow. Even my nightgown and robe.

The dress could go to the devil. I giggled at the sound of buttons popping and flying and took my first unencumbered breath of the day.

Wriggling out of underclothing, I made a dive for the tub, forced by the heat to enter in stages. Scented steam engulfed me as I sank clear to my ears.

It was glorious.

"Yes?" I said when someone knocked. A woman opened the door and stepped in. Before I could think about how startling it was to see a strange female, she said, "I am Hanna, the innkeeper's wife. Master wants to talk to you and he says it cannot wait. I have a screen that will provide privacy for you, and I will remain as your chaperone."

"All-all right."

She carried in a trifold screen and placed it in front of the bath. Once that was done, she brought a tray and placed a bowl of stew, a spoon, a napkin, and a steaming cup of tea on a second stool beside the tub.

Facing me, her eyes wide, she asked in a low voice, "You are Zoë?"

"Yes," I said.

She stared. "We were told you would come." She spoke softly, as though she didn't want to be overheard.

I watched, amazed, as her eyes filled with tears. "All my life I have heard the legends, the prophecies, but I never really believed." She swiped at her eyes. "My mother was from the city; she said it was nonsense, and if I allowed myself to get caught up in it, all I would find would be deep trouble. But my grandmother on my father's side was farm folk, and she believed. She collected the dust and hid it in jars under the foundations. I haven't seen those jars since I was a little girl, but I remember how the dust glittered and sent out rainbows. I am sorry I didn't believe."

"I-I don't know what you're talking about," I managed.

Uneasiness washed over me. It was the way she stared. It reminded me of the priest at the Schloss when he laid a hand on my head and prayed for my health.

She started to say something else, but a firm knock on the door stopped her. "Are you ready yet, Frau Schmidt?"

A flicker of fear passed across her face as she stepped quickly away. "Yes, sir, you can come in," she said, and took up a position beside the window.

"Zoë?"

His voice, like sunlight, was so warm it could make daffodils open. I glanced at Hanna, who had erased all trace of her earlier emotion. "Yes?"

"May I come in and talk to you?"

"Yes, come in," I said. "Sir," I added.

I couldn't see him but I heard his step. "I brought these," he said.

The innkeeper's wife moved out of sight. When she returned, she was holding the book and the velvet bag. She placed them on the bed.

"Oh," I said. "I left those in the carriage. Thank you."

"Of course," he said. "Have you tried the stew?"

I hadn't. I picked up the spoon and had a bite. It was a delicious brew of potatoes, beef, carrots, and other savory things. "It's good," I said.

I heard him drag something across the floor. The chair, probably.

Hanna was here to watch over me and the screen hid me from view. Still, I was mortified to be naked in the same room as an adult man—my husband, true, but nevertheless a stranger.

"I'm sorry for barging in," he said. "It's unforgivable, but I wanted to say goodbye. You could eat while we talk, if you like. You must be starving."

Food. Who cared about food? He was leaving. "Good-goodbye? You're going away?"

"Oh, Zoë." He sounded tired. "I don't want to. It's the last thing I want to do. But I must. I'm putting you in the hands of the men you saw outside. They will protect you to the death."

"But—" There was nothing I could say. Nobody argued with this man. I'd seen that clearly.

"They will take you to one of my homes, where you will be safe. I will join you as soon as I can."

I had so many questions. Who was he? Why had he married me? Was he evil like my mother said…good…or something else? Why had our house been attacked? What had Frau Schmidt been talking about? Dust that glittered, and prophecies?

Glancing at the woman, I knew instinctively that she didn't want me to reveal what she had said, and I was still too timid, too awestruck, to query Robert Louis. This left me with few choices. For now, I would put myself in his hands and do whatever he decreed.

Chapter 15

And so, my long journey began.

Fifteen mounted men surrounded the carriage. We traveled by night on rutted roads that were hardly more than paths, the horses' bits muffled with cloth to make our movement as quiet as possible. Each day before dawn we stopped at remote, dilapidated inns, where we were welcomed in such a way that I was certain we were expected. The carriage and horses were whisked off and I was shown to a room where I spent every minute until it was time to leave.

At each one, I ran the gauntlet of stares and whispers from the innkeepers and their wives, and a certain odd deference. The wives curtseyed. I saw more tears.

At the fourth inn, I rose early after a restless night. When I looked out the window, I saw the innkeeper and his wife standing on a nearby rise, their arms lifted above their heads, their faces turned towards the fading stars. I heard them speaking, but couldn't make out the words. She sobbed, and her husband appeared to be comforting her.

Just before we left, as I waited in the carriage for the men to mount up, the woman leaned in with a basket of bread and plums and a flask of tea. "We know you will bring her," she whispered, her gaze wide and haunted. "Nobody has had even a glimpse of her in eighteen years, but she will come out of hiding now that you have. I know she will. She will come to be with you. To protect you. She will clear away the dust and we will be forgiven for our sins."

I had no idea how to reply. At that moment the men set out and the carriage driver sent the horse trotting along with them. "Thank you for the food," I called. She remained standing by the steps, staring after me.

We avoided villages and towns, but once, the men chose to ride directly through the center of an abandoned village. Doors hung askew, windows were broken, weeds grew everywhere. The main road was rutted and overgrown. The only life we saw were birds and a couple of skinny feral dogs that growled and ran from us.

The mountains retreated into the northern horizon and our route descended into flatter land crisscrossed with rivers and lakes. The road petered out near the last inn. We left the carriage and I rode upon a horse, sitting in front of a burly black-bearded fellow with a gold hoop dangling from his left earlobe. Winding around his wrist and forearm like a bracelet was a purple, blue, and green tattoo of a snake, its tail tucked into its mouth.

Day by day, it grew colder. Snowdrifts piled in shaded spaces and weighted the branches of crowded spruce trees, but if ever I shivered, my pirate-protector draped his rich dark green cloak over my legs and across my chest so that nothing but my face was visible, and lent me the substantial warmth of his own body. The other men packed in close, a rider on either side though our path was narrow, others stretched before and behind. I'd read of such things. In the olden days, a "tail" of men accompanied Highland chieftains wherever they went. Having my own "tail" caused me to feel more certain than ever that Robert Louis was in truth the man I imagined him to be. I knew very well the Stevenson family was from Edinburgh rather than the High-lands, but the fantasy I lived in those days was too romantic, too bewitching to quash beneath the weight of reason. Knowing myself a fool for doing it, I nevertheless fabricated a detailed epic of love, danger, and the valiant hero who would give his life to protect his ladylove.

In time we came to a body of water that stretched as far as I could see, and which brought the distinct smell of the ocean to my nose. Huge ferries—the biggest ships I'd ever seen—made regular toll runs across the water, which the men simply called *The Sound*, but as we sat upon our horses looking down at the busy port, they decided crossing on one of those ferries was too risky, and chose instead to hire a private fisherman's seaworthy boat. He and his crew took us across at night, well north and out of sight of the ferry route; we reached land without incident or bad weather, before dawn.

Our travels, always doggedly south, now ranged through flat farmland that slowly lifted into hills and forests, uneventfully, for days and days. Monotony set in. I missed the sheer, cragged mountains I had grown up with and the smell of alpine air, not to mention Teófilo.

The adventure was wearing thin. Had I really longed to travel when I was younger? Now I only wished for respite.

My wish was granted in the dismal grey of dawn, a replica of countless dawns before it, as I traversed between dreams and waking, my head lolling against Blackbeard's chest. A quietly spoken order invaded my sleep; the horse beneath me drew up with a snort.

"Here at last." Blackbeard spoke with an accent I'd decided could be Spanish. "And you have been very brave, my gossamer princess." Leaping backward off the rear of his mount, he bowed in courtly fashion, sweeping out his cloak on one arm. I couldn't help laughing, as I'm sure he intended. He grasped me as I dismounted, steadying me around the waist. How good he smelled to me by this time, all sweat, leather, and cigarette smoke. How kind he'd been. He strolled with me, towering at my side like a cathedral; as my gaze left his face to take in my surroundings, I nearly gasped.

The rising sun cast vermilion light across the landscape. A formidable castle, in great red majesty, stood before us. It was more accurately a fortress, complete with window slits, a high battlement like that I'd left—though no gargoyles—and, wonder of wonders, a wide moat filled with water. A wooden drawbridge creaked and groaned as it lowered.

I had stepped back in time to King Arthur's Camelot.

Which naturally left me wondering…did Lancelot ride even now to join me?

Chapter 16

If I could have foreseen my fate, I might have protested that day at the chapel. I might have tried to flee into the forest or refuse my suitor's offer of marriage. From the moment I saw him striding over the hill towards my home, I was changed, and though my time at his fortress was not unpleasant, it was empty...of him. My first thought each day was the fervent wish that he would appear. Even my fears that he wasn't who he seemed, that he could, in fact, be violent, maybe murderous, could not stem the desire to be in the same room with him, to have those luminous brown eyes resting upon me.

My days were no longer solitary and I was not left to my own devices. Women lived here, three of them—a novelty in itself. They waited in a line for me that first morning as I crossed the lowered drawbridge with my bearded protector. The most elegant spoke. "I am Clotilda," she said. "Your husband's mother." Bending slightly, for she was tall and I short, she kissed me on each cheek. "That makes me your mother too. Your second mother." She took my hand from Blackbeard's and led me beneath a high lancet arch into a courtyard. Sweeping out one long, graceful arm festooned with creamy lace, she said, "This is my son's home, and now it is yours. He calls it *Möglichkeit*. Welcome, Zoë."

I fell in love with her instantly as I now suppose, at the advanced age of seventeen, is very common with twelve-year-old girls. She was the epitome of refinement and charm, in every aspect matching or surpassing my interior vision of the word "lady." Her head rested upon a neck I could only term swan-like. She kept her hair, of a lustrous brown like Robert Louis's, combed into a luxuriant pompadour, a velvet bow tucked at the back. Her white sloping shoulders, lovely bosom, and tiny waist were set off by a low-necked, form-fitting gown that fell to her ankles. When she gestured, the movement of her hands was reminiscent of a gentle ripple on the surface of a lake.

"Will he…will he come?" I ventured.

Her dark, radiant eyes reminded me of him. "As soon as he can." She touched the hair at my temple. "The moment it is safe, my dear."

As we crossed the flagstones to a set of double oak doors, she introduced me to the other women. "This is your sister-in-law," she said, clasping the younger woman's forearm. I guessed her to be in her twenties. Unlike her mother and brother, she was blonde and blue-eyed, with skin so fragile I detected a faint network of bluish veins beneath the surface.

"Beata." She curtseyed, holding out her embroidered skirts.

"I am Zoë," I returned, feeling the need to say something. I didn't attempt a curtsey since I'd never been taught how and, anyway, I was wearing trousers.

"This is Dagmar," Clotilda continued, motioning to the other woman. "She provides our meals, each more delicious than the last."

"Oh, *meine dame*." Dagmar tittered. A spotless apron draped the front of her homespun dress. Curtseying, she said, "*Willkommen, Fräulein*—er, Frau—"

"Never mind, Dagmar," Clotilda said.

I couldn't stop my eyes going wide at the formal and unfamiliar title given to married women. But I was married; Clotilda was my mother-in-law. I squared my shoulders and pretended I was comfortable with the term.

"Let's not stand around in the cold," Clotilda said briskly. "Dagmar, if you will direct the men to the kitchens, Beata and I will show Zoë her room. Would you bring tea when you can?"

"Of course, *meine dame*." Dagmar bobbed her head and scurried towards the drawbridge.

"You have had a long and tiring journey." Clotilda stroked my hair lightly. "Now you shall rest. We are going to do our best to make you happy here."

"Why does he call this place *Möglichkeit?*" I asked.

Her smile was tinged with sadness. "Because he believes in the possibility of things."

As Beata opened the door and we entered, I heard horses' hooves clatter against wood and, at last, the easy, stress-released laughter of the men as Dagmar invited them in for food and drink.

Chapter 17

CLOTILDA GAVE ME A SOUTHERN-FACING BEDROOM, CONTAINING A HUGE poster bed buried beneath vividly embroidered pillows and blankets, accented by a forest green spread. An exquisitely painted Japanese screen stood in one corner with a shiny brass tub tucked discreetly behind. The painting on the front of the screen depicted an Oriental woman in a fancy kimono, bent into an obsequious bow, arms outstretched, one hand holding an elaborate fan. Before her crouched a snarling tiger. The impression it gave was that the beast had just decided to reject her homage and was preparing to pounce. I could almost see its tail flick in anticipation.

There was a rocking chair, a freestanding mirror, a chest of drawers, a gargantuan wardrobe that swallowed my pitiful collection of clothing like a whale consuming plankton, and two nightstands, all made of cherrywood, I learned later. Each of the nightstands supported matching porcelain lamps. Thick Oriental carpets cushioned the stone floor and, on the east wall, a fireplace offered warmth and cheer.

The Schloss had been luxurious, but my bedroom small and austere. This was a palace by comparison.

"What have we here?" Clotilda asked that first night as she perched on the edge of the bed and glanced into my velvet bag.

I flushed a hundred shades of red. *My friend. Teófilo. The gargoyle from my roof.* No answer would do.

"Never mind," she said with a discerning glance, and pulled the drawstring, closing the bag. "I'll put it in the drawer so it is always near," and she did. She picked up my book. "This is everything you brought?" She opened the cover and thumbed through the pages. "A bag and a book?" Her rippling touch stilled.

"*'Being sent to the South is not much good unless you take your soul with you,'*" she read aloud. "*'And my soul is rarely with me here. I don't see much beauty. I have lost the key; I can only be placid and inert, and see the bright days go past uselessly one after another...'*"

She paused. Without looking up, she said, "My son feels this way sometimes. His responsibilities are...very difficult...and do not suit him." She did look up then. "He would much rather be here with you, Zoë. You make everything he does worthwhile."

How I loved her for saying that. She didn't have to. Some mothers would be jealous. Yet...I didn't believe her. How could I make anything worthwhile to a man such as he? I was a child, a skinny runt of a girl with no shape and baby-fine hair. He hadn't known I existed a month ago. Though my mind didn't believe, my soul fantasized.

I'd had a bath. Beata had combed my hair; it draped my shoulders, clean and glossy, like copper turned halfway to liquid. I'd been stuffed with sugared tea, slices of hot rye bread, and preserved peaches spiced with cinnamon and ginger. At Clotilda's invitation, I squirreled beneath the feather comforter.

When she left, she turned down the lamps but didn't snuff them. She kissed my forehead and tucked the blankets in around my shoulders. "Sleep well, *bienchen.*"

I did. I slept many hours, and did not dream.

Chapter 18

CLOTILDA WOULDN'T ALLOW ME TO LEAVE THE CONFINES OF THE FORTRESS.
I didn't mind, though the forest, pressing close to the walls, did call
out to me.

There was much to do inside. I helped Dagmar with the cooking
and baking, and the hours I spent with Clotilda and Beata in the
gardens, mulching and making decisions about spring planting, were
distracting and carefree. I loved being in the company of women—
perhaps I should say sane women. They had the supernatural ability to
discern almost every emotion and thought simply by observing me.
Years later, I learned to call this ability "empathy."

"Tell me about your life, Zoë," Clotilda asked as she opened a jar of
quartered apples and dumped them into a heavy ceramic bowl already
prepared with a rich pile of cinnamon, sugar, and cubes of butter.

"There's nothing to tell."

"Loneliness can create great things, I think."

How had she garnered that I was lonely?

"I understand you were tutored," Beata said as we cuddled kittens
in their basket by the fire. "What was your favorite subject?"

"Nature."

"You could be a botanist." Beata held a bottle of warm milk to the
weaker, smaller one's mouth. Latching on with her tiny white claws,
she drank happily. "That would be a wonderful thing."

All I'd said was "Nature." Yet she made my deepest desire seem plausible.

"Festival time in a week, Madam Zoë," Dagmar announced as she drew a sheet of golden rolls from her oven. The smell had drawn me—yeast and flour rising into the wonder of bread, a scent finer than almost any other in the world.

"Festival?"

"It's a tradition we have around here." She placed the rolls on the counter and wiped her hands on her pinstriped apron. "We call it *Skuldfest*. As the year draws to a close, we celebrate the unknowable future and do everything we can to placate the Norns so our destinies will be good."

"My tutor said only ignorant people believe in those legends. He called them silly. Skuld. She was the third Norn, wasn't she? Urd, Verdandi, and Skuld. Past, Present, and Future…?"

"Your tutor must be one of those science-loving sorts." Dagmar frowned as she plucked the hot rolls into a basket lined with a yellow and white checkered cloth. "True, it's an insignificant, local celebration. Actually, the Master—your husband—started it himself oh, about twenty years ago. Folk hereabouts look forward to it all year, and I wouldn't recommend going around calling it, or the people who take part in it, ignorant."

"That was rude. I'm sorry. I didn't think it was ignorant, but whenever I showed interest in something, he would make fun of me, so I would pretend I didn't think much of it either and then read about it in secret. Can I go?"

"Well, why not? You are part of our little world now." Dagmar's smile told me I was forgiven. "We'll dance and sing and feast, and wear our best costumes. I hope there's cheese. I know it isn't good for my digestion, but I do love it. You've never seen such fun. We'll light candles and pray for a fruitful year. The men wear masks with ram's horns and act like fools. So do the women, with their giggling."

She buttered a roll. It was pretty—three strips of dough woven into a perfect braid. And it was delicious. Soft and fluffy inside, with a crisp, buttery crust. I did enjoy the food she made. Clotilda was right—each meal was more delicious than the last.

"This Schloss sits right in the midst of our oldest legends," she told me. "It was here that witches and Valkyries were born." She proceeded to describe the Brocken, the highest mountain in the area, which was home to a fearsome gathering of witches every May Eve, and upon which lived magical rainbow giants that would sometimes lure unwitting hikers to their deaths. Dagmar told me countless stories of the Harz—she claimed it was the inspiration for most of the stories written by the Brothers Grimm.

"Oh, no," Clotilda cried at dinner that night when Dagmar brought up the festival. "You didn't tell Zoë she could go, did you?"

"Why, of course I did, Mistress." Dagmar's brows peaked. "Shouldn't I have?"

"No, no, you shouldn't, because she can't. It's far too dangerous."

"But can we not take guards with us?"

"Mama, perhaps it would be all right," Beata said. "If we go early, and stay just a little while."

Clotilda glanced at each of us. "Oh, he would forbid it if he were here. I know he would. It's a terrible risk."

I chewed my lower lip. Tears pressed against the back of my eyes, wanting to burst free, but I would never do that to Clotilda. For the first time this awesome fortress, that which Robert Louis called *Possibility*, closed in around me like a prison.

Beata voiced my inner thought. "Must she spend the rest of her life behind these walls? Punishment for doing nothing wrong. Is that what he wants for her?"

A fiery blush crept up Clotilda's translucent cheeks. She wrung her napkin in both hands.

"It's all right," I said quickly. Better to never see the light of day again than cause this wonderful woman anguish.

"No, it isn't," she returned in an oddly muffled voice. "You will go to *Skuldfest*. We'll all go. And we'll have a splendid time."

Chapter 19

Dagmar, an accomplished seamstress, made me several new outfits during those weeks—dresses similar to Clotilda's, though not low-necked or as sophisticated. Now that it was decided we would attend the winter festival, she eagerly went to work on a dirndl for me, cutting and sewing the dress out of supple black fabric with a square cut neckline, filled in with pleated ice-blue silk and three large blossoms, one yellow, one pink, and one purple. The skirt was full, fashioned to drape over three layers of stiff petticoats, and topped with an ice-blue silk pinafore. She found a black velvet belt and took it in so it would fit me. It was covered in gold tracery and tiny bells on a chain. The final touch was a large-brimmed black hat trimmed with braiding and a yellow silk flower. When I tried on the ensemble for the final fitting, I believed I outshone the sun.

No matter how many pins Beata used, none would hold my fine hair. An hour or so before we were to leave for the festival, she heated her round irons and transformed my straight locks into a lively profusion of waves and curls.

The girl staring from the mirror, hat tipped jauntily, reminded me of a picture I'd seen in my history book of Marie Antoinette. I didn't say anything of course, but for the first time in my life I considered myself, if not pretty, certainly passable.

If only Robert Louis could see me.

Dagmar was still stitching together my mask as Beata finished with my hair. Clotilda thought the mask would help keep me safe from unwanted attention. It was made of black velvet, with silk blossoms beside each eye, one of yellow and one of purple. Wearing it made me feel older, and mysterious. My three female friends were going to wear masks too, so I wouldn't stand out.

Just before we left, I opened the nightstand drawer. "I wish you were here," I whispered, brushing my fingers over the velvet bag. Almost wordlessly, I added, "I have not forgotten you, Teófilo."

Reverently touching the torn front cover of my Robert Louis Stevenson biography, I blew out the lamps, and left.

I'D NEVER BEEN TO A VILLAGE, OTHER THAN THE LONG-DESERTED ONES we'd gone through on our way to *Möglichkeit*, but I kept that to myself as I covertly examined the quaint houses with their thatch, and the shops, roofed with neat rounded tiles. Most of the shop windows were decorated with painted flower boxes and swinging wooden signs over the doors. *Apothecary. Millinery. Beer.* Someone had shoveled snow into discreet piles.

The cobbled market square was crowded with revelers. The women wore traditional costumes similar to mine. Some had on masks. Apparently, it was the custom for all the men to wear masks to this event. If that was so then men were everywhere, far outnumbering the women.

Colored paper shades turned the streetlamps to pastel rainbows, and there were many torches. Every now and then fireworks shot across the sky in dazzling sparks of red-blue, green-gold, and purple. A bonfire burned at the center of the square. I kept sniffing and sniffing for with each step a new smell introduced itself—sharp burning pine… sizzling meat…fried pastries…perfume…beer.

Street vendors offered food and drink. Clotilda bought us grilled sausages on hard rolls topped with sweet mustard, and cups of *glue-hwein*, which she said would help keep us warm.

The time came to beg mercy from the three Norns, who represented not past, present, and future as I had been told but more accurately fate, being, and necessity, although Dagmar said that was too simple a definition as well. Intertwining arms with our neighbors, we slid into a skipping sort of dance around the bonfire. On my right danced Beata and on my left Blackbeard, grinning his very white smile, and quite fearsome he looked beneath a huge ram's-horn crown. Those who knew the words sang to the omnipotent Fates, who tended and watered the sacred tree *Yggdrasil* and the *Urdrbrunnen*, the well holding the honey-water of life. The song seemed to hinge around pleading and forgiveness...of being given another chance—a chance that would not be squandered.

Despite my hat, mask, and the typical dress, I felt I was receiving special attention. Had I dribbled mustard on myself? When I glanced down and ran my hands over the material, everything seemed as clean as when we'd left the Schloss.

One unmasked woman gaped with such frowning intensity it left me blushing. Her male partner dragged her away. I wasn't certain, but it looked as though she'd begun to weep.

Why did the sight of me cause so many women to cry?

Perhaps the *gluehwein* affected my thinking, or maybe it was that I had never felt so free and unjudged. Blackbeard whispered jokes in my ear and I couldn't stop giggling. Clotilda gave me a startled glance from her place in the dance and I bit my lip, trying to force a return of propriety.

The musicians began playing more lively music and the circle broke. People milled and stumbled. Men seized women and pulled them into wild dancing. My grip on Beata's hand was severed and Blackbeard hoisted me away, swinging and twirling me like a top.

From the darkness of night came an undulating cloth dragon, its gold glittering scales reflecting the torchlight. I couldn't get a proper look at it because Blackbeard wouldn't give me a chance with all his circling. Every time it came into view it moved as things do in dreams, slow, detailed, the bottom edges of its fabric skin flapping as the line of people underneath swayed closer.

"Here she is," a male cried, very close.

I tried to discern the cause of the excitement, but the crowd had grown too thick. All I could see were masks. The shouts were deafening.

Blackbeard's grin vanished. He fumbled with his cape and, again with the slowness of a dream, I saw his hand emerge from the folds holding a long-barreled pistol. As I gawked, he smashed me against his broad stomach and backed away, taking me with him.

I didn't know whether to fight or assist him. The folds of his cloak hampered my ability to see.

"Get her," I heard—a voice of desperation.

"Stop it—leave us be!" This was a female. It sounded like Clotilda.

Blackbeard was locked in a fight for his life—and, perhaps, mine. His body jerked. I heard metallic scraping sounds, like steel on steel. We ran. His big hand gripped my delicate silk collar. I had no choice but to stumble along and try to keep on my feet.

A blast lit the night, nearly bursting my eardrums.

I fell—or was pulled down.

Something heavy fell on top of me.

I couldn't see, hear…or breathe.

There was only silence.

Chapter 20

I LAY ON THE GROUND, HELPLESSLY GASPING. A WHITE-FACED CLOTILDA knelt and seized my hand. Shadows moved restlessly. I couldn't tell what they were. I didn't care. Those first minutes I only cared about breathing.

"Hurry," a man said.

"We must go, *schätzlein*," Clotilda said urgently.

I sat up. Blackbeard sprawled beside me, mouth agape, eyes staring, blood pulsing from his temple. I wanted to weep, but I was too terrified.

The shadows came closer and became our grim-faced guards, brandishing pistols and knives.

"Where's Beata?" I asked as I rose to my feet.

"Safe—I think. Come, let's get you to the carriage."

"Wait—" One of the guards, a small, wiry man, rolled Blackbeard to one side then the other in order to free his great cloak. This he draped over my shoulders. "To help disguise you," he said before melting away.

We slipped through the dark like wolves, stealthily, our guards' knives intermittently catching the gleam of moonlight like a wolf's teeth.

"What happened?" I asked.

"Shh. They're everywhere, searching for us."

We found the carriage—it was not where we had left it before—and slipped in. Beata and Dagmar were inside already. Beata clasped my hands. Dagmar muttered prayers.

The guards mounted their horses and the driver spoke quietly to the dray. We moved through the night.

Behind us, fireworks continued to shower the heavens in merry color.

Chapter 21

Clotilda was too distraught to bother with questions. Beata supported her mother as they entered the Schloss.

"What happened?" I asked Dagmar, but she threw up her arms and wouldn't meet my eyes. "Not for me to explain. I must make tea for *meine dame.*" She left me.

"Best go to your room," one of the guards said as he unwound thick rope from a double hook beside the entrance to the fortress. The portcullis squealed as it descended. Four other men outside strained to raise the drawbridge. It didn't look like they believed the danger was over.

"But..." Nobody paid me any attention. I was in the way. Yet I deserved an explanation. Poor Blackbeard was dead. I could have died too—could the gunshot that killed him have been meant for me?

The men entered the courtyard and the portcullis finished descending with a thud. They pushed the heavy doors shut, barred them, and then moved off, talking among themselves. One, the short man who'd wrapped Blackbeard's cloak around me, threw me a glance. "There's nothing you can do," he said. I couldn't make out any details about him other than his height and build. Night disguised his hair color, his expression—everything that made a human individual. "Don't worry, young miss—we'll protect you."

"*Hist—*" One of the others grabbed his arm.

"Sorry."

They walked off, but the second one turned back long enough to say, "Please go to your chamber and stay there."

THE SCHLOSS SEEMED TOO SILENT. SOMEONE HAD LIT THE LAMPS AND THE fire in my room though, so it was pleasant and warm.

I saw myself reflected in the mirror, still swathed in the dark green cloak. It made me sad. I grieved for Blackbeard who, I assumed, still lay, abandoned, in the forest. Someone had to fetch him for a decent burial.

It was a sorry end to what I'd thought a harmless little adventure. I'd never experienced anything like the fun of dancing, eating, laughing with strangers, and sharing an invisible bond, like we were all in the same boat, to use a turn of phrase, linked through our human condition.

I'd also enjoyed feeling pretty. I tossed the cloak onto the bed and looked at my reflection. Dampness had unraveled the curls Beata had painstakingly created. My hair lay straight and tangled, and the dress's delicate silk collar was twisted and torn. Dirt smudged the ice-blue apron. My face had lost the transparent blush it acquired before we left. It now looked pale, thin, and dirty—my eyes big and dark.

Not ready to let the pleasure I'd felt slip fully into the past, I poured water and washed my face and hands. Picking up the silver-plated brush, I untangled my hair. I straightened the collar as best I could and scrubbed at the apron with a washcloth.

I was still pale…but passable. There was an echo of what I'd briefly acquired.

It was very late. Nothing to do now but put on my nightgown and go to bed.

As I turned from the mirror, the first blast struck the walls. My room was at the rear of the fortress. The sound was distant, the trembling slight, but I heard. And I knew what it was.

Chapter 22

Clotilda, Beata, and Dagmar came to my room. We huddled on the bed, listening to crashes and thuds.

"This fortress has stood for hundreds of years," Clotilda assured me. "It has repelled sieges before."

"Why are we being attacked?" I sensed their reluctance to hear the question, but I could no longer hold back. "I am shot at. The Schloss where I grew up—and this one—have been bombed. We traveled like fugitives all the way to *Möglichkeit*. People cry when they see me!"

"Hush, child." Clotilda kissed me on the forehead and patted my hand.

"No." I jumped off the bed. "You know what's going on—I'm the only one who doesn't."

"Tell her, Mama," Beata said.

Clotilda tensed her lips and shook her head. "Zoë…my son…his position is the sort that makes enemies. It's just too complicated. Rest assured, *schatzi*, our safety is utmost on his mind. We sent a messenger to him from the festival itself. He'll come, and rout these evil men, I promise."

"Like before." I couldn't quite pinpoint the problem but something about her explanation didn't square.

My suspicions were cut off when the fighting escalated. A cannon-ball struck and we could tell it was closer. Somehow it had cleared the outer walls. The floor shuddered. Six porcelain dolls along the top of the mantel rattled. One fell and shattered on the tiles in front of the fireplace.

"Mama!" Beata cried.

Clotilda embraced her daughter. Dagmar pulled out her rosary, closed her eyes, and frantically crossed herself, mumbling, "*Misericordias Domini…miserere nostri.*"

Another blast rocked the chamber, and another. Two more dolls fell and broke. A set of sleigh bells hanging by the window chimed.

The door crashed open. One of the guards ran in, his face blackened by gunpowder. A stench of smoke entered with him. "All is lost. Come —to the passage—the walls are destroyed!"

I heard Beata sob as we raced through the corridors. I had no idea where the guard meant to take us, but Clotilda seemed to know. We descended several flights of stairs, retreating to the rear of the fortress. The halls narrowed and darkened. They smelled dank, long-abandoned. At last, we entered a small round chamber with no furniture and only one window. Blue-green spruce branches almost touched the glass. This room must sit right up against the wall.

Clotilda pushed a wooden panel beneath the window. It appeared exactly as the others, yet a cleverly hidden trapdoor slid open in the floor.

"Hurry." The guard knelt by the opening as one by one we descended an iron ladder. "Good luck," he added, making no move to join us.

"Isn't he coming?" I discerned a hint of mounting hysteria in my voice and swallowed.

"He must close the door," Clotilda said.

"But he'll be killed," I whispered. "They'll all…"

No one answered. The door slid shut, locking us in darkness. Clotilda struck a match against the stone wall and lit a lantern. Her face, in the dim flickering light, seemed pallid, the set of her lips nervous.

"Follow me," she said.

Chapter 23

The lantern revealed an eerie passageway, casting light where we stood, turning to impenetrable black within a few steps. The rough stone walls ran with water in places. My shoes squished against soggy earth. It smelled close and damp and green. Not a sunlit meadow green, which I've always equated with pure warm joy. The green smell of this underground tunnel was tinged with moss, mold, and slimy wet creatures. It was cold. The earth pressed in like it wanted to crush us. Sounds echoed—our breathing, footsteps, the brush of clothing, Beata's quiet sobs, Dagmar's whispered prayers. Only Clotilda kept quiet. I sensed she was mustering her strength.

Just as I wondered how long we would be stuck in this claustrophobic wormhole, I realized the light coming from the lantern was dimmer. Beata and Dagmar's features were easier to see. Pale, aqueous light pierced the darkness and I heard a muffled, continuous roar that sounded like rushing water.

The passage veered to the right. We clambered over loose rocks and our tight breathless corridor unfurled into a cavern so vast I could not see the ceiling or the far walls. Intermittent squeaks and fluttering betrayed the presence of bats.

A cataract of water flowed across the cave mouth as smoothly as what might pour from the lip of a pitcher. Early morning light filtered through, white and shining, dancing like a party of drunken sprites against the walls.

"Where are we?" I asked.

"About a mile from the Schloss," Clotilda said.

"Wish I'd brought food," Dagmar said.

Clotilda dropped onto a boulder, sighing, and pushed back her damp hair. I'd never seen her disheveled or tired. It made her even more likeable, more human. "He'll come," she said, with no hint of doubt.

Beata settled at her mother's feet. I knew by now that she was twenty-six. I had often wondered why she never married, since she was quite pretty and congenial, but as usual, I didn't ask. The way she pressed against Clotilda's legs made her seem much younger. Clotilda absently stroked her daughter's head.

I walked to the cave mouth. The torrent poured into a lake, surrounded by pines, firs, and patches of snow.

None of us had brought cloaks. I still wore the fancy festival dress. Goose bumps rose on my legs and the back of my neck. I rubbed my arms and faced something I'd pushed away ever since we raced from my bedroom with the guard.

I'd left behind Teófilo and my book about Stevenson.

My only possessions. All in the world that connected me to my precious memories.

"Teófilo," I whispered.

I leaned my head against the cold wet rock and closed my eyes.

A horse whinnied.

I opened my eyes and stared into *his* face, distorted by the fall of water between us.

Chapter 24

He stepped through and stood beside me.

"Zoë. Zoë."

I couldn't speak.

Robert Louis grasped my arms. His eyes were wide and in them, I saw fear. The entire world was locked in his gaze.

He lifted his hands and cupped my cheeks. His warm palms made me realize how cold I was. I began to believe him not a dream.

Next thing I knew he'd pulled me to his chest, burying me in warm wool, the scent of tobacco, and the frantic hammering of his heart. Instead of all the logical things I might be thinking, my mind ridiculously focused on how he'd come through the waterfall without getting wet.

"Zoë," he whispered.

At last, the something that had frozen inside when Blackbeard drew his pistol, broke…and melted. The terror I'd harnessed rushed like soundless wind and I began to shake. I squeezed my eyelids tightly shut and lifted my arms—high, for he was tall compared to me —and wrapped them around his neck. My feet left the ground as he picked me up, saying something, but I couldn't sort out the words. It was a murmur of reassurance and, I suppose, it didn't matter what he said. Still, I wish I could remember.

After a moment I felt strong enough to stand on my own. I swiped at the tears on my cheeks and released a volley of rage and fear.

"We forgot to bring coats and food. We're wet—and—and I think the guards are dead. We were attacked—and they—they killed Blackbeard—"

"Blackbeard?" He shook his head.

"The big guard—with the—with the black beard—"

"Oh. Amos." His demeanor grew even more grief-stricken.

My mouth snapped shut. Amos. Blackbeard had a name. I blushed to my very scalp and turned away. "I'm grateful to be alive," I whispered.

Chancing a glance, fearful of what I might see written on his face, I was instead shocked again into silence. He was terribly pale and trembling. He reached out, seized my hand, and, covering it with his other, rubbed hard, sending warmth in a magical renewing drench clear to my core.

"But you…you're not hurt?" He touched my cheekbone, reminding me of the scrape I'd suffered earlier when I'd stumbled against the passage wall. "You're…all right?"

"Yes. Yes, I'm fine." I clenched my hands, horrified that I'd blamed him for what had happened.

Relief washed over him in a shudder. He closed his eyes, embraced me, and kissed the top of my head.

Fierce emotion shot through my body. All my life, I'd been a nuisance, a pest. Underfoot. A throwaway.

Now, for the first time, I mattered. I mattered to Robert Louis. More than his destroyed house, his murdered guards, more than anything. I was alive. Unharmed. And all was right with his world because of it.

Chapter 25

Robert Louis led us from the cave by way of a hollow beneath a rock ledge where one could slip through without getting wet. Outside, five mounted men escorted us away from that place. The first night we camped in a small clearing—the men set up tents for us women—and as we warmed ourselves by the fire, another rode in, leading four fresh horses.

Robert Louis met his man at the edge of the clearing. I watched from my spot by the fire, wondering what they were saying, especially when I saw Robert Louis's face relax into a brilliant smile. The man dug something out of his stuffed saddlebags and handed it over. I didn't have to wonder what it was for long; Robert Louis returned to the fire, sat beside me, and presented me with my velvet bag and Stevenson biography.

I wanted to hug him. I had done so in the cave, but embarrassment and timidity had since revived and I could barely meet his gaze.

Opening the velvet bag, I put my hand inside, filtering granite fragments through my fingers. Robert Louis opened the book, his smile lingering. Softly he quoted, in English, without looking at the page.

Be it granted me to behold you again in dying,
Hills of home! And to hear again the call;
Hear about the graves of the martyrs the peewees crying,
And hear no more at all.

I think my heart shivered to a complete stop.

He ran his fingertips down the side of my face, his gaze following his touch.

I swallowed—chokingly—and returned my own quote, also in English, one which I thought matched his.

The hue of Highland rivers
Careering, full and cool,
From sable on to golden,
From rapid on to pool—
The hue of heather-honey,
The hue of honey-bees,
Shall tinge her golden shoulder,
Shall gild her tawny knees.

If I had experienced doubts, in my bed in the dark of night, about this man's identity, they now vanished. He was Robert Louis Balfour Stevenson...resurrected through some incomprehensible magic. Journeyed from the dead to be my guardian angel. He even spoke English with an accent I was sure must have its source in Scotland.

The fears my mother had tried to plant in my mind floated away with the sparks off the fire.

I opened my mouth to shout his name, to see his eyes light with pride at my perspicacity, but no words formed. Yes, I wanted to cry out, *You're Robert Louis Stevenson!* And no, I didn't. Both urges were so strong they left me mute. My throat squeezed shut. I realized what I was afraid of.

Breaking the spell.

Teófilo died and Robert Louis appeared. My life had shattered then glued itself feebly together that day the soldiers attacked my home. I'd given Fate another chance because of this man. It was magic, him appearing and taking me away.

If I asked, if I said his name aloud, I might wake up. The magic might end.

The practical side of me offered another avenue. *Just a little while longer*, it advised. *Ask him tomorrow—maybe next week.*

His head tilted. "Do you know the book inside and out?" He placed it with care into my hands.

I stroked the torn cover, wishing for the millionth time that it could be restored, so I could at least say to myself, *Here is proof. Do you see? You are he and he is you.* "Much of it."

Earlier, he had gone off a little way with his mother. I watched them, noting their serious expressions. I assumed she was telling him about the attack, but perhaps not, because after he regarded the fire for a moment, he said, "Zoë, those men who bombed your home had false information that I was there. It was me they hoped to harm or kill. The same thing happened at *Möglichkeit*. You've been unlucky enough to be in both places when they came after me. I'm the cause of you being frightened and distressed, and I am so sorry."

"Is that why—why women cry when they see me?"

He looked away, back into the fire. "These rural folk are simple people. They get up with the sun and go to bed with the moon, and they are weaned on tales of witches and magic. I cannot say what goes on in their minds. I hope you won't let their mystic beliefs get you down. Our people love their legends."

Firelight glinted in his eyes. I felt certain he was not telling me everything. He probably thought me too immature, incapable of understanding grim reality.

Is it the same magic that brought you back to life? I wanted to say. *If so, I believe in magic too.*

We sat there a long time after the others retired. Together we watched the fire die. Above us, the full moons of winter voyaged across the black-ink sky, and I heard music—nothing like Mozart or Chopin or anything normally called music. I believe the sound came from the movement of the earth, a tingling love song conducted between it and the heavens and every growing thing, and was something that could never be heard except on very rare occasions of perfect harmony.

Chapter 26

CLOTILDA, BEATA, AND DAGMAR LEFT US AFTER THREE DAYS. ROBERT Louis explained that they would travel to one of his homes in the city, in order to give the impression that everything was fine. If asked, they would offer subterfuges concerning his whereabouts.

Clotilda hugged me and kissed my cheeks. "Take care, my darling. Put absolute faith in my son."

I failed to stifle tears. "I will miss you. Thank you. Thank you for everything."

"We will see each other again," she promised.

Dagmar slipped a few chocolates into my pocket and Beata said she would show me the wonders of the city when these troubles were over.

They and three of Robert Louis's men took the eastbound road. The rest of us melted into the forest and journeyed single-file southward along a deer track.

Yes, I know the first night after Robert Louis found us in the water cave and brought us away, I resolved to trust him. After all, my mother was crazy, while his mother...I had never known anyone with such a level head. Logic demanded I put faith in Clotilda rather than the incoherent woman who had borne me, yet...doubts and fears returned, however reluctantly. At night they roused and nibbled at my senses.

You're nothing but payment, my mother had said. *They will never let you go.*

Even if I didn't want to listen to my mother's warnings, there had also been the day I'd eavesdropped on the servants in the kitchen. *You don't think anybody cares about her, do you?* one of them had said scornfully, adding, *Especially him?*

I knew I was the her, and Robert Louis was the him.

Lying on frozen ground did not contribute to peaceful sleep. I spent hours pondering my situation. At last, I realized what didn't strike true about the explanations Clotilda and Robert Louis had given me. Clotilda said *Möglichkeit* was under siege because of her son. She claimed he had enemies. Robert Louis said something similar.

But he hadn't been there—nor had he been at my childhood home when it was attacked. The only person in common with both sites during both attacks was me.

The other nagging thing was my mother. She had sought me out. I witnessed her desperate struggle to communicate. She battled to get her message across and I felt compelled to give it consideration.

My home had been assaulted, not once but twice. Who were the attackers? What did they want? Why was it safe for Clotilda and Beata to go to the city but not me?

Throughout this adventure I'd denied what my innermost instincts screamed. I was the target of the attacks. Everyone wanted to protect me from this knowledge.

But truth it was, and if so, I must overcome my innate reluctance to confront, and discover why.

Chapter 27

Surprisingly, Robert Louis stayed with us as we traveled, always south, sticking to forests and back roads, journeying by night and concealing ourselves by day at certain out-of-the-way inns where he was treated like royalty, his every soft-spoken request instantly fulfilled.

One early morning, shortly after we'd arrived at an inn and the horses had been led away to be curried and fed, we had a scare. A company of armed men rode into the courtyard, their horses' hooves clattering against the cobblestones. Robert Louis slipped to the window, eyes narrowing, nostrils flaring like a hungry carnivore scenting meat. He ordered me in a low, urgent voice to follow the innkeeper's wife. That woman led me into the kitchen and struggled with the lid on a big chest as the men swung off their horses and inter-rogated the innkeeper.

"Has anyone come this morning?" I heard one ask sharply.

"No, *Herr Rittmeister*," the innkeeper replied.

I heard shuffling—drawers opening, chairs scraping on the floor.

"*Meine Dame,*" the innkeeper's wife whispered. "Get into the chest."

I heard no more as the heavy lid closed. I lay in darkness, legs curled against stomach, barely able to breathe, and tried not to think about being locked in a box. Silence hummed. I lost track of time.

When the lid opened at last, I blinked, blinded by sudden light, and gulped deep breaths before even trying to determine who had found my hiding place. The innkeeper's wife come to release me…or the men Robert Louis obviously considered a threat?

Thankfully, it was Robert Louis himself. He helped me climb out, his face relieved but grave.

"What happened?" It seemed an oft-asked question, yet seldom was it answered to my satisfaction.

"Those men were searching for us." He offered me a chair at the kitchen table. "I believe they would have found us but for our hostess's quick thinking." He laughed and the stress melted from his face.

She stood by the oven. When he said this, her cheeks flushed and she tittered.

"What did you do?" I asked.

She waved dismissively. "*Ha*, nothing."

Robert Louis answered. "They came in here. I'm certain they would have opened the chest but just before they entered, she disrobed. They were so surprised—and she made quite a screeching fuss—that they retreated."

"Did they find you?" I asked.

"Oh, *gnädige Frau*," the woman said, "if they'd found him, he'd be swinging—"

"Enough, Frau Gontermann." Robert Louis turned to me. "Are you all right, Zoë?"

"Yes, sir."

He sat down. Frau Gontermann brought us strong coffee in big round earthenware cups. I stirred sugar into mine as Robert Louis continued. "I must ask you to be very brave, because we need to be more careful."

Whenever his eyes met mine like this, my doubts faded into nonexistence, only to rouse again when he wasn't by my side giving me the benefit of his poet's gaze.

"Why…" I struggled through trepidation, swallowed, and forced the words out quickly. "Why do these men keep following you? Why do they want to hurt you? I—it feels like they want me, too, for some reason."

I wanted to say, *If it's only you they want, wouldn't I be safer if we split up?* I couldn't think of a way to ask without it sounding like I didn't want to be with him.

Such a profound expression of sorrow and guilt swept over his face that I felt sick. What had I done? I never should have—

He held my hand. "This is the hardest question I have ever faced."

"Nev-never mind. I—I'm sorry—I—"

"It's all right, Zoë. This is my fault, not yours. I hoped—wanted—well, there's no help for it. They only want you because they think they can constrain me—break me, even—by threatening you."

"But—why? I'd never even met you when my home was attacked."

"Oh, but I have known you, Zoë, all your life." One hand held mine and the other raked through his hair, giving me the impression that he was nervous. "I held you when you were a baby, at your christening."

I gaped at him. I'm sure I looked quite the fool.

He frowned and seemed to make a decision. "We were betrothed before you were born. It was common knowledge. And because of it, you have been dragged into my troubles. I can never make this up to you." His gaze broke from mine and he closed his eyes. "I am so sorry. About everything. About more than I can say."

"But—" I stopped, hating myself for forcing him to speak of things that brought such sadness. I vowed then and there that I would never question him again. Screwing up my determination, I said, as calmly as I could, "Don't be sorry. I wouldn't want to be anyplace else but here. With you."

He smiled. "You're very kind."

"Sir?" One of the men stuck his head around the kitchen door. "We're not agreeing on the best route. Would you come?"

Robert Louis paused, glancing at me.

I nodded. "I'm fine."

Giving my hand one last squeeze, he left the kitchen.

Chapter 28

MY BOTTOM HAD RUN THE GAMUT OF PAIN. STIFF, SORE, AND FINALLY numb, it at last grew accustomed to constant nightly riding. Robert Louis taught me how to properly sit a horse and avoid the worst of the abrasion. As the days slipped by my body adjusted to life in the saddle and I experienced inordinate pride in my ability to travel for long hours without complaint, though I did worry that my legs might permanently bow like cowboys in the American Old West. Thankfully, the man who raided *Möglichkeit* after the siege brought more than Teófilo and my precious book. I now had trousers and a long leather coat, split up the back so I could wear it while riding. One of the others purchased a man's felt hat in a village we passed. When I donned it, I resembled a boy more than a girl, and was delighted by Robert Louis's approving grin.

I longed to be no trouble, to be someone he could admire.

The Harz mountains became a distant memory as we wandered through farmland, then up again into hills and deep forests. The land was beautiful, cloaked as it was in snow, and often, in the distance, we saw castles topped by spired turrets. When our route brought us near roads or towns, we traveled quietly, alert to any sound of approaching wagons or horses. If we did hear something we simply became part of the forest. Dressed as we were in mottled brown and white, it wasn't hard. One time however, during a thick muffling snowfall, a group of about twenty men, riding hard, nearly surprised us. I glimpsed the leader's face as they passed. Though shadowed by a visored military cap, one eye covered with a black patch, it was mesmerizing. Frightening. Thick white scars gnarled it into a grotesque distortion. His hands, encased in leather gauntlets, held the reins lightly, yet gave the impression of ruthless determination, though this might have been caused by the merciless whipping of an already lathered horse.

I shivered then forced myself into stillness, afraid I might reveal our position.

We crept out of hiding. "Karl von Bäumer," Robert Louis said quietly. "They've sent their best."

"He is an enemy?"

"Oh, yes, to both of us. He has recently been given a promotion. That makes him even more dangerous, for he will want to prove himself. Von Bäumer cannot be allowed to capture us."

Later, as we roasted a hare upon a small campfire, I felt him studying me. I hoped my face was clean.

"What do you want to do with your life?" he asked. "Is there a field in which you excel?" His regard was attentive, as though my answer held great interest for him. "Something you would enjoy, something fulfilling?"

"I—I thought maybe…I'd like to work…with trees—somehow."

He made an adjustment to the spit so dinner wouldn't burn then returned his gaze to me, murmuring, "It is perfect. Trees. We must make it happen."

"Well, but—"

"Yes, Zoë?"

"I—I—" My face felt as though it might be boiling. I couldn't say it —*Won't I have to keep your house and bear children?*

Reaching over the flames, he plucked a golden leg off the hare and gave it to me. "Careful. Don't scald yourself."

I took it with a grateful smile. I was starving as usual. Dagmar had wondered if I had a tapeworm, for I ate and ate without ever fleshing out. Oh, I remember every moment of that night, even now. There's nothing that wakes the appetite like being out of doors for hours, trapping your food, spitting it and smelling it roast, hearing the fat drip and sizzle. I still do it sometimes, for it brings back those days, but now…I'm not so skinny.

Chapter 29

From time to time, I wondered if Robert Louis meant us to continue this journey forever. I was torn, sometimes weary of being cold, dirty, and hungry, and sometimes enthralled by the adventure.

One night we crossed a river on a flatbed ferry just beyond the reach of the torchlight glimmering above us on a stone bridge. We heard men up there talking among themselves—soldiers, one of the guards whispered. I prayed our horses wouldn't give us away, and they didn't, being content with feedbags. Robert Louis tried to pay the farmer after we reached the far side, but the man shook his head, penniless as he obviously was, grinned, and set his long pole into the mud, shoving off and vanishing into darkness.

We had navigated too many streams and rivers on our journey to keep track of, especially in the beginning. There was always a ferryman waiting to transport us. I thought it serendipity, until one of Robert Louis's men told me that the proprietors of every inn we sheltered at sent word ahead to the next crossing. It would have taken only one to betray us, but none ever did. For some reason, these country people trusted Robert Louis, and were willing to risk all in order to help him. The realization helped me with my trust, as well.

The rest of that night we rode beneath the intermittent glow of our two moons, the jagged fracture in the farthest accentuated by racing clouds in a rising wind. At dawn we entered countryside blanketed in fresh snow.

What remains vivid in memory is what happened as a frigid silver-blue morning descended around us. We were discussing how long it would take to reach the nearest friendly inn. The men always seemed to know exactly where these could be found. My stomach growled in anticipation of breakfast.

We came alongside a dense mixed forest. Since it was early and no one seemed to be about, we kept to the outer perimeter where the going was easier. I spotted a grey granite wall running through the depths of the winter-stripped trees. Obviously neglected, it rose quite high and forbidding in places and in others was crumbled nearly to the ground. As we rode along, I glimpsed a scrawl of charcoal too faded to read but for one word—*schwein*.

Robert Louis angled us closer, finding a faint path among the trees.

Hair lifted on my scalp as a couple of ravens shrieked and darted up from a roofless, half-disintegrated white building that hugged an iron-barred, chained, and padlocked gate. My mare shook her head, shied, and chewed the bit. She abruptly halted, her front legs stiff and unyielding. I had to force her to go on.

No one spoke now of inns or breakfast. A feeling of disquiet passed invisibly between us. My senses heightened to an acute pitch.

The wall accompanied us like a huge grey open eye. Yes, it felt like the wall was a living, malevolent entity. Breathing. Biding its time. I wanted to ask what it was and why it was there, yet my mouth was too dry. I was too afraid.

In the spots where the wall had collapsed, I could see through. There was no house or castle as I had assumed there would be, but rather a flat open arena. On the far side was a white square tower with a pointed dark roof, which reminded me of the fairy tale *Rapunzel*.

We came into a small clearing. It held just one thing—a tiny, round building of faded wood. Several gaping holes marred its snow-covered dome, shaped like an onion. Off to the left, a depression in the snow suggested another path. Robert Louis made his way there and we followed. Where were we going? I didn't know. No one spoke, so I didn't either.

The path was short, emerging into another clearing, one that contained a rectangular brick building with a dilapidated chimney.

Smoke had not escaped through it in a long time, if the bird nests poking out the top were any indication.

Robert Louis dismounted. He stepped over some debris, broken stones and such, and approached the open maw—once a doorway—directly beneath the chimney. There was an evergreen wreath dotted with holly berries and a purple ribbon propped against the edge, and a cairn of round pebbles. There were several of these doorless openings, all obscured by snowdrifts.

My hands clenched on the reins. I stood in the stirrups and forced myself to look away, searching for something to ease these irrational fears. There were no people here, of that I felt certain. Still, I was terri-fied. I wanted to shout, *Don't go in there!*

Because the trees on the west side of this clearing were thinner and leafless, and a lot of the grey wall toppled into low piles of rubble, I could see almost all of the area it once contained. Wind keened softly as it blew through an inner fence made of solid posts and barbed wire.

Two fences. Had they kept something in, or out? Along the oppo-site wall, beyond a ditch and spaced at regular intervals, I saw the remains of three towers like the one I'd noticed earlier. In the center of this large, flat expanse, two uniform rows of cement foundations thrust through the snow, a double line of naked poplars between them. At the far end there was a large white structure. From here I could tell little more than that the windows were shattered and the door swung in the cold morning breeze.

My gaze returned to Robert Louis. One of his hands was pressed against the wall by the doorway. His head was turned down. I couldn't tell if his eyes were open or shut.

"Come, Miss." A fellow by the name of Hubert swung his horse away and I reluctantly followed. We stopped at the far edge of the clearing. One of the men remained, holding Robert Louis's horse.

The whole morning had become icy-bleak and desolate. Then something happened that made the hair rise on my scalp and sent a terrible shiver racing down my spine.

The poplars.

As the cold breeze heightened into moaning wind, I heard their clear whisper.

Beware this place, Zoë.

The sky darkened.

Robert Louis entered the building.

Chapter 30

A HALF-HOUR PASSED BEFORE MY HUSBAND—*MY HUSBAND*—HOW HARD IT was to use that title—reappeared, walking haltingly, stumbling once over the rubble. As he took the reins from his man, he paused, pressing a hand over his eyes, and stood a moment, motionless. Then he and his guard mounted and rode to us.

I didn't like his expression. I was familiar with his thoughtful gravity, but there was anguish in the set of his mouth that I'd never seen before. The eyes that I considered beautiful beyond compare, expressive, inviting, concerned, sincere and direct, were shuttered. Closed. Blank.

I wanted to cry. Where was he, the man I'd adored from the time I'd first read *A Child's Garden of Verses*? Where had he gone in that half-hour? He was injured in some way, by the place he'd just left. Why hadn't I heeded the warning of the trees? I should have whipped my horse back to the building. I should have insisted that he come away with me—I should have forced the issue.

Glaring at the cold, sterile building, I barely suppressed the urge to spit. Indeed, I had been clairvoyant when I'd imagined the malevolence of the wall. Robert Louis still breathed, moved, and guided his horse, but I wasn't sure if he still lived.

Screwing up every iota of courage I could muster, I reached out and touched the back of his hand.

For an instant I wasn't sure if he knew who I was. His eyes closed tightly and his mouth tightened.

I withdrew. I'd angered him. I shouldn't have presumed…

His hand came out and seized mine so hard it nearly cracked the bones. He loosened his grip after a moment, but didn't let go. I stared at him, fearful, worried, castigating myself for making whatever had happened worse.

I could not name the emotion that flooded across his face. Then, *Teófilo*, I thought. I wasn't sure why my old friend entered my mind at that moment. Perhaps because Teófilo had looked at me like that when I'd been unhappy about something, or frightened, or lonely. Ardent, is what I'd call it now. I didn't have that word then.

"Zoë," he whispered.

And he continued to hold my hand, almost desperately, as we traveled away from that terrible place.

Chapter 31

I'D WASHED, EATEN, AND SLEPT. THE ROOM I'D BEEN GIVEN AT THIS INN held a battered old dressing table complete with a splotched mirror. Though by almost anyone's standards I'd been living in poor conditions, exposed to the elements, stuck in a saddle for hours on end, normal sleeping patterns disrupted, I didn't look bad. And I stared at myself most critically. There was a becoming bloom to my cheeks I couldn't remember ever seeing before. The skin beneath my eyes had lost the purple-tinged shadows that had always been there. My cheekbones didn't seem to stick out quite so painfully. Could I actually be gaining weight?

Plucking my brush from the saddlebag, I untangled my wet hair until it dried to the hue of a copper pfennig.

Cold white moonlight sparkled against the snow outside. I snuffed the candle so the moonlight could come in. It blanketed the room in shadow and light, like the inside of a cloud that's thinking about becoming stormy.

We would be leaving soon. Robert Louis wanted to put the Alps behind us.

A knock sounded softly against the door. "Zoë?"

I rose. "I'll be ready in a minute." I ran to the saddlebags and shoved my hairbrush inside.

There was a pause. "May I speak to you?"

I opened the door. "Of course." I gestured to the dressing table stool, the only thing resembling a chair in the room, and rushed to relight the candle.

He sat and so did I, on the edge of the bed, bracing my hands on my leather-covered knees.

How quiet and pale he looked. Tired, too. "Did you sleep?" I asked.

"No." He lit a cigarette. "Have you studied history, Zoë?"

I swallowed, suddenly nervous. "Well," I stammered, "it wasn't especially my fa-favorite subject."

"Trees were."

"Ye-yes. My tutor didn't like history either, so we didn't spend much time on it."

"That's too bad. History is more important than we sometimes realize. Understanding our history can help us avoid making the same mistakes as our ancestors. You see, Zoë, the key to our future is found actually, in our past."

I nodded, even as I wondered if I should say something. I propped my left ankle on my right knee and fiddled with the lacing on the front of my boot.

"Humans are the only creatures on earth who willfully torture others of their own kind," he said, not looking at me now but at the floor. "Who, without remorse, use and injure others to benefit themselves. Who kill…" his voice dropped to a near whisper, and it sent a shiver through me, "for pleasure."

I thought of that silent grey wall. The decayed brick building.

He sighed, lifting his shoulders and rolling his head from side to side as though he was in pain. I got up and crossed to him, extending my hand gingerly, ready to retreat at the slightest sign of annoyance, and rubbed the back of his neck.

His eyes closed and he dropped his head forward. "Oh, Zoë. If it weren't for you, I don't know that I could go on."

What have I done for you? I almost asked, but bit back the question. It was too nice to feel needed and important. How vulnerable the back of his neck seemed. From the front he was a man who inspired confidence, but from this angle he seemed younger. Someone who could have fears and insecurities like me. Someone who could make mistakes, who could weep.

"All human beings must be equal," he said after a moment. "Equal in dignity and importance. Equal in their choices."

I paused in my rubbing, but he didn't move, so I started again. "Yes," I said hesitantly. "That's logical. All mankind—"

"No." His head swiveled and he stared at me, his eyes as dark and deep as underwater caves, yet brilliant like the dazzle of sunstruck gems. That was what I thought then. Now I consider the comparison flawed, for gems are dead things. What made Robert Louis's eyes unique was their fierce and uncompromising life. "No, Zoë. *Not* mankind. *All* human beings. Too much evil has been done with those kinds of phrases."

I backed away but he caught my forearm. "Humans have lost their humanity," he said. "If we don't reclaim it now, it's the end. For all of us."

"What are we if n-not human?" I dreaded showing a lack of wit, but the passion in his face and voice demanded that I give my all to understanding.

"Mechanical devices. Faulty instruments, no connection to anything, no reason to breathe. I see it in their eyes—there's nothing. They're dead but they don't know. The earth gasps but they can't hear. We're poisoned, Zoë. I know it because of you."

"M-me?"

"I was dying…like they are. I swear…I'll live up to you. You and I will return humanity. We can—if you will help me. But it has to be your choice. That's everything. Never accept any less, Zoë. Will you promise? Never do anything that isn't your choice."

Chapter 32

Only a couple of things stand out in my memory about the next part of our journey. For days we rode south, headed for the ominous mountains that would surely prove our greatest challenge, I thought at the time. We would not be able to use any of the established routes and so our journey would be much more treacherous, especially at this time of year. The men purchased heavier clothing and blankets for the horses. The Alps never seemed to get any closer, then suddenly we were climbing, and the night sky, when it wasn't cloudy, had too many stars to comprehend.

"Do you know Arcturus, the red star?" Robert Louis asked our first night in the mountains. We had walked away from our fire to see the heavens more clearly.

"No."

"Follow the handle on the Big Dipper." He pointed.

"Ursa Major," I whispered.

"Yes, see?"

I followed the trail of his finger down the handle and a little farther. There was no mistaking the star. Its brilliance was hard to miss at this altitude.

"Do you see?"

"Yes. It really is red."

"Arcturus has been my guiding light for a long time. I follow it as men followed King Arthur and his sword Excalibur."

My tutor had not wanted to spend time on the silly legend of a king, a sword, a chalice, and adultery. I'd had to read about Arthur and his knights on the sly by pilfering books from the big library I wasn't allowed to use. The story sparked my imagination. The round table! The Grail! Lancelot and Guinevere! Poor, heartbroken Arthur!

"The name Arcturus has a loose meaning of guardian bear, and Arthur was known as the Bear of Britain." He paused for a long time. "I would like to live up to him, if I can."

He gazed at the stars and I gazed at his shadowy profile. *You have*, I wanted to say. *You and he are the same. Brave and true.* But I was too timid.

The weather worsened. The passes were most dangerous, for they were heavily guarded. Robert Louis used a mixture of bribery, deceit, and stealth to bring us through without being caught, but there was a confrontation on our last night, when we had almost achieved our goal. Robert Louis and his men fought fiercely and bravely. Still, we barely escaped, and three died. He only fought because he was forced. He fought to protect me, his men, and our freedom. I want that clearly understood.

One morning while we waited for his scouts to return, Robert Louis and I walked out onto a bluff. A frozen river ran beneath us through a gorge, catching and reflecting the newborn sunlight in a blinding glitter. On the opposite side stood a white castle, rising out of the mountain upon which it had been built. Early morning mist drifted around the pointed turrets, round towers, and battlements. The castle loomed protectively over its village, a quiet place of tiled roofs and evergreens. In spring and summer, it surely blazed with every flower imaginable, but currently all lay dormant beneath a glistening quilt of snow.

"It's so pretty," I said.

He took my mittened hand in his. "At one time," he said, his breath floating in steamy clouds, "a duke or prince would have lived there. Maybe even a king, whose life would be dedicated to a noble goal. He followed a hero's journey."

"What was the goal?"

"Rescuing the princess from the dragon, of course." His mouth curved into the smile that made my heart beat faster. "Through her rescue, he saved himself, the world, and every creature, past, present, and future. He gained honor, joy…and true love." He tilted his head to look down at me, still smiling, and rubbed my hand.

I was suddenly breathless.

"The princess is the guardian of mystery," he said. "That is why the dragon imprisons her, to seize the enigma she holds in trust. Our noble paladin proves his worth when he risks everything, even death, for her sake, knowing his defeat is never the end, for another knight will always come forward. Only the purest, the worthiest, will triumph. When the true champion frees the princess from the dragon's lair, she will share her mystery, gift him with joy, and unite with him to make one sublime creation. Their symmetry will bring fertility, growth, and plenty. Our birthright of endless happiness will be restored."

Robert Louis turned his gaze to the white castle. I kept mine on him.

"We have the misfortune of living in a world that has done away with magic. Now everything is handled with paperwork and policy, punishment and manipulation. I'm no longer sure the hero's call can penetrate the noise, Zoë. The noise and the lies. I'm afraid I've destroyed our last hope. I destroyed our last hero."

I didn't understand what he meant, but I hated the hopelessness I saw in his eyes. "Who knows?" I said, squeezing his hand. "Magic could still be there, invisible right now, but there. Maybe it's just waiting."

Rays of sunlight flared against the mullioned windows in the fairy castle.

He met my gaze and smiled. It was so tender I found myself blinking back tears.

"For a wise princess?" he asked.

"And the truest knight."

Chapter 33

I wondered what would happen when we reached the end of solid ground, but I should have known Robert Louis wouldn't let a little thing like the ocean stop him. Nothing, it seemed, could thwart this man—bombs, soldiers combing the countryside, winter weather, or the Alps. Certainly not an ocean. A few of his men left us outside of a place called Foggia and we didn't see them for several days. They returned on tired horses and gave him their news out of my hearing, news that caused him to frown. Nevertheless, we mounted, rode on, and eventually rendezvoused with a ferry on a very dark night, at a very distant shore from where I grew up. An obsequious sailor transported us to an anchored ship.

Apparently, this was not the spot Robert Louis had hoped for, but it was what we got. We waited until the deepest part of the night to attempt sailing through a strait, which Robert Louis said was our only obstacle to open sea, and well-guarded. Originally the space had stretched a comfortable seventy-five kilometers wide, but the governments on each side built snakelike piers that contracted the passage down to a mere five. Revolving floodlights on both sides kept the channel lit up, but one of the sailors explained that on every fourth sweep the lights fell out of rhythm, giving a talented steersman a moment in time to maneuver a ship through undetected. The men furled the sails and rowed, dipping the oars soundlessly. I chewed my lip and clenched the rail as pools of light came closer…closer…but we outran their reach by seconds.

When morning came the sun unveiled a vast world of water. We saw no ships, people, or land. Only marine life.

I must admit it was pleasant to sleep at night on a cot and forego endless hours in a saddle. Luckily, life at sea never caused me a queasy stomach. I was too enthralled by everything to have time for illness—dolphins chittering and grinning, flying seabirds, one whale sighting, and a climate that grew clearer and warmer with each passing day.

The world grew more colorful. Sunrises exploded, washed through in blues, golds, and roses. The sunsets were shimmery green and purple.

Robert Louis's health improved. I had agonized about him, especially in the bitter mountain passes, for a raspy cough refused to clear —and how could it, given such conditions? I blamed myself every time I heard that painful sound. He should have been in bed, with mustard packs and soup. Instead, he risked his health and life to personally escort me…I still didn't know where. As we continued and the air acquired spring softness, his cough faded and color appeared in his cheeks. I gloried in performing little tasks for him…bringing cups of Earl Grey so he needn't rise from his comfortable deck chair…fetching blankets as evening fell…reading aloud from the only book—my RLS biography, though reading to him about his own life did feel odd. I avoided the last pages, which described his death, and concentrated on snatches of poetry and adventure.

The first experience can never be repeated. The first love, the first sunrise, the first South Sea island, are memories apart and touched a virginity of sense.

He listened, never interrupting my irregular narration. Sometimes I thought he'd fallen asleep, but then he would comment, laugh, or tell me to "go on."

One evening as I read, a horrible sickening realization occurred. I wondered where my mind had been not to think of it before.

Trusty, dusky, vivid, true,
With eyes of gold and bramble-dew,
Steel-true and blade-straight,
The great artificer
Made my mate.

I stared at those devastating words, my stomach twisting inside out.

Honour, anger, valour, fire;
A love that life could never tire,
Death quench or evil stir,
The mighty master
Gave to her.
Numbness settled over me like suffocation.
Robert Louis couldn't have married me.
He was already married.

Chapter 34

"Zoë?"

His voice faintly penetrated the roar in my ears.

"You stopped," he said. His eyes were warm and lustrous. "Is anything wrong?"

Fanny, I wanted to scream. *Fanny Osbourne, that's what's wrong. As if you don't know.*

But how could I? He'd been so kind. I had no right to expect anything.

"N-no. Nothing."

The way one brow lifted, accompanied by his extended silence, told me he observed every expression I couldn't hide. "Your eyes just turned as green as the sea where we're going," he said, "and the color left your face. I've been lazy, sitting here letting you bring me things. Can I get something for you? Tea...coffee? Are you tired of reading? I hope not...I enjoy it so much." He paused. "I feel my life is starting over—I like this one much better."

I searched his face for the slightest sign of duplicity, but there was none. He smiled, reached out, and squeezed my hand.

"N-no—well, maybe I'm a little tired of reading for now." I almost whispered because I didn't trust my voice.

"Tomorrow we'll reach the archipelago," he said. "Three more days and we'll be on my island."

"You-you have an island?"

"It isn't really mine. I have a house there. I call it '*Naiskos,*' my little temple."

"What is it like?"

His face acquired a sort of faraway pleasure as he gazed beyond the rail at the sunset. "It's—well, Zoë, you'll have to experience it yourself. It's like no place else on earth, and I'm not a poet."

Not a poet. *Not a poet!*

Night after night in my sorrow
The stars stood over the sea,
Till lo! I looked in the dusk
And a star had come down to me.

I almost laughed out loud.

Chapter 35

WHAT CAN I SAY OF THE MOMENT WE APPROACHED OUR HAVEN? WE sailed south then east and gradually north, through the Cyclades and into the Sporades, the whole time seeing only two other vessels in the distance. Three dolphins adopted our ship and leaped, sharing enthusiastic chatter the entire way.

The islands we passed were mountainous, beach-rimmed, forested places. We spotted tiny silver threads I imagined might be gigantic waterfalls, fishing boats in quaint harbors, and the peculiar but lovely cube-shaped houses with shutters, roofs, and doors painted vivid hues of green, blue, yellow, or red.

We stopped at none of them. Robert Louis's excitement grew, betraying itself in his constant pacing. He pushed the sailors to *hurry, hurry.*

Navigating around the southeast tip, we kept the island—"his island"—on our left, sailing swiftly past a coastal city. Once that fell behind, a curved stretch of forest rose steeply from a shoreline and water of iridescent blue-green. We followed the coast almost to its northern edge—the island at this point seemingly deserted. I saw only our dolphins, a couple of seals lazing on rocks, and birds—the flash of kingfishers, gulls, and spindly-legged, snowy white herons.

The men guided our ship into a shallow cove. The water here was a phosphorescent aquamarine, reflective and transparent at the same time. While the sailors made anchor, we scrambled to bundle our belongings—this didn't take me but a moment—and congregated on deck.

Robert Louis's pleasure was as evident as if he were young Jim Hawkins accepting Long John Silver's version of life before the apple barrel.

Beyond the prismatic waves and white powder beach, upward from a dense forest of pine, high on the cliffs of a craggy wooded mountain, a house sprawled, managing to be both naturally flowing and arrogantly prominent, with its white walls, majestic pillars, and red-tiled roof. Trees rose around it like a close-drawn cloak. Below, on the lower slopes, stood a dusky green olive grove.

"Oh…" I managed.

"They've lowered the boat." Robert Louis tugged at my arm. "Let's go, Zoë."

I followed him over the side on a rope ladder. One of the sailors rowed us to the beach and we tumbled out.

The air was a glorious mix of sea, fish, purity, and pine—a completely different pine scent than the one at my childhood mountain home.

The sailor returned to the boat. The others waved from the deck and the ship slowly made its way out of the cove and headed south, probably to the city we'd passed.

Robert Louis seized my hand. "Come on," he cried. "*Naiskos* awaits!"

We headed across the beach towards what appeared to be an impenetrable clump of scrub backed by a stand of well-formed *Arbutus andrachne*, but I soon saw the path leading neatly through the foliage and into the forest.

The wood through which we hiked was filled not only with pine and cypress but several variations of *Arbutus* and even the occasional *Castanea sativa*. The path wound upward and I was soon panting. I paused to catch my breath, letting Robert Louis go a little ahead. I placed both palms against a twisted old plane tree, which looked, from the size of it, as though it could easily have lived a thousand years or more. As though of their own accord, my hands scraped around the trunk. I pressed my ear and chest against its ancient, hard flesh and listened to it exhale.

Zoë…

"Zoë?"

I opened my eyes. Robert Louis stood there, his white cotton shirt billowing, a half-smile on his face. "That's the oldest tree on the island," he said. "They say it's been around since before Paris stole Helen and Greece warred ten years with Troy."

I'd felt its age. Not it—her. The tree had a female soul. *I'll be back*, I promised, with a last lingering touch, then rejoined my husband on the trail.

"No one knows about *Naiskos*," he told me. "Not even my family." He swept out one arm as we walked, encompassing the entire island. "You can explore, swim in the sea, climb the trees." He stopped and clasped my shoulders, grinning. "You're safe here, Zoë."

"Are you safe, too?"

"Yes. This is a safe place for both of us."

I longed to ask why he'd gone to all this trouble for me...but I kept silent. I knew asking such a question would be self-denigrating, and I felt he would be disappointed.

I breathed in the soft air. Robert Louis regarded me tenderly. The sea breeze tormented the upper pine branches, making them sough and whisper.

We've been waiting for you, Zoë.

I understood then the attraction of that brown liquid my father and tutor had so eagerly drunk. Jäger, he'd called it.

My alcohol was this moment in time.

Chapter 36

The house was enclosed in layer upon layer of terraces. There were no fortifications of any sort. The forest path led us to an arched trellis built into a low rock wall, and we simply stepped beneath it into Paradise.

The trellis was heavily draped with deep red bougainvillea, filling my senses with color and movement, and lending to a nagging sensation that I'd fallen into a fantasy realm.

We passed a circular fountain. A naked, marble woman rose in the center, one graceful hand resting on the horns of a small stag, the other holding a tipped amphora from which water flowed.

"Artemis," Robert Louis said when he saw me staring. I blushed but he didn't appear to notice and went on pointing out various blooms, even picking one for me.

"*Dahlia Variabilis*," I muttered, running my fingertips over the tubular petals nestled around a central disc and fanning into a perfectly symmetric circle. "Pompon."

He laughed, took the blossom from me, and tucked the stem behind my ear. "What's important about this particular flower is that it brings out the pink in your cheeks."

The gardens were magnificent. May I say only that, if I promise to describe them later? But for now, the house commandeered my attention.

A line of twelve white pillars, at least seven meters high, stretched in both directions. We climbed shallow marble steps that encompassed the entire length of the main façade. A heavenly scent swirled from a flowering lime tree.

"Look, Zoë," he said softly, and turned me.

Right below me stretched the terraced gardens with their riotous color, scent, and trickling fountains. Beyond that, the forest swept down, down, and down to the blue-green-purple sea, crashing against boulders at the shoreline in a distant white froth. Three puffball clouds floated on a horizon of cobalt blue.

He spoke close to my ear. "You'll be happy here."

So many sensations did I struggle to sort through, so many scents and sights, that I hardly heard him.

"Master!" The shriek jerked me back into my body and I swung around.

A plump, older woman bustled towards us, holding out her hands and grinning so hugely I could see that two of her teeth—one on top and one on the bottom—were missing. Her grey-streaked hair was pulled back tightly. Wrinkles, whether from age or the sun, covered her cheeks—lightly by the ears, deepening next to the mouth.

My senses continued to sponge up other impressions—a tiled mosaic floor, chaise lounges, tables, the echo of her swift footsteps, a high vaulted ceiling, and behind her, the floating diaphanous movement of sheer white draperies fluttering shyly between a second row of pillars. Someone somewhere plucked a stringed instrument.

"Elena." Robert Louis extended his arms and caught the woman in an exuberant embrace.

"Home at last," she cried, then pushed away from him and studied him critically. "And not a moment too soon. You have been coughing, haven't you? And you're pale as the belly of a cuttlefish." She shook her head. "Those cold wet climates aren't good for your lungs, how many times must I tell you? You should never go there."

She turned her gaze to me, propped fists on hips, and examined me from head to toe, her thick black brows lifting.

"This is Zoë." Robert Louis rested one arm across the woman's shoulders. "Zoë, this is Elena. She takes care of things when I'm not here."

"Hello," I said. "I'm happy to meet you."

Her guarded expression disappeared into another grin. "And I you, *despinís* Zoë. *Hero polí.*"

I twisted my fingers behind my back and wondered what to say.

"She is pleased to meet you," Robert Louis said. He pulled me towards the drifting white curtains. "Don't tease her, Elena. And it isn't *despinís*—it's *kiria.*"

"*Kiria*—" Shock blossomed across the woman's face, but she masked it quickly. "You must be hungry. I have just made phyllo pastries filled with cheese and honey. Ouzo, Master?" she added, sending him a sly look. "Or retsina?"

"Have you any raki?"

"Of course, of course. I keep all things in readiness for you, though you never let me know you are coming."

He laughed. "We'll be right in."

"She'll feed you until you think you're going to explode," he said after she left, "but I look forward to seeing you well fed."

We slipped between the draperies. A cool, dim corridor curved to the left and right. Before us lay a circular sunken room. Crescent-shaped sofas surrounded a round stone hearth. There were shelves of books and knickknacks. An enormous fresco covered a portion of the wall—blue swallows fluttering amidst tall blooms, and behind them, a waterfall. The opposite wall was—how should I describe it—part of the mountain, separated from the room by nothing more than glass. I saw the roots of growing things, and soil, and over it all grew deep green ivy. An exotic bird perched on a bar stuck right through the glass and into the earth. It preened as we came in, and made a clicking sound.

"It's—it's..." I could find no proper word.

"Cool in the summer." Robert Louis pulled a book from the shelf. "Plenty of reading material, even for you. Let me show you your bedroom."

I followed him along the corridor to a suite shaped in a half-circle. One entered by opening a set of etched glass doors and as I stepped in, I actually gasped.

Three pillars supported a domed ceiling, magnificently painted with two sickle moons above a blue night sea covered in mist. Shorter pillars ran around the perimeter. White draperies floated between them, creating a fluttery, insubstantial wall between the bedroom and the terraced gardens. Green ivy twined from pots at the base of each pillar, rising to the ceiling. The bed, covered in white and crowned with a wrought-ivy iron frame, was arranged against the far side of the room. More white gossamer draped from this frame, partially veiling the bed from view, and crystal vases crammed with hyacinths stood on each nightstand.

A breeze moved the curtains, lazily beckoning. I took a step. Two. One of the panels drifted across the arm of a cushioned chair as though inviting me to sit.

The floor was fashioned of deep blue tiles surrounding a massive golden star.

"Do you like it?" Robert Louis asked.

He leaned against the doorjamb, arms crossed over his chest. His stance reminded me overwhelmingly of the picture that had once graced the front of my book.

"It's like a beautiful dream."

He crossed the space between us and put his arms around me, lifting me clear off the floor in an embrace so tight I couldn't breathe— not that I cared.

"That's exactly what I tried to create," he said, replacing me on the tiles. "Your dressing room and the bath are hidden away in here."

He pointed. I hadn't noticed it before, but to the left of the entry there was another door. When I opened it, I saw drawers, wardrobes, and a trifold screen.

"Master?" Elena stuck her inquisitive face around the edge of the open door. "Are you going to starve this child?"

"No, no." Robert held out his hand and I took it. "Of course not," he added, giving me a look so tender I nearly melted into the floor.

I will make you brooches and toys for your delight
Of bird-song at morning and star-shine at night.
I will make a palace fit for you and me
Of green days in forests and blue days at sea.

Chapter 37

It was hard to sleep that first night.

It turned out I could have walls. An ingenious track system along the upper edge of the ceiling supported screens. These could be pulled, accordion-style, closing in the room. Winter nights on the island, though not cold as I knew cold, were chilly, so I did use them, leaving one south-facing screen pushed back. For hours I lay in the white feather bed, listening to the fountain music, watching moonlight and water reflections play across the sheer draperies. The fabric moved in the night breezes like a sensuous woman enticing a man. I wondered if I would ever have enough courage or beauty to move in such ways.

Every now and then the scent of some flower drifted in. I thought I recognized myrtle. That particular plant was presumed to bring good fortune to newly married couples.

Wrapping myself in the long white robe Elena had provided, I left the room and stepped onto the nearest terrace.

A fountain stood close by. Earlier, I had admired it and Robert Louis told me it depicted Aphrodite and Eros riding a dolphin, and was a copy of an ancient statue preserved in a Greek museum. The murmur of water splattering from the dolphin's mouth seemed the most reassuring and happy of sounds.

One of Robert Louis's peacocks screeched wistfully.

The moons, in their first quarter phase, rode the sky like two wide grins, providing just enough of a glow to dimly illuminate the steps leading to the next garden level. Cool, still air intensified the heady aroma of countless flowers. I descended and roamed, tracing velvet blooms, the rims of stone pots, scrolled backrests on benches, and letting ice-cold water flow over my fingers, reveling in the sensory stimulation.

It occurred to me that I would resemble a phantom to anyone who happened to glance out from the house. Moonlit, floating among the flowers, what else could I be? Perhaps one of the *anthousai*, or a celestial nymph.

I am happy to blame the moons for what I did next—lifting my arms and dancing, robe fluttering around my ankles, soaring bell-like then folding in softly. Feeling the moonlight play upon my skin, I recalled that here in the Greek islands, the nearest moon, the one that had been with us the longest, was once worshipped as a living entity in temples that must have looked much like *Naiskos*.

I don't know how long I fluttered through the gardens before I saw him. I wasn't even sure anymore where I was.

He sat in a chair on a terrace staring out to sea, and didn't notice or hear me. Exaltation hummed through my blood when I saw him. I nearly cried out and started to run to him, but something stopped me. His stillness, perhaps, or the forward tilt of his head, or the hunched set of his shoulders.

Resting one hand on the head of a white stone gryphon, I watched, hardly breathing.

Robert Louis could not be termed a beautiful man. Physical frailty made his body almost ghostlike, but the poetry that ran through his blood created an impression of motion, air, and music—far more precious and lasting than any simply beautiful thing.

None of that ephemeral magic was visible now. He sat motionless, one hand cupped around a half-full wineglass, the other resting in his lap. I sensed his bare, undisguised grief. I saw it in the way he held himself.

I'd seen this before, the first time at that abhorrent place on our journey south. That place—the mere sight of which sent icicles through my soul—where the poplars whispered warning. When he came out of the abandoned building, he stumbled. Grabbing his mount's stirrup, he bent as though gripped in pain. When he rode to us, I saw the agony in his eyes. I could tell he'd been weeping—his eyes were red and his lashes wet. I will never forget the way his face looked that day, and I hated myself for not knowing how to comfort him.

It happened again when we looked across a frozen gorge at a white castle, sparkling like it was dusted in fairy glitter. *We live in a world that has done away with magic,* he said. *Now everything is paperwork and punishment.*

My heart wept for his sorrow.

I destroyed our last hero.

Absurd. Robert Louis could never destroy anyone or anything.

But he believed he had.

I watched his suffering and didn't know what to do. On our long southbound journey, he never talked about himself. He always steered our conversations around me…my interests…my desires…

He must know me thoroughly by now, yet as I stood by the motionless stone gryphon, watching the equally still man, I realized that for all my book knowledge of the poet and writer, I knew nothing of him at all.

Chapter 38

"I have a gift for you," Robert Louis said the next morning.

I gazed up at him from my seat at the well-scrubbed kitchen table. Elena had spread a feast before me. Crusty bread and a dish of herb-seasoned olive oil to dunk it in, black and green olives, sliced tomatoes and cucumbers. She set down a mug of steaming coffee and a bowl of sugar as he came in.

Last night's despair had vanished, or was hidden. He looked tired, but otherwise at peace. I wanted to ask what caused such sadness, but I knew I wouldn't. I didn't have the guts, any more than I had the guts to ask about Fanny. My propensity to stifle questions, to stutter, to allow myself to be borne on the wave of life like a cork in a fast river, was frustrating, even infuriating, but I didn't know how to change it. My fears, and years of conditioning, held me prisoner.

He wore one of his loose white shirts, tucked into the waist of black trousers. It looked good next to his dark hair, still damp from his morning ablutions and tucked behind his ears. Though Elena thought him too pale and thin, I saw a big difference from the man who had first appeared among the dead soldiers at my home. His shoulders seemed more squared, and right now his eyes gleamed—not with fever, but something born of hard-won tranquility.

Dropping into the chair beside me, he held out his gift, a book tied with ribbon. I took it and untied the bow.

Robert Louis Stevenson, Poems. First Edition.

My eyes met his. He returned my gaze steadily, a smile playing about his mouth. His eyes narrowed as I continued to stare, but he didn't blink or turn away. For my part I couldn't hide my feelings.

"What is it, Mistress?"

I felt like I was swimming out of depthless blue water. My lungs involuntarily sucked in air as I turned away from him to face Elena. "A-a book." I gave it to her, and could only pray the silent, observant man sitting beside me didn't notice the trembling in my fingers.

His hand gripped my shoulder and squeezed. *It's all right*, it seemed to say. *Everything is all right.* I wanted to meet his gaze, but was too afraid. I hated being so vulnerable...so damnably childlike, so incapable of hiding my feelings. Robert Louis, a grown man, had traveled. He had lived. He had loved. Whatever I offered was...pathetic.

At that moment I would have given anything to be older and beautiful. To be a woman Robert Louis Balfour Stevenson could admire. Could...love.

But not even on this enchanted island could I conjure such a spell.

Chapter 39

Everything was perfect, which should have given me warning. I should have known my happiness would end, and prepared myself.

A week passed. I spent many joyous hours exploring. I retraced the forest path we'd come up and spoke at length to the gigantic plane tree. Soon I felt myself on the way to making a new friend—friendships with trees, I knew, could not be rushed. Those who possess the secrets of the earth and all of earth's history take their time. Perhaps friendships between humans would do better as well, if forged more slowly.

At the cove, I splashed barefoot through foamy water and wet sand. I watched spiny spider crabs scramble among the rocks and redshanks forage for delicacies. I examined at ecstatic length three tiny seahorses clinging to greenery in the shoals, and finally, I climbed boulders, found a comfortable spot, and reveled in an ever-changing view.

One day I fell asleep up there, the tangy, dusky scent of tamarisk filling my senses, and didn't wake until a clap of thunder brought me upright in a heart-stomping hurry. As I scrambled down to the sand it started to rain, huge heavy drops that stung when they struck and immediately soaked me through. Lightning flashed. The air crackled. The hair on my scalp lifted and I felt certain some nearby tree had met a fiery end. I ran home, slipping on dirt transformed to mud, and endured a lecture from Elena about the need to be alert for such things.

When Robert Louis saw me, he started laughing. I was mud-splattered to the knees, hair plastered to my skull, shivery from cold. When I thought of how I must look, I couldn't help laughing too. Fetching a big soft towel, he threw it around me, scrubbing away the water and warming me clear to my bones.

Elena was more practical. She steeped herb tea and prepared a bowl of rizogalo, claiming a full belly prevented chills.

"Have you looked at yourself lately?" Robert Louis held the edges of the towel, effectively imprisoning me in front of him.

"Looked at myself?" Gazing into his face, I was reminded of a phrase William Ernest Henley had written about him.

Lean, large-boned, curved of beak, and touched with race,
Broad-lipped, rich-tinted, mutable as the sea,
The brown eyes radiant with vivacity...

"I can hardly remember the girl who stared down from the roof of that monstrosity of a house." He tightened his grip on the towel, bringing me a hair's-breadth closer.

I was a willing, though timid, prisoner.

His brows lifted. His grin widened. "You're red as boiled lobster, and by hell getting fat."

My face suffused with heat. I slapped a hand over my mouth and struggled but he wouldn't release me, and to make matters worse, I glimpsed Elena laughing as well.

"You don't believe me?" He pulled me into the dining room we never used, and pinioned me before the big round mirror over the sideboard. "There." He stabbed the air with his index finger.

The sunburned girl looking back at me was a virtual stranger. Sun and salt water had bleached my hair into a hundred shades of blonde and copper. My eyes seemed greener, nearly as transparent as the sea in which I spent so much time. What had transformed them from their usual dullness? It must be this new color baked into my skin. I saw that Robert Louis was right—my cheeks had filled out. I no longer resembled a starveling orphan. If I should name what I reminded myself of, it would be a starfish. I don't know why, but something... maybe the various parts put together...looked as though they'd been fashioned in the sea.

He bent so his head was level with mine, and kissed my cheek. The mirror framed us, me copper-headed and him dark.

"You're a beautiful girl, Zoë."

I love you. I almost said it. My mouth opened. But in the end, I couldn't.

Looking back, I think I did say it, without words. As I gazed into his reflected eyes and saw him smiling, carefree, nary a hint of the persistent sadness that so often hung over him like an invisible cloud, a sharp stab of joy raced through me. Such overwhelming rapture can't be hidden. It pours forth like a newly opened bottle of champagne, frothing, bubbling, sparkling in the light.

Robert Louis was a man who would never miss nor misunderstand such things.

Chapter 40

We had a cozy dinner, Elena, her bearded husband Demetri, who'd been playing the *santoúri* when we first arrived, Robert Louis, and myself, feasting on broiled mussels with oregano, dolmades, marinated olives, kadaifi, the local cheese pie, and wine—retsina for Robert Louis. I was given only a little wine in a tiny crystal goblet.

Robert Louis excused himself after eating, which was unusual. He generally sat at the table smoking one cigarette after another, drinking strong coffee, and playing backgammon with Demetri while Elena and I washed the dishes.

I didn't think I'd ever seen the expression I glimpsed on his face either—a mixture of anticipation and wariness.

My senses roused.

After the dishes were put away and Elena had made herself comfortable at the kitchen table with her husband, I wandered off with some excuse about reading, but I couldn't concentrate. The forest sent whispers I couldn't quite decipher, which made my nerves sing stridently. Finally, I left the villa for a stroll in the gardens.

That's where I saw them.

Robert Louis.

A woman.

Walking together, hand in hand among the flowers, the low-riding deep red sun washing them in rosy light.

How many times had I read of Fanny as striking rather than beautiful, brown-eyed and haired like Robert Louis, vivid and selfish? This woman, though dark like Fanny, was heartbreakingly beautiful. A goddess. She was everything I would never be. And the way Robert Louis walked beside her, half-turned towards her, struck me like a physical blow. So absorbed was he that I sensed, had he seen me standing there above them, it might not even register.

I felt as frozen as the woman in the fountain behind me.

The couple stopped and faced each other. Robert Louis gazed down into this gorgeous creature's face. She returned his gaze. He brought her hand to his lips and kissed it. Her arms lifted, crept around his neck. He embraced her tightly, burying his face against her shoulder.

I heard her crying.

They broke apart. She pushed him with one hand then turned and ran, stumbling, quickly vanishing.

As miserable as I felt, I suspected Robert Louis was in worse shape. He stared after her, every line and feature infused with grief.

And when I rose the next morning, he was gone.

Chapter 41

ROBERT LOUIS HAD DECIDED AT THE LAST MINUTE THAT HE'D NEGLECTED his affairs for too long, and had gone off to "sort out the bungling of others," Elena said irritably as she handed me a note.

Scribbled handwriting on crackly parchment.

Dearest Zoë,

I must leave, but I promise to return as soon as I can. Be happy. Watch out for the crabs—they pinch. And be wary of jellyfish. I'll miss you, Zoë. Every night I will look up at the stars and think of you watching them too.

My heart sank as I folded the note and tucked it into my RLS biography, for those words suggested he would be gone a long time.

The sea lost its translucent shimmer. The trees were inanimate objects swaying without will in the force of breezes, the sounds they made not voices but the meaningless brush of leaf against leaf. The sun was hot, not intoxicating. I had no appetite, not even for Elena's honey-sesame cakes. She clucked and muttered but didn't try to make me eat.

Damned woman. This was her fault. Robert Louis would never have left but for her. He'd grown happier and happier—until she came. Useless, pretty woman—teary and whiny. What had she been blubbering about anyway?

Maybe me. Maybe she had demanded to know who I was, why I was living in his home with him. Maybe she was jealous.

129

Jerking a weed out of the forget-me-nots, I crushed it and flung it away before stomping along the terraces, immersed in angry fantasies.

At length I came to the terrace where I'd seen Robert Louis that first night, staring out to sea beneath the sickle moons. I dropped onto his chair and tried to capture the smell of him, but all I could detect with any certainty was jasmine and hints of pine.

My parents had betrothed me to him when I was a baby. Robert Louis was meant for me. We were promised to each other. And I *wanted* to be with him. I wanted him to miss me as much as I missed him.

Littering the surface of a small glass-topped table was an ashtray full of cigarette butts, an open, upside-down book, and an empty wine glass. I picked up the book and read the page he'd left it turned to.

With love's light wings did I o'erperch these walls;

For stony limits cannot hold love out,

And what love can do, that dares love attempt.

I read those three lines again…and again…and again.

And was still sitting in Robert Louis's chair reading when the sun set.

Chapter 42

"WOULD YOU HELP ME, ELENA?"

"Of course, *barbouni.*" She spoke without hesitation as she wiped her hands on a dishcloth. Later I learned she was calling me a red fish, but at the time, I thought it was a word for baby because it sounded somewhat like the Italian *bambini.*

"Would you help me learn a play?"

"A play—what play?"

"Romeo and Juliet. I want to be Juliet. Do you think Demetri would be Romeo?"

"Yes, yes, he will—if I tell him to. And who shall I be?"

"The friar. You get to say this: '*And flecked darkness like a drunkard reels, From forth day's path and Titan's fiery wheels!*'"

"What does it mean, Mistress?"

"Well, that night flees the day I suppose. Do you think we could do it? I-I want to perform it for...my husband."

"Ah." She acquired a thoughtful expression. "He would like that." She presented me with her wide, unselfconscious grin. "But he could return tomorrow."

"He could?" I hadn't considered that possibility. "Could he, really?"

"Well, not if he's truly taking care of business, and not just...bah."

What had she started to say? Instantly I wondered if he'd gone to be with that woman. "Elena…"

"Yes, *barbouni?*"

I choked. There was my pride…and even stronger, fear. I didn't want to know the truth. "Never mind."

"Let me call Demetri. He'll make a poor Romeo…"

She shrugged.

WE REHEARSED ALL AFTERNOON UNTIL DEMETRI COMPLAINED OF starvation. Elena went off to the kitchen and I returned to Robert Louis's terrace, gaining a small measure of comfort from sitting in his chair and holding the round velvet pillow he'd left there.

I'd stared at the sea and clouds, pondered life, and suffered terrible longing for about forty-five minutes when I heard the sound of Elena's bell, letting me know dinner was ready.

With a heavy sigh, I stretched, rose from the chair…and saw her.

That woman. *Fanny,* my mind supplied. *Fanny Osbourne… Stevenson.*

Misery was an immediate bone-wrenching surge of unendurable pain. But the next second I realized with an equally precipitous tingling swell of joy that he was not with her.

She strolled on a lower terrace level, built right on a cliff edge. Pausing at the retaining wall, she lifted a gardenia to her nose and gazed out to sea.

She reminded me a bit of Clotilda, with the same elegance of movement and a voluptuous body veiled rather than covered by a floaty, sleeveless red gown. Last time I saw her, her hair had been up in a twist, leaving the back of her neck bare. Today it spilled freely. She was flawless—the living embodiment of the Artemis statue.

Why was she here? Did she live in another part of the villa? Why else would she be here, so far from any village or city?

The bell rang again.

I gripped the edge of the ivy-covered wall that separated my terrace from hers.

She straightened. Her head lifted and she turned so suddenly I didn't have a chance to duck. She stared, a long, measured gaze in which I discerned that her eyes were brilliant blue.

Fright battled anticipation. I wanted to flee, but gripped the wall harder and forced myself to stay put. I was his wife. I was almost thirteen years old, and we had been betrothed all that time. Now we were married. I would not run.

As it turned out, I didn't have to. She did. Dropping the gardenia, she bent her head and hurried away, disappearing swiftly around a bend in the path.

Chapter 43

It was difficult to speak Juliet's lines to Demetri—a grey-stubbled, watery-eyed, overly plump, yellow toothed man in his fifties who smelled of garlic and cigarettes and whose fingernails were always dirty.

We used one of the terraces for the balcony scene. I stood above, leaning over the edge among the flowers, and Demetri blinked up at me from below. Elena sat on a ledge with the book so she could prompt her husband. He needed much prompting.

"'What man art thou that,'" I quoted, "'thus bescreened in night,
So stumblest on my council?'"

Demetri stepped forward, supposedly into a circle of light, and pressed both leathery hands against his chest as we'd coached him.

"'By a name,'" he wheezed,
"'I know not how to tell thee who I am.
My name, dear saint, is hateful to myself,
Because it is an enemy to thee.
Had I it written, I would tear the word.'"

I leaned farther over the edge, propped on my elbows.

"'My ears have yet not drunk a hundred words
Of thy tongue's uttering, yet I know the sound.
Art thou not Romeo, and a Montague?'"

He knelt, clumsily and grunting, onto one knee. "'*Neither, fair maid, if either thee dislike.*'"

"'*How camest thou hither, tell me,*'" I said, "'*and wherefore? The orchard walls are high and hard to climb, And the place death, considering who thou art, If any of my kinsmen find thee here.*'"

His next line was my favorite. I wanted it to ring into the cloudless blue heavens like a paean.

"'*With love's light wings did I—*'"

Demetri stopped. Scratched his armpit. Sent Elena a sideways glance.

"'*o'erperch these walls!*'" she whispered loudly.

"Oh right, right," he muttered. "'*O'erperch these walls; For stony,*' ah, um…" He stood up laboriously. "What the hell do I say next? Do I have to beg, woman?"

"If you would learn the lines, I wouldn't have to repeat them over and over, would I?"

"Why don't we stop—" I began.

"I've had about enough of you," Demetri interrupted. "How did I get dragged into this? I'm a gardener. Do you see these hands? Not a damned poet nor an actor. None of it makes sense anyway."

Elena dropped the book and rose, planting her hands on her hips. "You'll do this because Mistress Zoë wants it and that's good enough for you. Have you forgotten how much Master has done for us? Well?"

"Demetri—Elena—"

Their argument rose in pitch.

"'*O gentle Romeo,*'" I muttered.

"'*If thou dost love, pronounce it faithfully. Or if thou thinkest I am too quickly won, I'll frown, and be perverse, and say thee nay.*'"

Just then there was the oddest rustle…like the patter of leaves against the flagstones, but not exactly. And a muffled trill, mostly lost beneath Elena and Demetri's bickering.

Yet when I listened, and searched, one way then the other, I saw nothing.

Chapter 44

Two months passed with no word from Robert Louis. In all honesty, I didn't know if he was alive or dead.

And so came my thirteenth birthday.

It was my habit to swim most mornings in the cove, then have a light lunch and siesta. Afterwards, Elena, Demetri, and I practiced the play until dinner. Demetri was marginally better than in the beginning. I think I succeeded in hiding my frustration. After all, he *was* a gardener, and hadn't had much in the way of schooling.

I swam in an outfit Elena had come up with somewhere. It was white, with a short skirt and shoulder straps that crisscrossed in back. I thought it quite flattering except for the vee neck, which made my obvious lack more obvious. Clotilda and Beata were well endowed, as was my Schloss mother and Elena, and though I could hardly bear to admit it, so was the mysterious woman I'd seen with Robert Louis. I must be the only female on the face of the earth, barring children, who lacked breasts.

Since I only ever saw Elena and Demetri, I told myself it hardly mattered. The brunette in the lovely red gown had gone away or hidden herself. Once since that day I'd seen her, but she'd been far off, standing on a rock outcropping at the edge of the sea.

If Robert Louis intended to return, wouldn't he at least write?

Draping a towel over my shoulders, I hiked to the cove, dropped the towel on the sand, and dove in from one of the boulders. Turquoise water enveloped me like a cool silk cocoon. Swimming made me forget dejection and loneliness. A friendly dolphin had allowed me to touch its nose, and we'd swum together, playing among the coral and seaweed. It always grinned as though it wanted to tell me a funny secret.

I spent most of my time underwater. In those days, I would have liked to possess gills. I loved watching plants beneath the surface swaying gracefully, as though dancing to music I couldn't hear.

It seemed wrong, allowing this momentous passage from child into teenager to pass without remark. But I'd thought about it, and had decided not to tell Elena. Without Robert Louis to hail the occasion, I found I simply didn't care—any celebration would make me sadder because of his absence.

My dolphin appeared and nudged my ribs. Looking up, I noticed a shadow on the surface and decided to investigate. It might be one of those sudden storms. I'd learned to respect them.

Streamlining my body, I headed up, blowing air from my lungs. My dolphin zipped beside me and we broke the surface together in a small explosion, the dolphin chittering happily as it turned a somersault in the air.

I hardly noticed its antics, for I found myself staring directly at Robert Louis's startled face.

Chapter 45

ROBERT LOUIS...RETURNED AT LAST...ON MY BIRTHDAY.

"Zoë," he cried.

I waved and swam to the side of his boat, climbing the rope ladder a sailor threw over. The moment I reached the deck, I was wrapped in my husband's arms.

"Zoë," he whispered.

"You-you're getting wet." I tried to wriggle free.

"Who cares?" He laughed. The sound of it was freer, easier than I had ever heard. He did put me away from him, but only by the length of his arm, and looked me over, shaking his head.

"Do you know what I thought?" he said. "That I'd finally seen a mermaid. I've always secretly believed in them. You shine like a star, Zoë."

I cringed. "Ha-have I changed or something?"

He snorted. "Your skin is brown as topaz and I swear your hair has a thousand colors. Coral and copper and bronze and white. It's longer too. You're all gems from the ocean, Zoë, even your sea-emerald eyes. I feel I've been gone years, not a month."

"Two months," I corrected severely.

His smile widened and he ran his hands over my upper arms, smoothing the gooseflesh. "I think this place agrees with you."

Did he see me as a woman now? The idea was enticing but scary.

"Come then," he said. "Let's go home."

As they dropped the dinghy over the side, two sailors gave me strange glances. One crossed himself.

I wanted to show off. I dove over the side and sliced with hardly a ripple into the sea.

He was laughing as I surfaced. "You've frightened these men. They think you're a mermaid, like I did…or worse, a siren." He shook his head and rubbed the stubble on his cheeks. "If you'd seen the way you came out of that water. Zoë…are you sure you're mortal?"

I giggled.

ELENA GAVE HER TRADITIONAL SCREECH WHEN SHE SAW ROBERT LOUIS trudging up the stone steps, his black coat draped over one shoulder and me clutching his free hand as though I feared he might vanish. The peacocks went off flapping and crying and Demetri came at a run.

She soon had my husband tucked at the kitchen table with ouzo and *mousakás*, and promised us some of her special *giaoúrti kai méli*.

"You'll bust me wide open," Robert Louis complained.

"Don't talk her out of her yoghurt and honey," Demetri hissed. "If she wants to make it for you."

Robert Louis laughed and fired a cigarette. "It's good to be home." He leaned his chair back and impaled me with a stare. "Is there something you would like to say?"

"N-no." I played with the corner of the towel draped over my shoulders.

"Oh, I think there is, if you want your birthday present."

"How did you know?" I whispered, feeling the flame of my cheeks.

Elena snorted. "As if there's anyone—"

Robert Louis's withering glance stopped her cold. "You think I would miss your birthday?" he asked mildly.

"You knew it too?" I asked Elena.

"Yes, *kiria* Zoë…Master told us before he left."

"But you didn't say anything."

Her grin showed off the spaces in her gums as though she was proud of missing teeth.

"Now…" Robert Louis placed his cigarette on the edge of the ashtray and dug in his pockets, first his shirt, then his trousers, then he reached for his coat as I grew increasingly agitated. "What did I do with that? Ah."

He tossed a small container from hand to hand. "Do you want it?"

"Well…yes."

"She didn't sound sure to me. Did she sound sure to you, Demetri?"

"Oh aye, she sounded sure. Give it to her before she pops."

Reaching out quickly, Robert Louis grabbed my hand. He slipped the container into it, closed my fingers around it and, looking quite satisfied, sat back and picked up his cigarette.

I opened my fist. It was a box—not anything ordinary like cardboard, but delicate scented sandalwood, painstakingly carved with flourishes and ivy. The lid was shaped into the profile of an elephant. I removed it carefully.

Two blue-white gems rested on a black velvet bed, their shape plump and rounded, like beads of water.

On either side of those nestled two deeply purple stones, cut into the shape of hearts. Silver filigree wound around and through, linking all the stones together and forming a ring.

"For…me?" I whispered.

"There is only one of these in the world. Only one, for Zoë."

I met his intent, solemn gaze. "Come," he said, gesturing.

I rose and circled the table. Removing the ring from the box, he held it up. "It is far past time you had a wedding ring." He tilted it from side to side. "See how they change?"

I nodded, still not sure I could trust my voice. The two gems in the middle were translucently white with a bluish cast, but when tilted, more colors shyly appeared and disappeared, purple and pink and green.

"Rainbow moonstones." He pointed to one of the purple hearts. "These are goldstone, a miracle of invention. See what happens when the light hits them?"

I was enraptured. The purple hearts glittered like virgin snow when struck by sunlight. Layers upon layers upon even more layers of minuscule diamonds.

He slipped it onto the middle finger of my left hand. It fit perfectly.

"For you and no one else. Moonstones for my Zoë, to draw down moon magic, to protect her and guide her. See the crack in the one on the right?"

"Yes."

"Like the fracture in *L'ombre Moon*."

"*L'ombre Moon*…?"

"When it first came, that is what we humans called it. Shadow Moon. That name fell into disfavor, but I like it."

"I do, too."

"What do you think the hearts mean?"

"I don't know." I had an idea. The fear of being wrong kept me silent, but my heart soared and sang like a joyful canary replaying his words. *My Zoë. My Zoë.*

"Loyalty and love." He touched the one on the right. "This one is you. This one," he touched the left, "is me. Twin hearts. As long as you wear this ring, Zoë, we will never be separated."

"We'll always be together?"

"Always."

Chapter 46

EVERY GIRL SHOULD HAVE A BIRTHDAY LIKE MY THIRTEENTH, AT LEAST THE way it began. I've had good birthdays since, but never another touched by the kind of magic only a child at the precipice of adulthood can fully appreciate.

At twilight, I supervised the lighting of the terrace where we would perform *Highlights from Romeo and Juliet*. Colored wax paper around candles created bewitching pools of purple, green, and blue.

Demetri kept Robert Louis busy drinking the locally made retsina and talking about the gardens, the weather, and politics.

Slipping to my bedroom, mulling over what I could wear, I turned up the lamp by the door and froze.

A gown lay on my bed—the most beautiful gown I had ever seen, of a period I could not name, but like something women would have worn in Shakespeare's time. It was the color of aged cream, inset with lace and tiny pearls across the bodice; these were repeated at the pointed ends of the long, close-fitting sleeves. An apron panel of fine lacework draped down the front.

Half-fearfully, I swept it into my arms. It was no chimera but real, inviting me to put it on and accept the dream. An ingenious cap of pearls glimmered on my pillow, sewn together with fine, fragile thread that would disappear in my hair.

Elena. Who else? She provided everything I wore. I blinked away tears. This must be her birthday gift, and the reason for that sly grin. I stripped and stepped into the fantasy. It was impossible to deal with the lacing up the back, but I did the best I could. The dress was slightly too big; even so, the bodice gave the impression that I had a bosom, set off by lace, pearls, and a collar that rose stiffly on the nape of my neck.

I brushed my hair a hundred distinctly counted strokes, and settled over it the cap of pearls. Since coming to this island, my hair had acquired a tendency to wave. The longer it grew, the more it waved. I can still bring to mind with great clarity my awed reflection in the mirror that night. The shy peek of luminous pearls through my hair, waves cascading down my back, the wondrous cream-lace dress setting off the darker, sunbaked sheen of my skin…and on my middle finger the milky, blue-green moonstones and purple glittering of gold-stone hearts in my brand-new wedding ring.

On the floor by the bed lay a pair of slippers in the same shade as the dress. They were too big. I decided to leave them and go barefoot.

I floated along the corridor, holding up the heavy hem so I wouldn't trip, and peeked into the kitchen, not wanting Robert Louis to see me. There was no sign of him or Demetri. Only Elena, drying plates.

"Where are they?" I whispered from the hall.

She glanced my direction and stilled. "They've gone off to inspect the hibiscus. What are you wearing?" Without looking at the plate she'd been drying, she set it on the counter.

"Oh, Elena. Thank you." I ran into the kitchen and threw my arms around her neck. "It's so beautiful. Would you tighten the laces?"

"What? What is this?" She backed away. "Where—where did you get that dress?"

Her skin had gone sort of greenish. Her eyes were wide. She looked horrified.

"You didn't put it in my room?"

She hardly seemed able to tear her gaze from the gown, but at last she did. "It was in your room?"

"On my bed. I—I thought you—"

"Oh no. Not me. No. But—but it must have been—" She shook her head, touching the damp dishcloth to her cheeks. "*Ise poli omorfi, kiria Zoë.*"

"What's that?"

"Beautiful. You are beautiful."

Chapter 47

WHEN YOU LOVE SOMEONE, THEY ARE BEAUTIFUL TO YOU. IT DOESN'T
matter if they have a wart on their nose or a gap between their teeth or
are bald. Even if they have leprosy, they are beautiful. Robert Louis
was not a handsome man. He was painfully thin. There were usually
shadows beneath his eyes suggesting ill health, and he couldn't grow
much of a beard—only the mustache. But for me, he was the zenith,
the essence, the marrow, of beauty.

I knew it was Elena's love that made her call me beautiful. But I
decided, just for this night, to believe.

Together we went off in search of my husband and hers. I held my
head high, moving with, I hoped, sophistication and grace.

We found them just as they approached the terrace where we'd
strung the colored lights. Robert Louis, hands stuffed into trouser
pockets, was bent over, admiring them. He turned at the sound of our
footsteps. Oddly, Elena grasped my arm in a reassuring manner then
stepped away, going quickly to his side.

As she had done, so did he go still and silent.

"It was on her bed," Elena said in a low voice. She rested her
plump hand on his forearm. "Waiting for her. A gift."

I gazed at him, half-smiling, expecting him to exclaim, if not at my
beauty, at least at the gown's. I held out the skirt and twirled.

He swallowed visibly and I thought...I was almost certain a

shudder ran over him. As I stood there, slow, terrible horror numbing and freezing me, his eyes filled with tears. He covered his face with his hands as though the sight of me was too awful to bear.

Every nerve screamed to run. Just run from this wretched mistake —whatever it was. I turned, the breath a vile fire in my throat. Tears filled my eyes too, hot and acidic. But before I could escape, he grabbed my arm.

"Zoë."

Lifting one hand, he swiped impatiently at the tears on his cheeks.

"I—I must apologize." His voice broke, but strengthened as he continued. "I know it—it looks like I'm upset...but the truth is, I've simply never seen anything so beautiful as you in that dress."

He smiled, a little shakily.

"Oh," I breathed. "Thank you."

He brought my hand to his lips and kissed it. I'd watched him do that to the gorgeous brunette woman.

I'd never seen his eyes so luminous. They really were beyond description.

Chapter 48

"'*What's here? A cup, closed in my true love's hand?*
   Poison, I see, hath been his timeless end.
   O churl! drunk all, and left no friendly drop
   To help me after? I will kiss thy lips.
   Haply some poison yet doth hang on them
   To make me die with a restorative.'"

I kissed Demetri, not on his lips but next to them. "'*Thy lips are warm!*'"

Elena struck the flagstones with her stick. Hand over mouth, she called, "'*Lead, boy! Which way!*'"

"'*Yea, noise?*'" I looked up from my Romeo. "'*Then I'll be brief. O happy dagger! This is thy sheath; there rust, and let me die.*'"

I prostrated myself over Demetri's wheezing chest as Elena spoke Romeo and Juliet's sad finis, and surreptitiously peeked at our audience of one. He watched Elena, grave of face, a handkerchief wadded in one fist.

When the last words were spoken, he leaped to his feet, clapping furiously, and kissed us all on both cheeks—even Demetri.

"Spectacular," he cried. "Absolutely glowing! The best presentation of Romeo and Juliet ever produced."

That couldn't be right, not with Demetri's lackluster performance, mumbled lines, and those annoyed clucking sounds Elena made whenever he forgot something—which was almost constantly.

But I no longer detected any hint of grief or despair on my husband's face.

We had a splash of ouzo to celebrate. Elena and Demetri went inside for yoghurt and honey—Demetri's favorite delicacy, and one his wife had promised him if he did this favor for Mistress Zoë.

Robert Louis and I sat on a bench, blanketed in shimmering, colorful candlelight. The way he looked at me made my heart stutter like my voice, and my breath catch as if there were nails in my throat. He brushed his fingertips along my hair, over the back of my hand, and gently along the line of my jaw.

The moons rose, purely white and only a little lopsided.

"I cannot believe you talked Demetri into that," he said, laughing. "You're a witch, Zoë."

Willing to follow fickle bravery farther than ever before, I said, "Witch? I thought I was a mermaid. A star."

"And maybe a sorceress. This stage you created makes me feel like I'm swimming in a rainbow. Come. Jump in. Let us drink color until we are refashioned into an aurora borealis."

This, from the man who had once claimed he was no poet. If only it didn't have to remind me so poignantly of Teófilo, with his talk of rainbows and happiness.

I laughed, feeling tipsy, though Elena had allowed me exactly three sips of liquor. The blood zinged in my veins. Flushes surged and retreated through my cheeks, rearing when he looked at me, fading when his gaze wandered. "I've been in it since I met you," I stated… then bit my lip.

"You're happy?" He frowned. It worried him then. He'd taken this course of action but wasn't certain it had been right for me.

Oh, how could I express such happiness? "Yes." *Only one thing could make me happier*, I longed to say. *If you kissed me.* I felt courageous tonight, but hadn't yet reached that apex.

He smiled and coiled a tendril of my hair around his finger.

As I look back, I know I didn't plan to ask the question. It simply gave birth to itself from the enchanted light and perfection of the moment. "How did you return to life?"

His head tilted in that endearing way, which at this moment made tears burn behind my eyes. He smiled hesitantly. "What do you mean?"

"You—I read that you died in 1894. But you're here. The books were lying, weren't they? They lied about your birth, too, or else you would be…two hundred and forty-one years old."

"I don't understand, Zoë."

Dragging mettle to the surface, I did what I'd longed to do since the day I'd first seen him. I touched his face. First his jaw, then his temple, the soft edge of his hair, his cheek. How many times, before it was destroyed, had I caressed the picture of his face on the cover of my book? Hundreds. He said nothing while I did this. I met his steady gaze. "You *are* him…you're…*him*. Robert Louis Stevenson."

He studied me, his eyes weighing all I revealed and all I tried to keep hidden. Gently he said, "If only I were, Zoë. I'd give anything to be whatever would make you happy."

Everything within me stopped. The blood flow, the heart, I think even my brain stopped. When he spoke again, though his voice was as soft as it could be, it echoed.

"I am…Odenwylde."

He must have seen the resultant devastation, though I made no movement. I did not cry out. He was a man of sensitivity and wisdom.

He rubbed my hands then pulled me against him, pressing my cheek to his shoulder. "Bastien Jäger-Abelard. I thought you knew."

My mind rejected these names. He was lying. Perhaps to keep himself—or me—safe. He couldn't tell the truth. It was, for some reason, too dangerous. That must be the answer.

I have never known such joy and grief intermixed at the same moment—joy from the ring, the night, the dress, his homecoming. Grief at his lie. I clung to him. Breathed in the smell of him, of cigarettes and retsina and him, the scent of books. Of living poetry.

Odenwylde.

Bastien.

I'm ashamed to admit that at length I fell asleep there against his chest, my tears dampening his shirt.

You leaned to me, I leaned to you,
Our course was smooth as flight—
We steered—a heel-touch to the left,
A heel-touch to the right.
We swung our way through flying men,

Your hand lay fast in mine,
We saw the shifting crowd dispart,
The level ice-reach shine.
I swear by yon swan-travelled lake,
By yon calm hill above,
I swear had we been drowned that day
We had been drowned in love.

Chapter 49

I had a vague memory of being carried to my bed, and a last, lingering kiss on the cheek, ticklish from the mustache.

It was a moment before I remembered.

Putting on a sleeveless dress, I went to the kitchen. Elena said my husband had been called away and would return this evening or tomorrow.

I felt lost. Fidgety and nervous, not satisfied with anything I set my hands to. At last, I walked to the cove and clambered over the boulders to a favorite secluded spot where I could watch the clouds and the rippling waves.

Maybe two hours had passed when he appeared on the small beach below. My husband, who called himself *Bastien of Odenwylde* emerged from the trees and crossed to the water. He wore his usual black trousers and white shirt, which rippled in the breeze. He was smoking. After a moment he threw his cigarette away, unbuttoned his shirt, and dropped it. His trousers followed and he walked naked into the sea, deeper and deeper, until he could dive under the surface.

How vulnerable he was, his fragile thin body, his grave expression —like he'd made a mess of things and didn't know how to fix them.

I had never loved him more.

He swam. At times I glimpsed him beneath the waves, his body a pale streak. He came up for air and dove again.

While he was underwater, the beautiful brunette appeared. I tensed as I watched her take up a position beside his discarded clothing, but I had no desire to make my presence known, to scream and scare her away. I can't explain why, even to this day, but I knew no jealousy as I watched her watch the water and wait for him, motionless except for her hair and a playful wind-flutter at the bottom edge of her dress.

Robert Louis—how could I think of him otherwise? rose to the surface and saw her. He swam closer, stood on the sea floor, and climbed out to her.

He stopped, his body streaming water.

She put her hands up and laid them on his chest.

And then they made love.

Chapter 50

I COULDN'T ERASE THE PICTURE. IT WAS SO DIFFERENT FROM THE UGLY scenes I'd clandestinely witnessed between my mother and father. Robert Louis, twined into and around the brunette, his hands seizing her hair, his mouth against her throat, made what I observed beautiful. Like poetry, music, or a painting—but better, because instead of still words on paper or inert pigments, it was love put to motion like a ballerina and her partner, or the musical wash of the sea.

It was the love dance I had witnessed at the Schloss between the downy birch tree and the wind, with Teófilo as the backdrop.

Why couldn't I have that? Yes, I'd vowed no man would ever touch me in such ways…but I was no longer a child pouring out her loneliness to a gargoyle. I was married, and heartrendingly in love.

The morning after, Robert Louis and Demetri rowed to the south end of the island for supplies. As soon as they were out of sight, I began a methodical search and eventually found my rival's home—a whitewashed cottage deep in the pine forest. I stood for a moment, taking it in, the door and window frames painted cobalt blue, a black and white cat sunning on the front porch, and the flowers hanging in pots. It was a peaceful, welcoming sanctuary.

I knocked.

"Bastien?" she called from within. I made no reply.

She opened the door, pushing a lock of hair from her eyes. A basket of cut flowers dangled from one arm.

Her smile faded into a careful, expressionless mask, taking with it the charming dimple beside her lips.

"May I come in?" I asked in German.

Her gaze faltered. She tucked her lower lip behind a set of even white teeth.

Everyone has flaws. Somewhere. Nobody is perfect. But I looked hard, and couldn't find a single one.

She inclined her head and stepped aside.

The vestibule opened into a room full of flowers and the scent of herbs. For an instant I thought I caught a faint scent of him.

"Sit," she said in English, gesturing to a sofa. "I've just made tea."

She returned with a tray. There were figs, cut in half, cubes of feta, a bowl of fat pistachios, a bunch of dewy grapes, a teapot, and two cups. She poured tea through a strainer and handed me a cup.

It was good tea, golden, with flavors of fruit and peppermint.

Her hair was pinned up but several dark tendrils coiled around her ears and against the back of her neck. She wore an apron over a home-spun dress with little cap sleeves. It was low cut—framing her breasts beneath the thin material. Throughout eternity man has idolized and idealized female breasts. I still don't understand why. What's so special about them? Perhaps the damned things symbolize the one time in his life he enjoyed unconditional love.

This woman, patiently awaiting whatever I meant to say or do, seemed everything…simply everything I wanted for Robert Louis. The perfect companion and mate.

Now that I'd come, I lost all my rehearsed words and started to cry.

She knelt by the sofa and clasped my hands. "Zoë," she whispered, and her own eyes filled with tears.

"You—you know who I am?" I asked, sniffling.

She picked up a napkin and gave it to me. I swiped at my nose.

"Yes." She took the napkin, folded it, and patted my face. Her fingers brushed over my lashes. The tears that filled her eyes spilled down her cheeks and even they were like drops of dew. Her skin didn't splotch, her eyes didn't redden. They grew even more incandescently blue. She wept like the goddess she was.

"Who are you?" I asked.

She sat beside me. "Phaedre."

The goddess had a name. "Phaedre. Beautiful. Like you."

She stroked my hair. "Not as beautiful as Zoë. Did you know your name means…life?"

I shook my head.

"Life," she said softly. "Your mother picked that name."

Her eyes darkened and she glanced at a potted lemon tree in the corner of the room. "I had a daughter," she said softly. "She would be just a little older than you."

Sun rays slanted through a set of blinds at the window, striping her face in light and shadow. "Is she…gone?"

Her lids dropped briefly. "She is dead."

"I—I'm sorry."

Phaedre patted my cheek. "I made her a dress…to wear when she married."

And I knew…why Elena had paled, why Robert Louis had wept. "The dress. It was…you…"

We sat without speaking.

She tightened her grip on my hand. "Zoë, I am going to tell you something that might be hard to understand. Not only are you the youngest person on earth that we know of, you may be the only female left who can have a baby…and because of that, you are very important."

She paused as I tried to make sense of the words. Why would she say such a thing? What did it mean?

"It's funny, isn't it?" she said. "That you can be just yourself, a girl, living a carefree life, and without your knowledge, you are the most important person in the world."

"I don't—what—what—"

"Oh, I'm sorry. Maybe he was right."

Horror spread through my solar plexus like the insidious creeping of a spider. Her sorrowful expression magnified the sensation. "Is that why…why my home was attacked? To kill me?"

She shook her head. "To capture you. There are many people… countries…who would give much to have you under their control, Zoë."

Things were becoming painfully clear. "That's why he married me."

"To give you his protection."

You don't think anybody cares about her, do you? the servant at my mountain home had said. *Especially him?*

He was protecting me...for his country. The valuable resource. The commodity. More than that—he was keeping track of me. Making sure no other country stole me away.

"Are you...are you his wife?" It seemed my body understood these things before my mind. It had started to tremble.

"It makes us sisters, in a way."

"I—I don't want a sister. I want you to go away."

She smiled sadly and cupped my cheek in her hand, but I knocked it off and rose to my feet. "He lied. We weren't betrothed. He just said that—to keep me quiet. I'm just a—a substitute—for your dead child."

"No, Zoë. You're hope to him. Do you understand? For the future. Hope...for life and dignity."

"But he doesn't—he doesn't love—he couldn't—he doesn't care— not when you—" I failed to stifle my sobs though I clenched my teeth and fists and muttered, "*Stop it, stop.*"

As I turned, there he was, in the doorway, staring from Phaedre to me and back again.

"What have you done?" he thundered.

I couldn't stand to be the subject of any argument between them.

I squirmed past him, evading his grasp, and ran.

Chapter 51

"Elena. Where is Zoë?"

By craning my neck, I could see him. He looked frantic. Darkness, delphiniums, and a terrace ledge disguised my presence.

"I don't know. It's been hours since I've seen her. What's wrong?"

"She found Phaedre."

"Oh."

"There's more. In the city, Demetri and I heard—"

The rest was lost as they disappeared beneath the pillars.

I watched the moons rise and breathed in the heady jasmine. I tried to slow the hammering of my heart and told myself, again and again, *it doesn't matter*.

"Zoë. Oh, Zoë."

I jumped. I hadn't heard him approach—no surprise when I saw he was barefoot.

He sat beside me on the bench.

"It was wrong of her to tell you. It should have been me. I wanted to protect you—to preserve your idealism, your innocence, as long as I possibly could. She thought you had the right to know everything— and you do, of course. She's right about that."

"It's true?"

He lit a cigarette, inhaled, and blew a cloud of smoke. "No woman that we know of has had a child in the last thirteen years, nor for some time before that. Your mother was the last."

I was asking him about marrying me when he was already married. But I didn't correct him. It was my fault for being unable to articulate what I needed.

"My mother…"

"Not the woman at the Schloss. She isn't your mother. That man isn't your father."

"He's not—he's not—" My hands fisted. The biggest surprise was only the lack of surprise I felt. That sweaty, smelly man wasn't my father. The woman who obsessively annihilated her eyebrow…was not my mother.

Relief flooded through me.

"He was hired to watch over you," Robert Louis said, "and to preserve the illusion." He threw the cigarette on the flagstones, where it smoldered. "Someone high up owed him or was being blackmailed by him. That's the only reason you were entrusted to such a fool. They were lamentable—the woman dosed with so many drugs it's surprising she could walk."

"Sometimes she couldn't," I said automatically, even as my heart swelled with pity. She wasn't crazy. She'd been drugged. "Why did they do that to her?"

"They wanted a woman around you—more illusion—but they didn't want to take a chance that she could reveal their plots and turn you against them."

"They…?"

"Our government. The scientists. They've been waiting, Zoë, impatiently waiting for you to grow up. The attack on your home—those were Russian paramilitary, attempting to kidnap you. But we were tipped off and I was sent to stop them. It gave me the chance I needed to get you out of there. If I hadn't, our own government would have soon come for you."

I wanted to ask who and where my real mother was, but the more pressing question had to be answered first. "What did they mean to do?"

Moonlight accented the repeated clench of his jaw. He rubbed his temple. "I'm only guessing. That department is very tight-lipped. But I have had some…experience with them. I am fairly certain they would have conducted experiments on you. They might have done even worse things. And if you actually proved fertile? There might have been a bidding war. Or they might have decided to keep you, which would give Germany superiority over every other government in the world, unless one of them produces a fertile girl."

"And how did…marrying me stop that?"

"I used the attack to justify taking you from the Schloss, and your pseudo father didn't dare try to stop me. He was terrified I would punish him for letting your location get out, and I ordered him to keep quiet. He managed to follow my orders for a few days, giving us a little precious time before the military came after us. I believed, if I could get you here, this would be a safe place for you. No one knows about it. You could live your whole life here, if necessary, and because we went through with that ceremony, I thought maybe I could convince them you're not fertile, if the worst happened and we were captured. I meant to tell them we have done everything possible to make a baby, without success. You're not a girl to them, Zoë, with her own feelings and a desire to care for trees. For some, you're the world's last hope, and that's bad enough. But for others, you're a means to an end—an end that doesn't have anything to do with infertility or the human race."

In the background, there rose an insistent whispered call, like rushing wind. I looked up—I knew I should pay attention, but I couldn't just now. I returned my gaze to him, detecting a tremble in his fingers as he ran a hand through his hair.

"They've given this crisis a catch-phrase. 'Profound necessity.' That name, all by itself, gives them unconditional authority to do whatever they want. Any challenge is instantly halted when they drag out those two words."

He stopped to draw breath, and, I suspected, to organize his thoughts.

"It's not too late. There are still women young enough to turn it all around. But every passing year takes us closer to the point of no return. Do you understand what I meant now, about the evil done with words and phrases? The men pulling the strings—mostly scientists— use words like swords. First, they heaped blame upon the second moon, then women, then the haze. They would have accused geese if they thought it would deflect the attacks on them."

I gazed at him, torn between what he was saying and the distant, urgent call from the downward slope of pines beyond the terraces.

"Haze?" I asked, because he paused, and I thought he was waiting for me to say something.

"You don't see it, do you?" His head tilted. "You've never mentioned it."

"See what?"

"The haze. More accurately, the dust."

I shook my head, puzzled. "I see dust. My mo—the woman at the Schloss was always complaining about how dusty everything was."

"This is a different kind of dust. Remember when we talked about the fracture in *L'ombre Moon?* It happened before you were born, not long after women stopped having children. When the moon cracked, something came out and spread over the world. That's the dust I'm talking about. One of the reasons you were taken to the Schloss was because it's almost nonexistent there. The wind blows much of it away, maybe. Do you remember your tutor asking you questions about the flora around the estate? He's the one who figured out you couldn't see it."

I thought about the odd questions my tutor had sometimes asked, and my attempts to avoid punishment by answering in a way I felt he wanted.

Hesitantly, I said, "I do see…something, sometimes. Rainbows, out of the corner of my eye. But if I try to look directly at them, they vanish." Teófilo saw them too. He was always going on about rainbows.

"People were frightened and angry when women suddenly stopped getting pregnant. They demanded answers. They thought the scientists were withholding the cure. There was violence. Truth is, scientists have no answers, but they won't admit it. To protect themselves, they enlisted religion. Science and religion are thought to be opposites, but they have worked together before to control people, quite successfully. With their alignment, what chance was there for truth to prevail? People were maneuvered into accepting, even embracing, their own deprivation, while those under the domes enjoy cutting-edge technology, space travel, computers, and satellites."

I knew nothing about space travel or what a computer was. I was only vaguely aware of the word "technology," and not sure what it meant, but I didn't interrupt.

"The ruse was successful. It became a matter of patriotism, and those who resisted were attacked, sometimes killed. There are only a few of us who know that nothing harmful has ever been found in the substance that came out of the moon. It doesn't store in our blood or organs. It doesn't collect in the lungs. There are no detectable metals or chemicals. The dust doesn't cause cancer or respiratory infections, emphysema or heart disease. And nothing, *nothing* has ever linked it to infertility. The only bad thing it does is clog up machinery. As soon as the gears and engines are cleaned, they gum up again. That's partly why rural people agreed to return to the old ways. Farm tools of bygone eras don't clog. Oil lamps and candles don't short out. The scientists and politicians claimed that the dust does the same thing to women's bodies. People believed. Why wouldn't they? They can't see how their current state makes them much easier to control."

He turned his head and stared sharply over the terraces towards the sea. For a moment I wondered if he'd at last heard the warning that was becoming louder, more insistent. But then he turned back and I saw that he hadn't.

"There are scientists who really believe the dust is to blame, and we just haven't determined how, yet. It's the timing, you see. Worldwide sterility started a few months before the crack in the moon. Some think the dust weakened what's left of the ozone layer around the earth, and allowed more radiation to get through. Glass domes were built in three cities, over government buildings and research facilities, designed to keep even minute particles of dust and radiation out. Scientists, high-ranking officials, and political leaders live their lives beneath those domes. Everyone else is on their own. They can wear air-filtering face masks but that's the extent of what our government has done to help them.

"Here's what they're hiding, Zoë. Every test indicates that we are still fertile. There is nothing physically wrong with any of us, men or women, and if the problem isn't physical, then what is it? When they were deciding what to do with you, many wanted you kept under one of their domes, in a hospital, but many others believed that might cause mental or emotional damage, and harm the chances of you getting pregnant in ways that we are less able to understand. In the end they chose a place that was high, clean, and very remote, and created the illusion of a normal life, a normal childhood, like the old days."

I rubbed my temples. It was hard to follow so many paths. My head ached. "We're going to disappear, like tigers and polar bears and sea mammals?"

His face was angry and sorrowful. "Ruthless, shortsighted politicians are lying to a populace that is too poor, apathetic, uneducated, and exhausted to fight." He lit another cigarette. It made my lungs hurt to see him smoking so much. "They don't seem to care that there will be no one left to dominate in a matter of fifty to seventy years. Oh, Zoë. There is so much to explain. I hardly know where to begin."

He threw the second cigarette down. It landed near the first one. Smoke rose, stinging my eyes.

"They used their profound necessity to pass laws about almost everything. You, for instance. There are laws specifically about you, giving them the legal right to do whatever they want with you. Another casualty is romance. Marriages are arranged by scientists now. They run tests and match couples they think have the best chance of conceiving. Usually, the couple have never even seen each other before their wedding day. You and I, our betrothal? They allowed it at the time because they trusted me. They thought I would follow their orders, lie to you, and hand you over without protest."

I felt helpless and hopeless. My dreams were shattered, and it must have showed. *What about Phaedre?* I wanted to ask.

He clasped my hand. "We can defeat them, you and I. There are others, too. Men and women are different, but that should never mean unequal. We are yin and yang. Symmetrical. A musical chorus, perfectly designed to bring out the beauty in each other. This is ancient knowledge, but it's been suppressed by those who couldn't care less if humans survive. All they care about is wealth, power, and control. They want to hold onto those things until the very end. I know they're building something in secret, probably ships to carry them to some other planet. Do you understand what I'm trying to say? Even faced with annihilation, they won't give up their need to control."

He took my other hand and brought them both to his chest. "We have to go beyond anything we've ever done to save ourselves. The fight itself will transform us. Your father taught me that. I am his heir to the transformation."

"You know my—my real father?"

His gaze faltered. "Not really. I shouldn't have said that. He inspired me, is what I meant."

Questions poured through my head—about my real mother...my

real father…what had caused humans to lose the ability to reproduce, and, oddly, underneath, the first movement from Beethoven's *Pastorale Symphony*, which I'd fallen in love with while eavesdropping on a party thrown by my "parents" at the Schloss. It wove quietly through everything Robert Louis said.

Once more, I heard the servant's words. *You don't think anybody cares about her, do you? Especially him?*

"Why…why are you doing this?" My voice rose. "You were already married…to Phaedre. I know you—you love her. Have you…made yourself their enemy…for me? Or…are you—are you lying to me, like you say they lied?"

He didn't have a chance to answer, because at that instant, the earth exploded and so did the sky.

EVOLUTION

May - June, 2091

Chapter 1

I SCREAMED.

Robert Louis grabbed me, pulled me to his chest, and turned his back to the cyclone. Wind whipped dust and dirt into my eyes and mouth. Monsters, standing upright like men but with black featureless faces and round greenish-reflective eyes, surrounded us, holding rifles with bayonets.

I heard Elena shriek.

The air thrummed in a rhythmical beating roar. Even through my terror I couldn't help noticing how flowers were being ripped out of their pots.

Three of the manlike creatures grabbed Robert Louis and tore us apart. He struggled. "Do you know who I am?" he shouted.

"Oh yes," one replied. Raising his weapon, he brought the butt-end smashing against my husband's skull.

He fell. They dragged him into the house.

Two others prodded me under the pillars and into the sunken library.

Robert Louis lay on the floor, pallid and still. Blood ran from a bruising gash on his temple. When I was released, I knelt, using the hem of my dress to blot the flow.

One of the beasts removed the thick greenish things he wore over his eyes then stripped off a black balaclava. He was indeed a man—

hair tufting out in spikes, black paint or charcoal smeared across his cheekbones.

I knew him. At first, I couldn't pinpoint from where, then it returned—the journey through my homeland, hiding during the day and riding by night. Once a company of soldiers nearly flushed us out. This man's grim expression and relentless lashing of a weary horse had frightened me.

Robert Louis had named him. Karl von Bäumer.

A rough white scar started on his forehead and ran through one eye, emerging beneath a black patch and deforming his cheek. "Secure," he said into a round nodule at his collar. He pressed his fingers to his right ear, listening and nodding, though all I heard was my own shallow breathing and thudding heartbeat. He came closer, his working eye squinted. The scars were countless and startling, some raised and some indented. As wounds, they must have been agonizing.

"Stand up."

I obeyed.

"You have the look of your mother."

I thought he meant to say something else, but the entry of another man stopped him.

"The transport is ready, *Herr Oberst*," the new soldier said as he peeled off his headgear. Clicking his heels, he bowed in the ancient military polonaise.

The man beside me nodded.

"He needs a doctor," I said.

Von Bäumer glanced at Robert Louis and sneered. "He won't die. The great Odenwylde will live to stand trial for his crimes."

Three black-shrouded, faceless men appeared in the doorway, their heavy guns pointed at my chest. Even I, a very, very ignorant girl, knew escape was impossible.

I was handcuffed along with Robert Louis, who groaned but remained unconscious. He was tossed carelessly onto a stretcher and we were taken through the forest, the trees whispering their alarm all the way.

A pulsating gigantic basilisk sat on the beach in the cove. My terrified struggles were futile—the soldiers dragged me to this thing and hoisted me into its heaving metal gut. When everyone had entered, the door slid shut and the throbbing increased to impossible levels. We lifted, me cringing, shuddering, chewing my lip until it bled.

The commandant grinned. In the dim light I fancied his scars came to life with their own grins that widened and narrowed as the shadows changed. "Never been in a helliglider, have you? They're fast as hell—hence the name—and when we switch on the stealth covenant, invisible. Not even illuminators can detect them. We can't use them much because of the way they scare the peasants, but we hauled one out of storage for you."

He pulled a knife from the holster at his waist and ran his thumb along the edge, hilt to tip. A thin line of blood formed. "Everyone had technology, you know. Some of us still do. But you commoners lost it, all because of a woman. One unholy woman and her followers. She sent her piss cloud, and now you're back to oil lamps and horse-drawn carriages, trying to appease the fertility gods. Just so you know, where we're taking you? That piss cloud is thicker. Try not to breathe too much when we get there, girl. We don't want your eggs getting smoggy after all we've done to keep them clean."

His men laughed as though this was very funny. Robert Louis woke soon after, but he couldn't speak; they'd gagged him with a thick white strip stretched tightly around his head. It looked painful, the way it bit into the edges of his mouth. He could only gaze at me and I at him.

We flew all night.

Chapter 2

FOR THE FIRST TIME IN MY LIFE, I ENTERED A CITY IN MY HOME COUNTRY. Faint, yellowish veils of dust drifted between ugly grey buildings. I was sure this must be the dust Robert Louis and our captor had spoken of. There were no plants. No trees. Through the oblong window, I saw two other flying machines, pricked by early morning sunlight. They darted from cloud to cloud like mechanical crickets playing hide and seek.

The transporting ship approached something that looked to me like a soap bubble sitting over a complex of buildings. We flew straight at it, fast, but just as I thought we would crash, a portal opened and we slipped through. The transport circled and landed on a platform ringed with blinking red lights. Our captors hustled us out and across a roof. Raised in the quiet of the mountains, I found the noise coming through the soaring dome as invasive as the thrust of a knife. I wanted to cover my ears but the soldiers had cuffed my hands behind my back.

We were taken down a set of stairs and into a corridor lit by some unseen artificial means. We stopped before a set of double doors. When they opened, we were pushed into a tiny cubicle. The doors closed; my stomach lurched as we dropped. It was all I could do to keep from collapsing into hysterics, but no one else seemed concerned, so I clenched my hands and swallowed stark terror.

Robert Louis's gaze seemed sadly reassuring.

The falling thing stopped gently. The doors opened. We exited and I found myself in a different corridor. People—mostly men, but a few women—were everywhere, some dressed in suits, some in long white coats and loose green trousers. A few wore caps with strings. All gaped at me. Once I turned to see an entire corridor full of people standing motionless, staring. Wherever we went, silence fell.

At a three-way juncture, the guards holding onto Robert Louis pushed him into a different corridor from the one I was led into.

"No," I cried. "Don't—don't separate us."

Von Bäumer laughed and put his face close to mine. "You two got close, didn't you? Tell me, girl. Are you pregnant?"

The other guard tilted his head, his expression intent. I didn't answer.

Now I was truly alone. They put me in a room and locked the door. There was a window, too thick to break nor would it open, but by scooting a footstool underneath I could look outside.

Two stories below, on the other side of the dome, a mob was screaming, fighting, shoving. Figures in black uniforms pushed them back with clubs.

I felt like most of the people were women, but it was hard to be certain because of the masks over their faces.

When I was spotted, framed by the window, the shouting died away. The crowd stopped fighting and stared. I stared back. There was an endless expanse of dead silence.

Then somebody screamed and the rest took it up. The shoving renewed. Faces were raised towards me. Some tore off their masks.

I left the stool and crossed to a corner. I sat on the floor, resting my shoulder and head against the cold wall, turning my face away from the room and my unimaginable future.

Chapter 3

The orderly who brought a tray of food said that Robert Louis—Odenwylde—would stand trial for treason, kidnapping, and murder. He said I couldn't attend, but since the courthouse was across the street, maybe I could see some of it if I looked out the window.

I understood the treason and kidnapping, but not the murder. Next time the man came, I asked.

"What—you think he isn't capable of taking lives?" One of his thin, squiggly brows lifted as he set the dinner tray on the table. "He's killed plenty—a man doesn't rise to his level without proving himself capable of carrying out any order, no matter how brutal. Brazil would like to see him extradited, but they'll have to wait their turn, won't they? We're trying him for the murder of three men in the mountain passes—soldiers under his own command who tried to stop him from taking you through. And no doubt they'll bring up the death of his child…again."

A gasp escaped before I could stop it.

"That's right." The orderly, wearing a tag on his breast pocket naming him "Franz Weber," smirked as he shook out a napkin. "His little daughter, only seven years old."

"No."

"The things he did to her don't bear speaking of. You're lucky, girl, that you didn't end up dead too." He shook his head and left, locking the heavy door behind him.

Other men came, garbed in white coats, stringed caps, and thin, tight, almost transparent gloves. They, along with two armed guards in grey uniforms and red berets, escorted me to a cold room containing a wheeled bed, two chairs, and a floor lamp. This wasn't a lamp in any familiar sense to me, but a tall, silver thing that glared like an unblinking eye.

I had to sit beneath its blinding light.

One of the white-coated men sat opposite me. He took a small round thing from a box and twisted it. It opened up rather like a flower blossom, and a flat edge formed at the bottom. It gave off a whirring sound. He set it on the metal table beside him. "Have you started your periods?"

I stared at him.

"Bleeding. Have you begun your monthly bleeding cycles?"

I shook my head.

"Do you know what I'm talking about?" He massaged the bridge of his nose.

"No."

"Well then, you haven't. No matter. They can be induced. It gives us more time anyway. Did Odenwylde have sexual intercourse with you?"

I saw in memory the lovemaking between Robert Louis and Phaedre on the sand in the cove. He had said that if we were ever captured, he hoped they would believe we had done that. "Yes."

His gaze sharpened. My face heated.

"You can't lie about these things, you know. The truth is too easily discovered."

"We did."

"We will see. Did he harm you?"

"No."

"Well, you didn't hesitate with that answer. I'm going to tell you something. The man who kidnapped you is being tried for the murder of his daughter."

"I know."

"Are you upset over his capture?"

"Of course. He's my—my husband."

"He's a criminal, and already married, so he couldn't be your husband too, could he? We don't allow that sort of thing here—not yet, anyway. Your loyalty is misplaced. He used his position to gain trust, and used that trust to commit high treason. He meant to sell you to whomever would pay the most. Hanging's too good for Odenwylde. He's betrayed everyone who ever knew him, even his own child. You ought to cooperate with us. We won't hurt you. As a matter of fact, you have our government to thank for the life you've lived. I've heard it was peaceful and clean—off in the mountains somewhere. There's plenty right here in this city who would have gladly traded places with you."

Tired and confused, I rubbed my eyes. *You're nothing but payment,* my Schloss "mother" had cried. *An experiment. They'll never let you go.*

Had she been speaking of Robert Louis…Odenwylde? Or these men who tried to make me hate him?

After they took me back to my room, I looked out the window. It was raining, but that didn't seem to affect the energy of the crowd. One woman standing apart from the others next to a streetlamp caught my eye. She wore no mask and did not take part in the frenzy, but stood as still as if carved of stone, leaning on a cane and bundled in a long brown coat with a hood. Dark spectacles were directed at my window. I stared back, struck by the image of calm immobility adjacent to such raving chaos.

Chapter 4

THE TRIAL BEGAN. MANACLED AND WEARING A VEST THE ORDERLY TOLD ME was bulletproof, Robert Louis was taken into a building just outside the dome. A courthouse, Franz explained. The screaming crowd had to be beaten off with clubs and threatened with bayonets.

The doors closed and I knew no more.

I was no longer certain of anything. Parts of what the white-coated man had said were true. Robert Louis had already been married when he went through the ceremony with me. It could be true that he'd planned to sell me to whomever might pay the most.

But I would never believe he murdered his child. Not the man who risked his precarious health to escort me to the island. And Phaedre— she never would have allowed her child's murderer to make love to her.

Yet there was the bowing and scraping I'd seen from my "father" and the servants. They'd spoken of his unquestioned authority. They'd mentioned hangings, firing squads. Odenwylde could not be crossed with impunity.

The white-coats came again. One rolled up the sleeve of the sweater I'd been given because it was always so cold in this place.

"What are you doing?" I tried to jerk free.

"Don't worry. This will simply relax you. We're going to examine you to see if you have indeed had sexual intercourse, as you say you have."

"No!"

It was no use. The guards stepped forward. I received the injection. Soon their voices echoed and my surroundings wavered like they were underwater. I pictured myself swimming with the dolphin in the turquoise cove at *Naiskos* until they lifted me and placed me on a wheeled stretcher. I was rolled through what felt like endless corridors, one harsh light after another floating above me. Franz called this "electricity." He said it had been around for a long time but because of the years with no births, people rejected heathen inventions and reverted to simpler lives, hoping to earn forgiveness from God before it was too late. That was how I'd been raised, he explained, in a clean, safe, pollution-free environment, to safeguard my mental health and physical fertility.

"My wife asks about you," he said. I thought about it as the white-coats strapped me down and bent to their work. "She asks what you look like, and if you can have babies. She says she'd give her right hand if she could have one. Women these days—ha, they're crazy. Babies. That's all they think about. I've heard they used to complain about getting pregnant. There were so many people, there was talk of mandatory birth control. Now women are barren and it's like their brains have snapped. Oh, it's important, I'll grant you. We're all going to die out aren't we, if they can't solve this. You know what you might be? The mother of the future—of the next human race. How does that sound, little girl?"

Chapter 5

Muffled chanting woke me.

"Death to Odenwylde! Death!"

According to the clock on the wall, it was nearly seven—morning or night, I didn't know. Whenever the white-coats injected me with their relaxing drug I felt groggy and disoriented for a couple of days.

"You're a virgin," they said after the first time. "Did you think you could hide it from us?" The older one scratched his ear. "Odenwylde. He's a strange one. To have in his possession a virgin—and possibly the only fertile female on earth, and not try to impregnate her. He might've gone down in history as the Father of the first-born child after the Barren Times." He shook his head and glanced at me queerly, as though he wondered if I were so disgusting that even to be the father of the first-born child after the "barren times" wasn't enough to spark Odenwylde's interest. Then he added, "Well, he tortured and slaughtered his only other offspring. I guess that says it all, doesn't it?"

Anger erupted. Everyone thought they knew everything about us, and they all thought the worst. "I was his wife only in name," I snapped. "He treated me like a beloved child. A daughter. He made me feel...loved."

The doctor stared at me, frowning, and I knew what he was thinking. That maybe Odenwylde had used me as a handy replacement for his dead daughter.

I crawled out of bed. The place between my legs was sore. I didn't inspect it. I had before and had seen nothing. It was just a generalized soreness. I never knew what they did while I was drugged. I could only hope I didn't act like my Schloss "mother."

Thoughts of her were disturbing. She'd lost her life, in essence, because of me. My chatty orderly said that the doctors very carefully monitored the drugs I received, because they didn't want me harmed. Had such care been taken with her? This deafening metallic world seemed to have discarded the rights and importance of the individual. Anyone, everyone was dispensable.

Except maybe…me.

Yet, important as I was, I was given no choices—not even about what food I ate.

It was a peculiar sensation—all my life I was nothing. Nobody cared about me except Teófilo. I was an unwanted little pest.

Now I was the cause of daily stampedes in the streets, the object of the doctors' fascination, the hope of the world.

Stepping onto the footstool, I viewed the street below. I'd become used to the throng milling between the courthouse and my building. They were mostly women in dingy coats, many wearing masks that covered their mouths, noses, and eyes. Once they realized which window was mine, they always kept watch, and whenever I appeared, they would scream and push and nearly trample each other. The only word I discerned in their cries was *baby*. Sometimes I was ordered to get down so the swarm would disperse. It never did though. Like a wave, it undulated between the courthouse and my prison, all day and all night. Before long I hardly noticed them…but for the one who appeared every now and then, always taking up a stance in the same spot, hands shoved into coat pockets, eyes hidden behind dark glasses, sometimes wearing a scarf over her nose and mouth.

Franz told me my room had special, very expensive filters on the air circulator. They didn't want to risk my health. My eggs, more specifically. "That damn dust," he said. "They're pretty sure it's to blame for this predicament. It came out of the second moon, you know, about the same time pregnancies everywhere stopped. They say since it was brought from outer space, we humans have no immunity to whatever poison it carries. It's like we're aboriginals being exposed to smallpox for the very first time. But here's something that makes no sense. Even unfertilized eggs harvested years before the sterility shriveled up and died. That's always made me wonder. I mean, they weren't exposed, were they? They were in sealed, sterile dishes, in deep freeze, in sanitary rooms." He shrugged. "I'm only a hospital aide, so what do I know? But I can't figure that one out."

He looked at me, his brow puckered, as though I ought to pontificate with something wise. He idly sprayed the table with disinfectant and wiped it with a cloth. "You ever hear about the London Smog?"

"No."

"I often think of it these days. It happened in the nineteen-fifties. It was yellow too, from what I've read. It coated the whole city and thousands of people died. That one was caused by smoke and fog mixing with pollution and something about the weather."

He leveled a gaze on me. Again, I had the sense that he wanted me to explain, or reassure him. Something.

"The Industrial Revolution, that's what brought people to their knees. It got worse and worse. That's why everyone agreed to dump their TVs and VR games and computers and cars and whatnot. Even electric cars still required parts that were mined and...oh, well. You don't know what I'm talking about."

He crossed to the window. "Those gas masks are all the fashion. Pink ones for the ladies, with flowers, but damn, I miss the days I could admire a woman's face."

He left the window, shaking his head. "What about Erin Aragon and her revolution? Anybody ever tell you about that?"

I shook my head.

"They say she did this. She's the reason women stopped bearing children. She brought the whole world to the edge, and now we're about to tip off. I've heard it was her who cracked that moon. She's the one who sent poison across the world and then disappeared. I've heard she hated men. Maybe she wants us to die out. If so, it looks like she's going to get her wish."

Nobody had given any thought to how I should occupy myself during those endless days. Finally, my orderly asked for and was given permission to provide something called a portable monitor. Through this flat black screen that, when activated, spoke and made pictures, I was able to see and learn more about the world than my tutor ever thought of teaching. It was fastened to the wall and I was given a device that turned it on and off and could scroll through various things called services. Every service displayed different content.

One day, after pressing a button, Robert Louis's face appeared. Close-up. Staring directly at me.

I cried out. I only realized after jumping up and beating on the front of the monitor that he could not see or hear me.

Whatever was relaying this image of him retreated. The angle widened. I was able to see more of where he was and who he was with.

"The defendant has admitted," said a man in a long black robe who paced before him, "that though he rose to the supreme rank of Generalinspekteur—a position of highest trust and command, he was the entire time secretly involved in the enemy faction known as *Chthonia*."

"Is that true, Herr Doktor Jäger-Abelard?" A man wearing a robe of dark red, seated in the midst of four other similarly gowned men, leaned forward, resting his forearms on the table in front of him.

"No," my husband said. "It is not true."

Tears flooded from my eyes but I allowed no sound, for I didn't want to miss a single word.

His voice. I hadn't expected to ever hear it again.

"Edify us if you will on the meaning of that word."

"Of the earth," Robert Louis replied.

"Yes…" The prosecutor—or defender, I didn't yet know which— hissed the "s" and allowed silence to reign for several heavy seconds. "That meaning will become pertinent in a moment, Herr Vorsitzender, but first, I would like to read for the court the defendant's heritage as head of the dynastic House of Odenwylde."

He retrieved a document and sipped water. "He was born Bastien Günther Jäger-Abelard. Who among us need have the ancient lineage of that family explained? Indeed, this court does not have the time it would take to hear even his many names." He glanced around as though he thought someone might ask. I hoped they would, for I knew nothing of the Jäger-Abelard family.

Another man, also robed in black and seated near Robert Louis, interrupted. "Herr Vorsitzender, there is absolutely no relevance in this."

The red-robed judge waved his hand. "Is it germane, Herr Staatsanwalt?"

"I believe it to be, Herr Vorsitzender."

"Make it brief."

Inclining his head, the prosecutor read from the document. "He received his doctorate from Johann Wolfgang Goethe Universität..." Here he paused, then added, with dripping contempt, "In social philosophy, before beginning his military education. Perhaps this explains his willingness to commit high treason against his mother-country, she who gave him everything—his prestigious standing, his expensive education, and not least, his rise to a position of absolute trust."

The seated man beside Robert Louis stood, pressing his fists against the table. "Herr Staatsanwalt rejects the basic rules of the courtroom, Herr Vorsitzender. Will you not put an end to this rant?"

"What is your purpose with this soliloquy, Herr Staatsanwalt?" the judge asked.

"It is imperative for our esteemed judges," here the prosecutor gestured to the five red-robed men seated before him, "to fully comprehend the magnitude of political betrayal the accused has perpe-trated upon our people and country. As titular head of the Odenwylde dynasty, the defendant had a hereditary obligation to serve to the full extent of his means, which are indeed many. Had he put his family's wealth and resources into the task of finding a cure for sterility—a legitimate cure—we might be witnessing the rebirth of nations right now instead of agonizing over the possible end of the human species."

"Are you patronizing me, Herr Staatsanwalt, or aggrandizing?" The judge's frown was severe. "If the defendant is convicted, it will be due to his actions as an adult. I will not stand for penalization of child-hood or schooling."

"As you wish, Herr Vorsitzender." The prosecutor replaced the document on the table. Though his "rant" had been cut short, he still looked satisfied.

The judge turned his attention to Robert Louis. "How old were you when you joined the association of Chthonia?"

"Thirty, Herr Vorsitzender."

"And you are now...forty-one?"

"Yes."

"Herr Vorsitzender, I would like to hear an explanation of why he joined that corps of outlaws," the prosecutor said.

Every word the prosecutor used was designed to denigrate Robert Louis. If I were in that room, I would hit him over and over until he could no longer speak.

Robert Louis sighed. He looked so tired. There was a bruise on his right cheekbone. His nose appeared swollen, and a scab marred the bridge. I could just make out a partially healed gash on his lower lip.

"Human rights," he said, so low the judge made him repeat it. He was then asked for more detail.

His hands, resting on the table, clenched. "Zoë cannot be treated like an incubator. Chthonia believes she, and every other human being, has the right to grow up normally, marry for love, and bear or not bear children in a purely natural manner."

"Ah, the 'nature' argument." The prosecutor's voice oozed disgust. "The defendant adheres to such a philosophy even when the continuation of our species may hinge on that girl. He maintains, quite selfishly, that she should be allowed to conduct her life at her own haphazard whimsy, against the indubitable law of profound necessity."

The judge regarded Robert Louis, brows lifted, waiting.

"Yes," my husband said.

How I loved him. I adored him. If only he could hear me, see me. I would tell him I wasn't listening to those who tried so hard to turn me against him. I would promise—

The prosecutor faced the judges. "Maybe the truth is that he wants the human species to end."

Robert Louis shook his head. "No. But I accept that it might be the natural course. And perhaps we deserve to die out, after the choices we have made."

Wearily, the defense stood again. "I request that last statement be stricken from the record, Herr Vorsitzender."

"Not at this time," the judge replied, after listening to indecipherable comments from his fellows.

"Perhaps he could defend his choices to the court?" The prosecutor scuffed the toe of his shoe against the floor. "The evidence suggests that he has plotted to eradicate the human race."

Robert Louis lifted a hand and rubbed his eyes.

"It is odd to hear him spout the importance of human rights, Herr Vorsitzender, since he so cruelly ripped away his daughter's. Did he not murder his child—nearly the last child born on this earth, and thus of extraordinary consequence, not only, one would assume, to her parents, but to the entire world?"

Robert Louis's shoulders hunched. He cradled his face in one hand as though his head was simply too heavy for his neck to support.

"Tell them," I whispered. "Tell them it isn't true. You could never hurt anyone—least of all your child—tell them."

"His wealth and position shielded him from paying for his daughter's murder—"

The defense counsel pushed back his chair with a squeal and rose. "Now Herr Staatsanwalt is dredging up old accusations that were never proven. I hope we do not lose sight of the years of loyalty the House of Odenwylde has given to his suzerain. Lest we forget, it was Seine Durchlaucht—yes, I will use his hereditary honorific—who led the pivotal raid that acquired the last pregnant woman! Without his intervention, we might not have her child safe in our custody." He banged his fist against the tabletop. "The purpose of this trial is to deal with the current charge of kidnapping, treason, and war crimes. Either Herr Staatsanwalt will follow procedure or I must demand all charges be with—"

"What he did is treason. He is a war criminal, Herr Vorsitzender, do not mistake it for anything else—"

"She is a human being!" Robert Louis lunged to his feet. "Not a lab rat. She has feelings. She wants to be an arborist. She has every right—"

The picture vanished. The courtroom disappeared into black and grey spinning circles.

I tapped the side of the monitor, and used the device to scroll through other services. They worked. I could watch a program on interior decorating, or I could phone in and purchase a pet, but the trial was gone.

Chapter 6

"THERE'S NOTHING WRONG WITH THE MONITOR," I WAS TOLD WHEN I asked for help. "Someone said something the government doesn't want us to hear. They probably won't show any more."

I affixed myself to the window. Every now and then, just enough to make me reel with anxiety and longing, I'd glimpse Robert Louis coming out of or going into the courthouse, manacled and dwarfed by a bullet-proof vest. Sometimes he almost had to be carried, which worried me. How could he defend himself if he couldn't even stand?

The white-coats continued their examinations. Once after I woke, my abdomen burned. To the right of my navel was a thick blood-spotted bandage over a blistering red incision that seemed to be glued shut.

"What did you do?" I asked when next they came.

"Nothing to worry about," my grey-haired doctor said. "We harvested a few eggs, not in the usual manner, but we felt an incision was safer, and we don't want anyone accusing us of anything. They appear to be viable, though we can't be sure until we inseminate them. We're hoping that because you're young and were raised in a place where there was very little dust, you haven't fallen victim to the syndrome. Who knows, Zoë? You may become the mother of a whole squad of babies—lots more healthy fertile girls. There's nothing wrong with the semen, you know. It's the eggs that won't take."

I stared at him, remembering Robert Louis's insistence that nothing was ever found to be wrong with either sex. Why did this doctor want me to believe females were to blame?

Something Robert Louis said at his trial rang through my mind. *Perhaps we deserve to die out, after the choices we have made.*

"Maybe women's eggs are the mark of our right to live," I said to the doctor. "If we can't keep our eggs healthy, maybe we lose that right."

"Looks like Odenwylde infected you with his oddball ideas. Too bad. You seem intelligent beyond your years. Strange you can't see him for what he is. A criminal. A murderer." He observed me intently. "Perhaps it's time you were told what he is truly guilty of."

"You won't turn me against him. Don't waste your time."

He dragged the chair close to the bed and sat. "The world was frantic. No test, no matter how sophisticated, could find anything. There was no germ, no bacteria, no residue of pesticide, and no answers. Women simply weren't conceiving. Year after year passed with no births. A man feels his mortality when he walks past a disintegrating schoolhouse. Anyway, Odenwylde and his wife—"

"Phaedre."

Shrugging, the doctor said, "Had a child. A girl. She died at the age of seven. She was the last, but for you. You were two and still with your mother."

My Schloss mother, or the real one? He continued, giving me no time to ask.

"In those days, Odenwylde was obsessive about his duty to the state. Unquestionably loyal. That dedication helped advance his career, but now it's generally believed his mind warped in the process."

"Blah, blah, blah," I said. "Are you a psychiatrist too?"

The man's jaw clenched and his gaze turned cold. Leaning forward, he enunciated each word as though it gave him great pleasure to destroy me. "He longed to be remembered as a German hero. He was willing to do anything to reach that goal. He conducted experiments on his daughter—Louisa, I believe her name was. Experiments rather like those we've administered to you, but not in a hospital setting. His were cruder and much less kind. After he induced premature menstruation with growth hormones, he raped her."

For a moment I lost my sight and hearing in a swirl of dizziness. *Lies,* I told myself savagely.

"Do you know what would have happened if she had conceived?" The doctor's voice drilled through my vertigo. "She almost certainly would have ruptured and bled to death. She was much too small to carry a baby."

Impossible. Like it was impossible that Robert Louis Balfour Stevenson, author of *Treasure Island* and *Master of Ballantrae*…had defeated death to come to me. Yet, I confess it—no matter how many times I heard him called Bastien or Odenwylde, my heart insisted he was my idol. My poet, reincarnated.

"Oh, Teófilo."

I didn't realize I'd said it aloud until the doctor frowned. "Teófilo?"

I hid my face in my hands. "Leave me alone."

"But I haven't told you everything. You want to be fully informed, don't you? Odenwylde dosed Louisa with various fertility drugs. One of the combinations he tried proved fatal. She suffered horribly—hemorrhaging, vomiting, diarrhea—a helpless child sacrificed to his desire for fame. Why do you think it is that people fear him so much? This is why. His utterly ruthless nature. There are some who believe him the actual reincarnation of another cold-blooded slaughterer in our past…but I don't believe in such ridiculous folderol."

My wedding ring glimmered up at me, the rainbow moonstones, goldstone hearts, and connective silver filigree. I twisted it round and round on my finger, wishing I could say I didn't either.

A birdie with a yellow bill
Hopped upon the window sill,
Cocked his shining eye and said:
'Ain't you 'shamed, you sleepy-head?'

If this tiresome white-coat was speaking truth—a notion I violently resisted—then my husband was not Robert Louis Stevenson, no matter how much I wished him to be. He was in truth Bastien Günther Jäger-Abelard of the House of Odenwylde, and deserved to be publicly hanged, as the ever-growing horde outside demanded.

Chapter 7

I no longer turned on the monitor and gave up staring out the window. I lay on the cot, sleeping, examining the ceiling, hearing his voice in memory.

We are yin and yang. A musical chorus, perfectly designed to bring out the beauty in each other.

Like trees and wind, that continual, ever-changing love-dance. What had happened? Why had we thrown such perfect happiness away?

Franz reported that I'd stopped eating. The white-coats conducted a humiliating invasive physical examination and pasted a black patch on my arm that sent nutrients directly into my blood…or so they said. That was the last time I saw the one who took such pleasure in recounting the details of Louisa's death.

I overheard two men talking in the corridor outside my room. The doctor who told me about Louisa was punished. His license was revoked and he was exiled from the safety of the glass dome.

More days passed. I don't know how many. One evening, as Franz came in with my dinner tray, he said, "Something's happened. But you have to get out of that bed if you want to hear what it is."

Lethargically, I obeyed.

"Oh, you'll perk up once I tell you." He set the tray on the table and plopped, loose-limbed, into one of the chairs. "It's about him." His smile was sly. "There's good news and bad. Which do you want first?"

I stared.

"All right, then." He shrugged. "He's been sentenced to death. Public hanging. That hasn't happened in over a hundred years— maybe longer. No appeals, either. They've dragged out some ancient law that gives them supreme authority." He nodded towards the street. "You'll have a bird's-eye view if you want. Ready for the good news?"

The question could hardly breach the freezing wall of agony that reared inside me. I whispered, "Yes."

"He wants to see you. It's his last request. But you won't be allowed to go unless you show some life. There's a few of these doctors —quacks, I call them—who believe a person can will themselves into the grave if they try hard enough. That's been discussed around here lately, just as it was when you were born. If they think you'll go into a worse funk by seeing him, they'll let him die without a glimpse of you. I assume you don't want that?"

I shook my head.

"Well, then, get up and eat. Prove you've got spirit, and don't let on I told you these things. When they broach the subject, act surprised. Otherwise, they might decide you're trying to fool them. Use your wits, girl."

I sat at the table and ate, though every bite made me gag and I felt queasy after. He watched without speaking. When I finished, he gave me a proud smile and whisked himself and the tray from the room.

Chapter 8

THE GUARDS HANDCUFFED AND BLINDFOLDED ME. WE DESCENDED IN AN elevator machine and walked for a long time. The air turned chilly, there was a damp, moldy smell, and I heard dripping water. It reminded me of the underground tunnel outside of *Möglichkeit*.

One of the guards removed the blindfold. He refused to take off the cuffs, but at least my hands were shackled in front. The second guard unlocked a rusty iron door with a big key on a ring filled with keys. Wherever this sad, neglected place was, it had the feel and smell of a mediaeval bygone age.

The door opened with an unhappy squeal onto thick darkness and a nauseating stench.

"Go on." The guard pointed with his chin. "And don't get creative."

I stepped in and the door rasped shut behind me.

One sob escaped. I silently cursed myself.

"Zoë? I'm in front of you. Keep coming. One more step."

My shin bumped against the edge of a cot. Little by little, I made out more details. It wasn't completely dark. Dim light filtered through thin slits high on the wall. My husband was a humped shadow, his arm outstretched. I fell onto the bed and grabbed his hand. His other arm pulled me to his chest, where I lay and wept.

"They won't give us much time," he said. "There's a candle on the floor by the bed."

Wiping my eyes, I looked and saw a candle stub. A book of matches lay beside it, empty but for one. I lit it and turned back to him.

"Oh." I felt sick. "Oh."

One of his eyes was swollen shut. His face held countless wounds and abrasions. He coughed painfully, half-retching, and spat blood into a filthy handkerchief. Even his lips were marred with bruises.

I feared touching him. But he lifted his hand and I put mine around it. His fingers were icy.

"Zoë. Oh, Zoë. Why couldn't they leave us alone?"

I tried to push damp hair off his hot forehead without hurting him.

"I've missed you." Another coughing fit sent him into a convulsion. When it subsided, he said, "I'll beat them to my own death if they don't hurry."

Another traitorous sob nearly burst free, but I bit it back.

"We were happy on the island, weren't we?" he asked. "Tell me you were happy, my Zoë."

"Because of you. I—I would be happy with you anywhere."

He smiled. It was almost negligible, but definitely there. "Have you ever heard of Pygmalion and Galatea?"

I had, but shook my head, sensing he wanted to tell the story.

"He carved a woman out of a block of marble then fell in love with her. Aphrodite, the goddess of love, felt pity and brought the statue to life."

His hand pressed against the side of my head. "You and I lived that myth. But you, the beautiful statue, brought the old sculptor to life."

"No. You—you did it."

"Maybe we gave life to each other. Do you remember asking me why I took you from your home and hid you away when I was already married?"

"Yes."

"It's because I love you, Zoë." Dropping his hand from my hair, he wove his fingers through mine. "I love your passion and intelligence. I love the way you observe life and the way you can hear what trees have to say. I have loved being in your company. There are so many things to love about you. Do you believe me?"

I nodded, too full of rage and agony to speak.

"Promise me something."

"Anything."

"Choose your own future. Right now, your enigma is locked inside, but it is there, and it can never be taken from you. It is a shimmer of blue embers. A whisper on a breeze. It's like a passing cloud, trembling with thunder." He paused, then said, almost inaudibly, "It carries the fragrance of beginnings. You have dazzled me, Zoë."

Even now, so tortured, so broken, the poet was undaunted.

But he wasn't thinking clearly. Choose my own future? I hadn't had any choices since the day I was born. It was childish fantasy to pretend otherwise.

"Why are they—accusing you of—those awful things? About your daughter?"

He stared, his eyes widening. Wretched anguish darkened his face. "They told you."

Shock crackled through me like I'd been struck by lightning. He should have denied it instantly. "You did—you *did* those things to your daughter?"

He said nothing.

"Tell me," I cried. "You couldn't have done...*that* to Louisa." I struck him in the chest with my fists.

His eyes closed. He swallowed. The involuntary grimace betrayed how much it hurt. "I haven't heard her name in so long."

"How could you be so good to me after that?" Tears spilled, splattering the back of my hands. I hadn't believed. But he didn't deny it. I had asked, and he didn't deny.

My heart broke. I felt it, like a teardrop striking stone.

Chapter 9

"I don't want to see you. They can do whatever they want to you."

He gripped my shoulders. "Will you listen?" he said, his voice unsteady and harsh. "This is for you alone."

His desperation overrode my misery. I nodded.

"Louisa died in my arms."

Sudden, overwhelming fear washed over me, in that primal instinctive way that knows beyond logic what is coming. I, the coward, wanted to flee, but he wouldn't relax his grip. "The last thing she said was *Papa*."

His voice broke.

Dread expanded. It was suffocating, escaping in gasps. "Don't—"

He cut me off. "You must hear. You must know. Before I die—*you must know*." His eyes glittered, from fever or maybe from the tale he shared. The air in his lungs rattled.

"Like I told you at *Naiskos*," he said, "no women were conceiving, and every test was inconclusive. No matter what they say, Zoë, nothing has ever been proven wrong with either men or women. There came a year of rage. Doctors and government officials were attacked. Women were told they were the problem. Their eggs. Their fault. Blaming them opened the door to repeating what we did not even fifty years ago. We turned a blind eye to the crimes we committed, and granted ourselves permission to commit them again."

He had to pause to catch his breath. I rubbed the back of his hand.

"Phaedre was pregnant. We tried not to hope, but there was no trouble. She gave birth at home, on the island, with only me and Elena to help. We decided to keep the baby a secret. We knew what would happen if people found out. Our daughter would become a sensation. She would never have any peace.

"For seven years, we succeeded. Not even my mother and sister knew. But Louisa wanted to meet her grandmother and aunt. We couldn't risk taking her to *Möglichkeit* nor could we risk bringing my mother and sister to the island. We finally decided to meet in a poor suburb of Athens, thinking that we wouldn't be noticed as long as we were careful. We were very careful, but a cleaning woman at the inn spotted Louisa one morning, and she told someone, and that person told someone, and he went straight to the tavern and our secret was out. We rushed Louisa home under cover and I returned to Berlin, hoping to contain things, but I couldn't."

His breathing was more labored. I didn't tell him to stop. I knew he wouldn't.

"A group of highly respected scientists came to me and asked if they could examine her and Phaedre. They assured me that I could be there, with them both, every step of the way. They pleaded with me. They told me they understood why I wanted to keep her a secret, said in my position, they would all have done the same. But what if they could learn something that would save the human race? Phaedre was willing. We asked Louisa. She was very brave, and wanted to help, so we brought her to Berlin. At first everything seemed fine. Phaedre had no complaints. She and I were present at every exam with Louisa. It was basic—temperature, weight, reflexes."

His eyes closed briefly. "Then Louisa complained of nightmares."

"I don't think I can—"

"Zoë, they'll come any second to take you away. Phaedre and I slept at the hospital with Louisa, but they drugged us. They did things to her. I should have known—I did know—what desperation will drive some men to do."

"No, no," I cried. "Please don't. I understand—"

"Do you?" He stared at me. "You understand…how I could sleep through that?"

My soul stilled in a way that felt like death. I knew then as if he'd said it aloud, and there was absolutely no way to lessen the pain. I knew that, too. "You were drugged." I stated the obvious, useless platitude.

The shake of his head negated my words. "What drug could be made that would keep me from knowing—"

He wept as though he'd just learned of the crime, and hadn't had eleven years to recover.

"That's why you let them believe…" I choked and couldn't speak for a moment. "Do you know that's why you've been sentenced to death? They're using Louisa to convict you, not the treason. It's the people. They're so angry, because they've been told…and you didn't do anything. You're not guilty. They are!"

"Zoë," he said, "I was her father."

"You saved—you *saved* me. And you've tried to help others, too."

He shook his head. "I failed to save you. Just like I failed Louisa."

I grabbed his shirt collar. "You're going to die. Because you tried to save me. What you have done, for so long, with that group. You were trying to make up for Louisa."

He stroked the side of my face.

"Will you forgive yourself?" I whispered.

His eyes closed, and I knew the answer.

Sudden banging on the door startled us both.

"One minute!" the guard shouted.

Chapter 10

"Do you remember when we saw the castle?" he asked.

"Yes."

"I wasn't the purest." He kissed my forehead. "Not the worthiest. But I promise you, Zoë. I promise another knight will come."

As the guard dragged me from him, sobbing and clutching at his hands, he whispered something that made me stop struggling and fall into silence.

Here he lies where he longed to be
Home is the sailor, home from the sea.

I held on to those words.

After they hanged him in the street outside my room.

METAMORPHOSIS
July, 2091 - 2095

Chapter 1

IT IS TRUE WHAT THEY SAY, THAT THE DEAD LIVE ON IN OUR MEMORIES. From time to time, Robert Louis appears in my dreams. I relive our adventures. We eat yoghurt and honey while Elena nods approvingly. We laugh at some anecdote from the biography. He weeps at the sight of me in his daughter's wedding dress, and tells me he wishes he could be everything I want him to be.

Together we gaze at the fairy castle across a frozen gorge. *When the true champion frees the princess from the dragon's lair, she will share her mystery. Their symmetry will bring fertility, growth, and plenty, and grant endless happiness to all creatures living upon the earth.*

Was it an ancient story…or one for our future?

"We are taking you to another city," one of my doctors said, a month after the hanging. "This one has become too dangerous. The people are revolting."

"They know you lied," I whispered.

He shrugged and left. He looked harried. He might not have heard me.

A new soldier came—a man in gleaming black knee-high boots and perfectly creased khaki jodhpurs. Medals, badges, patches, and ribbons covered his tailored jacket; a visored military cap shadowed his face. He handed the doctor a sheaf of documents then waited, stiff as an iron pole, hands folded behind his back. Only once did he glance at me. I felt his hate.

A warrior, through and through. An automaton—awakened each morning in some barrack to a whistle and the clipped bark of orders, falling asleep to the rhythmic flood of searchlights. Nurtured and trained to obey. To kill.

He went away but returned the next morning flanked by armed sentries. "Come," he ordered. I rose from the cot and awaited further instructions. None of the doctors were there to say farewell, nor was Franz.

I was taken through the corridors and up to the roof, where we boarded one of their terrifying helligliders. The two sentries sat on either side of me. I smelled their aftershave and the dry, fusty scent of their wool uniforms. Their leader sat in front beside the pilot. I glimpsed a segment of his cheek lit by reddish sunlight, one dark, precise sideburn, his ear, oddly vulnerable, the temple-piece of his opaque sunglasses, a squared shoulder, and one hand, resting on his thigh. His fingers drummed impatiently.

It startled and frightened me when he turned and leveled a blank black stare at my face. I felt lightheaded and helpless, like an insect being pierced with a pin. The set of his mouth was merciless. He looked like someone who had never smiled, never cried, never held a girl's hand or shared secrets with a friend.

One of the sentries shifted his rifle to his other shoulder and the leader turned away, leaving me to slowly regain my composure.

We landed. I was transferred into another conveyance, decorated on the front with our country's flag. The doors sealed and it lifted, zipping above the ground at such a pace that the passing landscape was no more than a blur. We came in due course to a grimy station house, where a new contingent of feldjäger stood in precise rows, their gun barrels bristling like a scourge of virulent bacillus. I was steered onto yet another transport, this one stretching into the distance like the body of a shiny metal snake. It was so long I could not see the end.

My warden, without ever speaking a word to me other than "come," climbed into the back seat of the vehicle we arrived in and was driven away. I didn't see him again.

The snake-like apparatus left the station and barreled through the night.

I spent little time wondering or caring where my journey would take me. I knew Robert Louis didn't want me to give up. Until the very end he believed I, along with some magical non-existent knight, could overcome everything. But I saw nothing left to fight for.

A hand shook me out of dreamless sleep. Everything was dark but for a tiny, blinding light held by a shrouded figure.

"Be quiet and come with me."

Obediently I rose and donned the coat thrust towards me. I followed the anonymous person off the snake, which appeared to have stopped in the middle of a vast, flat emptiness.

I was ushered into a fourth machine, one that carried me through the rest of the night and into morning.

Chapter 2

It took a long time to get here. I marvel at how much traveling I've done...I who once believed I would die without ever leaving the confines of my childhood estate.

Mountains again line the horizon, but in a country very far from the one in which I grew up.

This place is a well-kept secret. If my homeland knew of it, they would declare war and many would die.

The house is big, spread out, fashioned of something called "adobe," which blends into this wild, open landscape. Its construction makes it warm in winter and cool in summer, and reminds me a little of the whitewashed houses on Robert Louis's island, where I was so happy.

The land it sits on has many ecosystems. I could explore for the rest of my life and always find something new to study.

There are trees I never would have seen but for my special circumstances. I met the rarest of all, the bristlecones, *pinus longaeva*, which hold almost the entire world's history within their ancient rings.

The air here is dry, clean, and sharp, the heavens cobalt blue. Every morning I examine the sky but there is no sign of the nearly-transparent yellow dust I grew accustomed to seeing in my homeland's largest city.

It isn't logical, but sometimes I wish I could see the dust. In a strange way, seeing it would make me feel closer to my dead husband. He didn't fear it, and neither do I.

I walk every day…I sit on canyon rims, my legs dangling in space, and reminisce about looking down from the battlements at the Schloss, chattering with Teófilo. I admire the endless play of cloud shadows sweeping along the carved valley floor so very far below. I cradle my ring and wish the second heart could join me. He promised we would never be separated so long as I possessed this symbol of our union… but I suppose he wasn't able to predict the future.

Only his hopes for it.

Chapter 3

When I approached my high desert home for the first time, two people were standing outside waiting, as though they expected me.

My transport was a sort of conveyance for hire, I was told, sent from an enterprise called *Tour de Suite*. It called itself a "taxi." The uplifted wings on each side, round shape, and protruding antennas in front made me think of a ladybug, though it had no spots. It sped along an artery of blinking red sensors for several hours before slowing and making a right turn into the midst of a stately grove of ponderosa pines, the first I had ever seen. How I longed to get out and touch them, but the taxi drove on.

"Missing sensors," the automated voice informed me. "Lowering tires to compensate."

There was a grating sound then we were creeping along a dirt road punctuated with many rocks that made the going rough.

We climbed from flat, desolate land surrounded by distant lofty mountains into rolling foothills. Slowing at last, the pod turned onto a graveled drive and came to a stop. Behind the house, like a sheltering rampart, a snow-capped mountain soared, higher and more forbidding than the others pushing up against it.

"You may now exit," I was told by the voice that kept me company during the journey, patiently explaining what a "sensor" was, how it and the locator beacons kept the taxi in place, and informing me where we were going and how long it would take to arrive.

The side slid open. Scent rushed in. I could not put a name to what I smelled, but it was enchanting.

I got out, remaining close to the open door. If something happened, I would leap back in and send it flying.

The man and woman approached me. She walked slowly, using a cane. The man kept his hand on her elbow. The cane sparked a memory—I had to dig around but soon remembered the woman in the city where I was kept, standing adjacent to the mob. She had leaned on a cane.

"Hello, Zoë," the woman said.

Anger swept through me. Everyone always knew who I was. Yet I knew no one, and was constantly handed over to strangers without explanation or excuse.

"I've made tea," she added.

"And cinnamon bread," the man volunteered. His voice was deep and slightly hoarse. Though they both spoke the same language— English—his accent was different.

"I'm not much of a cook," she said, smiling, "but I think it turned out."

Silence fell.

"Who—who are you?" I managed. Perhaps it was rude.

"I'm so sorry," she replied, frowning. "They should have prepared you. It's inexcusable. My name is Maya. This is my husband, Nash."

"Why am I here?" I paused, but before there was time for them to reply, I added, "Am I your prisoner now?"

The woman's frown deepened. "Most certainly not," she said forcefully. "You are an honored guest. I am going to do my damndest, Zoë, to make sure you are never anyone's prisoner, ever again. You are very welcome here. Welcome and safe."

Tears filled her eyes. The man grabbed her hand. I could see he was worried. He didn't like her being upset. He didn't know what to do.

"Will you come in?" he said to me. "We will explain."

I took one step. The open panel snapped shut; gravel crunched beneath the tires as the taxi zoomed off, leaving behind a cloud of dust as it vanished down the dirt road.

"I guess so," I said faintly, staring after it.

A hand clamped onto my shoulder, startling me. It was the man, Nash. I cringed.

"I'm sorry," he said, removing his hand. "Don't be afraid, Zoë. You are safe with us. I promise."

His words actually made me feel safer. I wasn't sure why. The last time I'd been told I was safe was Robert Louis's island, and that's where I was captured.

They waited.

"I am a little hungry," I said.

Maya smiled with relief. Nash swept out his arm and they escorted me inside, careful to give me plenty of space.

$$\rule{6cm}{0.4pt}$$

Chapter 4

$$\rule{6cm}{0.4pt}$$

MY NEW HOSTS WERE IN THEIR SIXTIES. THE WOMAN WAS THE FIRST PERSON I'd ever seen with skin dark enough to suggest an ancestry from the hot climates near the equator. Her husband was something called Diné. I'd never heard of that.

In contrast, the color of Maya's eyes reminded me of the water in the cove at Robert Louis's island. Cane notwithstanding, she was intimidating—but my apprehension lessened when she smiled. Her short curly hair was white, and there was an indefinable sense of age about her, but her face had only a few lines. Nash's hair was black threaded with silver. It was very long. He kept it braided in two neat plaits. I grew to love watching Maya plait his hair and listening to them joke with each other. His face, with its deep lines, prominent cheekbones, straight black brows and bottomless black eyes, held quiet mystery that both drew and frightened me. In his spare movements and still expressions, there was a sense of contained wildness.

They took me on a tour of their home and showed me the bedroom where I would sleep. It was a normal room, rectangle-shaped but for a curved alcove on the north side with a big window. After that, they led me to the kitchen and we sat at a round table.

Feeling like a waif from a Dickens novel, I said stiffly, "Thank you." Maya merely smiled and held out a plate of crusty cinnamon bread. It was delicious.

After we finished our tea, she led me to the deck. Nash didn't join us. The land stretched, seemingly forever, in every direction, painting deep, inscrutable shadows as the sun lowered.

"What is that smell?" I was finally able to ask. "I…like it."

"You must mean sagebrush. We'll soon be inundated with blooming chamisa, which doesn't smell nearly as nice, but right now, sagebrush takes center stage. I'm so used to it I can hardly differentiate it from plain air anymore. Sagebrush is a wild desert shrub. *Artemisia californica.* The First People used it thousands of years ago for ailments —colds, coughs, cramps. They made teas and liniments—all kinds of things. I'm told it works wonders on pain. You know, Zoë, sometimes my old bones are so stiff in the mornings. I'm going to dig up a recipe and give it a try."

She stopped then laughed. "You're thinking you're stuck with someone who never shuts up, aren't you? A boring scientist who always has to overexplain and grandstand about Latin names and tedious facts."

I couldn't confess to this woman I'd just met that I'd fallen a little in love with her already. My face grew hot. "No, I—I don't think that. I—I would like to see the sagebrush."

"Look around you. It's everywhere. Carmen, our housekeeper, flavors almost all our meat with sage." She left me, descending the two steps separating the deck from open land. She bent and picked some, crushing the leaves in her palms as she came back. I held them to my nose. The smell was dusty and spicy at the same time, with a barbed aftereffect.

"You'll meet Carmen tomorrow, and her husband, Marco. Marco is our handyman. He takes care of the horses and—"

"Horses?"

She smiled, not missing my precipitous interest. "We have three. Mustangs. I hope you like to ride."

Growing up, I'd spent hours staring at pictures of horse breeds. I loved their beauty and elegance, their velvet noses and deep, soulful eyes. I'd become very fond of the horse I rode during my journey with Robert Louis.

"We are—this is California?" I asked, belatedly remembering what the Ladybug Pod had told me.

"Yes. Do you know where that is? One of the three westernmost territories of New North America."

I nodded. I'd come so far as that, then. No wonder it seemed strange, from the smell in the air to the different color of blue in the sky. "Along with Oregon and Washington," I said. "The United States."

"Ah, I was told you were a scholar. But this is no longer the United States. After the end of the chaos we endured for so long, the five states that seceded rejoined the rest of the country, but now we're called New North America."

She motioned to rustic chairs with arm rests. "Shall we sit awhile, Zoë? We could talk until you are ready for bed."

I nodded and we sat, side by side, half-turned towards each other.

"Your English is excellent," she said. "Who taught you?"

"A—a tutor. He came every day, for as long as I can remember." I wasn't ready to talk about how I yearned to read Robert Louis Stevenson's poetry in his own language.

"It's nice here," I said, comparing this place to the city I'd left. "Quiet. Peaceful. Big."

"That is partly why it was chosen for you."

"How do you even know of me?"

"Well." She drew in a deep breath as if to prepare herself. "That is a long story. I can't tell you everything in one sitting, but I'll make a run at it, okay?"

I nodded, though I wasn't clear on the meaning of her vernacular, and saw her in my mind running, holding out her cane like a weapon.

"I am your aunt. Your great-aunt. Nash and I have been searching for you for a very, very long time. Your whole life, in fact."

"Did you take me off that snake thing?"

"Snake thing?"

"Like the thing that brought me here, but it was long, like the handle on a soup ladle."

"Oh, a train."

Train. I'd seen a picture of a train in one of my history books, but it bore little resemblance to what I'd been transported in, which was sleek and maniacally fast. The one in the book moved on iron rails. Smoke and coal cinders billowed from the engine. I'd read that more often than not, those trains moved at the pace of a turtle and most anything could impede them. Snow. Tree limbs. Herds of sheep.

"We arranged for you to be taken from it," she said. "We stole you, in a way. Those who had you had no right to keep you like they did. So yes, we stole you off that train and brought you here."

"Where was I going before you took me?"

"We're not sure. To another secret place, no doubt. To hide you and keep you under their control. You were a valuable asset, not just financially, but biologically."

"This place…it is really safe?"

"They have no idea where you are," she said firmly. "There are very few who know of your presence here, and those who do are committed to keeping the secret."

"I don't understand why you, or anyone, cares what happens to me."

She drew in another measured breath. "America was at the forefront of the atrocities that nearly destroyed the world before you were born. The current, duly elected government is trying to reform itself, but we don't trust it, not yet. We brought you here without them knowing, to give you this space where you can live and decide for yourself what you want to do."

That didn't really answer my question.

Leaning closer, she said, "Besides that, you are my family, Zoë. If we have to be pedantic about it, we aren't related by blood, but we are family, nevertheless. Of course I care, deeply, what happens to you. I always have, and I always will."

I tried to smile, to indicate in some way that this meant something to me, but it was hard. I didn't know her. I wasn't sure why she said we were related. And everyone I thought was my family was taken from me, sooner or later. I didn't want to get attached.

"Nash and I," she said, "and the others who know, believe you have as much right as anyone to live your own life. To make your own choices. I know it doesn't seem like it. We brought you here without asking you, and now I hope you will stay. Will you, at least for a while? Perhaps until the uproar over your disappearance dies down?"

Nash and Maya must be part of the group mentioned at Robert Louis's trial. Chthonia. Her words were similar to what he'd said.

A sinking sensation twisted through my stomach. "Will it die down?" I asked, even as I thought, *Where would I go, anyway?*

"I hope so. Right now, almost every country is in uproar. Everyone thinks they know what needs to be done. There is much fighting, and I will be honest. The world is in danger of falling back under the thumb of dictators and authoritarian regimes. Our hope is that at some point, humans will accept their fate and choose to live out the rest of their lives with kindness, democracy, and respect."

I heard the doubt in her voice. "You are saying—because no babies are being born, everyone will die and we will be no more."

"That's right."

"Are you the woman I saw outside the window? In the city? There was a woman with a cane."

Surprise passed over her face. "Yes, that was me. I kept an eye on you as best I could while we plotted how to spirit you away. The man who brought your meals, Franz, he was with us. He felt so badly for you, Zoë."

The orderly. He'd been quite good at hiding those tender feelings. But when I thought about it, I realized he was the one who kept me going. He was the one who made it possible to see Robert Louis one last time.

I had more questions, but exhaustion was becoming harder to ignore as anxiety slowly gave way to trust.

"I think you're going to fall asleep right there in that chair. Why not get some rest? There's no hurry to know every detail."

I agreed and after the goodnights were spoken and I assured her I didn't need anything, I made my way to the bedroom they had provided. Nash was nowhere to be seen. Perhaps he had already retired.

A few lamps showed me the way, and my bedroom was illuminated by a single lamp on the bedside table. Maya had explained that things operated not through the "electricity" I'd encountered at the hospital, and not by the more familiar coal, oil, or candlelight, but sunshine. She explained that the roof absorbed the energy created by sunlight, stored it, and converted it into some kind of magic that powered everything. I only had to speak to turn lights on and off.

I washed my face in the little bathroom, changed into a nightgown that someone had left on the bed, and told the lamp to shut off—whispering *thank you* when it obeyed, then snorting at myself.

Just before I climbed into bed I glanced at the window in the alcove, stretching across the wall and even up onto the ceiling. A padded window seat and folded blanket invited me to sit and look out. Someone had closed the screens to give me privacy but I decided I wanted a glimpse of the heavens—something to ground me and make me feel I had not left the earth I knew. I crossed to the seat and, seeing no mechanism, tried ordering the screen to open. It worked, though not in any way I could have predicted. The screen seemed to disintegrate before my eyes, leaving glass so clear it was like there was no barrier at all.

What I saw was breathtaking. I realized how much I had unconsciously missed seeing stars. I hadn't, not since Robert Louis's island.

Where were Elena, Demetri, and beautiful Phaedre? Had they been swept up in the attack? If Phaedre was alive, did she know Robert Louis had been executed?

Noticing a clasp at the bottom of the window, I touched it and a section of the glass swung open. A breeze—the kind of breeze that always seems to rise at night in the desert, and which I would come to love, cooled my cheeks for the first time.

Far to the south a hulking mass of starless black spat wicked branches of lightning. The breeze brought a scent of rain.

Subdued voices rose to me, and I noticed two shadows in the deck chairs beyond my window, holding hands.

"It's like Fauna is alive again." I recognized the voice as Maya's. "Her mannerisms, and the way she speaks."

"Don't cry." This voice was Nash's.

"Why not?" Maya demanded. "Why shouldn't I cry? I miss them. I miss Erin. I miss Will. I miss everyone. That girl brings it all back like it happened an hour ago."

"I'm sorry," Nash said. "Go ahead and cry, Ádeezbaa'."

Their chairs were close enough that she could lean in and rest her cheek on his shoulder. I heard her quietly sob.

I returned to the bed and lay a long while, pondering many things.

Chapter 5

In the days that followed, it became my habit to have coffee on the deck, sometimes alone, sometimes with Maya. I learned that Nash rose earlier than we did, and went off somewhere on horseback. Maya said he liked to commune with the dawn in solitude.

I loved listening to the wood on the deck creak and pop as the sun rose. I loved watching the sky blaze with color, and breathing the addictive scent of sagebrush. I didn't think I would ever take these things for granted. In the first days, as I learned more, I witnessed with breathless wonder a herd of wild horses gallop past on their way for a bath and a morning drink at a deep blue lake south of the house. The stallion was a glossy chestnut mustang with a white star on his forehead. Our mustangs grew restless when the wild ones galloped past, and called to them from the stable. Nash explained that when births stopped, small towns and farms were abandoned in favor of cities and human companionship. Farmers turned their horses loose to fend for themselves. Over the passage of time, the mustang herds blended with other breeds.

On day four, a fresh breeze through the open window and the cry of a bird I could not name woke me. There was no more than the slightest violet light on the horizon. I had been wanting to get up early and explore before anyone else, but I guess I was catching up on rest, and slept later than I ever had at *Naiskos* or the Schloss. With this breeze teasing me and the bird calling, I decided to dress and go walking. I would slip away to the far side of the stables, where I'd noticed a stand of ponderosa pines, and see what they had to say.

I went onto the deck. A coyote howled in the distance, saying hello to the day before curling up to sleep, and I saw the bird that had awakened me, soaring in high circles. It was big, with a reddish cast to its feathers. A raptor, I decided.

As I approached the stables, I smelled horses and manure. The big heavy door was open. I heard nickering.

Nash was there, tightening the girth on a beautiful tricolored mustang in the center aisle.

"Morning, Zoë," he said without surprise.

"I—wanted to see the horses."

"Here they are." He left the horse and patted the forehead of another, still in its stall. "This is Mustang Sally. She hasn't been ridden in a while, and I know she would love to get out." He crossed to another stall. "This is Retro, named because he reminds me of a toy horse my granny gave me when I was little." Returning to the horse he'd saddled, he said, "This is Curm, short for Curmudgeon. Self-explanatory."

"I don't know that word."

"It's usually reserved for grumpy old men. Curm is cranky and likes to test his rider until he gets the wind in his nose. Then he's happy, and gentle as a lamb. Have you ever ridden, or will this be a new experience?"

Memories flooded of Robert Louis, his men, and our flight through multiple countries. "I have ridden," I said quietly.

He frowned, and I wondered what I'd given away.

"Would you like to join me?"

I nodded. "I would, if you don't mind."

"I'll show you some of the area. Let's give you Sally, all right?"

I could see he was intrigued by my familiarity with saddling a horse, but he asked no questions. A few minutes later, we rode out, side by side.

He showed me many things. We didn't return to the house until well past lunchtime, but I never felt hungry or tired, and even forgot my grief temporarily.

After that day, we often rode together as the sun came up. I felt at ease with Nash in a way I didn't think I had ever felt with anyone before. He never asked uncomfortable questions or tried to get me to talk about my past.

He showed me his favorite places. Canyons, lakes, forests, and overlooks. We drank water from streams and picked wildflowers for Maya, who couldn't really ride anymore, with her arthritis.

Whenever we talked, which was rare, it was about nothing in particular. He asked only one question in those days as my horizons expanded and I learned more and more about my new home.

"You like trees?"

I nodded, and he said there was something I should see. Back at the house—a ranch was what they called it—we turned the horses out to pasture then he led me to a concrete landing pad hidden in the fold of a hill, where he kept a contraption called an aerocopter. I was apprehensive, remembering the dreadful helliglider, but Nash's flying machine was solid, quiet, and smooth, powered, as most everything at the ranch, by sunlight.

He coaxed me into the passenger seat and the aerocopter lifted. I could see the ranch, the stables, and had a bird's eye view of the mountains all around us. As he flew over a range he called the Sierra Nevada, he recounted how his best friend died flying him to his grandmother, long ago. He said he felt so helpless and guilty that he became a pilot so he would never have to ask for that kind of help again.

He landed in a meadow on the other side of the range and introduced me to the giant sequoias, the glorious *Sequoiadendron giganteum*, and *Pinus lambertiana*, the sugar pines, that produced cones longer than my forearm. I had read about them both, naturally, and had dreamed of seeing them in reality, though I never thought for a moment I ever would. The trees I ran to were as excited to see me as I was them. They welcomed me in sonorous, rumbling voices.

I gathered enough courage to ask a question of my own.

"Who is Fauna?"

Nash's piercing gaze shot to me and his brows lowered.

"The—the first night, I—I heard you and Maya talking."

"Maya can explain more eloquently than I can." He must have seen the disappointment on my face because he added, "She was beautiful and strange. She was…more deer than human. In certain light, I could see antlers." He looked away and his jaw hardened.

I was too shocked to reply.

Once he saw how enamored I was with the sequoias, nothing

would satisfy him but to take me to the bristlecones, *Pinus longaeva*, and, in that empathetic way that came naturally to him, he left me alone with them. I placed my arms around one, then ran to another, and another, listening to their haunting stories. They had many.

They greeted me by name, in voices of the truly ancient, the watchers of our earth. I pictured their dryads as wise old men who walked with gnarled staffs. They had long white beards and glowing eyes.

Their memories showed me a harrowing catastrophe, thousands of years in the past and far, far away over the ocean. A volcano that blanketed the world in smoke and ash for many years, and destroyed a hundred civilizations. The ash from that volcano fell upon these trees and sank into their rings. It was there still. I tasted it when I touched the bark.

It changed your history, Zoë, one of them told me. *You are descended from that volcano.*

Now you are here with us, another said, and I thought for an instant that the contorted bark was curling around my fingers. *We will keep you in our rings, and never forget you. You will live on and on, until the end of all that is.*

Chapter 6

A month passed. Nash asked me if I was ready for another visit to the sequoias, and I eagerly agreed.

The couple exchanged a glance as we were leaving. It seemed filled with silent communication, so I wasn't as surprised as I might have been when, after we ate our picnic lunch, he brought an object out of an inner pocket of his jacket—a flat, triangular-shaped prism of glass or polished stone. He spoke a word I did not understand and it expanded on his palm into a hexagonal pyramid. My heart beat erratically, for it was purple and glittery, like the hearts on my ring.

"We were going to give you this later," he said, "after we got to know each other better, but Maya felt the time was right, at least to introduce you." He glanced into the canopy of leaves. "The light is good, and you feel safe here, with these trees, correct?"

I nodded.

"Come then, let's sit on this limb."

The limb had fallen off one of the sequoias. It was enormous. It would have crushed anyone with the misfortune of being under it when it dropped. But today it was a comfortable, mossy bench in the midst of this awe-inspiring grove. I felt the nearest trees listening. I knew they would pass our conversation on to others farther away, through their roots and in the wind.

He set the pyramid on the limb between us. "Right now, it's

imprinted on me, but after it's cleared, it can be imprinted onto you—to your touch, your fingerprints, your breath, your eyes. Your DNA, to be more specific. It will be completely yours, and will obey only you."

I didn't know what he meant, but nodded anyway.

"Show Fauna," he said to the pyramid. A beam of white light shot upward from the tip and a detailed scene formed around us, seemingly as real as if we were in another place. There was an oak tree to my right, and a chair, and a slender girl sitting upon the chair. She had long, light brown hair and soft green eyes. She was smiling up at someone and holding his hand—it looked like a man's hand—but I couldn't see more of that person than his hand and a bit of his forearm. The scene blurred at the edges. The only truly clear thing was the girl, the chair, and the oak trunk behind the chair.

As for the girl's face, it was so clear I could see the shadows from the leaves play over her forehead and cheeks. I could feel the breeze and smell the scent of the oak. I reached out to touch this girl, but my hand went through her.

"Fauna," I whispered. I wasn't sure why I was so moved. I didn't know who Fauna was.

"Once the crystal is imprinted to you, you can see her whenever you wish," Nash said. "You can see most anything. All you have to do is ask."

"Thank you," I said. *But who is she? Why will I want to see her?*

I bit back the questions. I would try to be like Nash, and let things happen organically.

Chapter 7

I COULD HARDLY WAIT FOR BEDTIME, WHEN I COULD BE ALONE WITH THE crystal pyramid, which was now unlocked from Nash and imprinted upon me.

I helped Carmen, the cook and housekeeper, prepare dinner. She made her specialty, seared pork with cauliflower, flavored with sage. Accompanying it was Nash's favorite sage onion stuffing. Lastly, she taught me how to create a citrusy walnut phyllo baklava for after dinner, with coffee.

I was reminded of grizzled old Demetri, and how he'd loved Elena's phyllo desserts.

He had pushed through his comfort zone to play Romeo. I blinked away tears, wishing I could see him again and kiss his weathered cheek.

Maya had gone over the rudiments of the pyramid. "Let's say you want to know more about sage. You only have to ask. Tell it to show you California sagebrush."

Threads of gold spiraled around the pyramid as the light shot upward from the tip. Nash told me that would happen for a while, until the pyramid "learned" my brain.

Open land formed around me, covered in sagebrush—green and fernlike, as it was in springtime. Whichever way I turned my head, that area became clear, even to the fragrance.

"Now ask it to define the sage," Maya said.

"Define California sagebrush," I repeated, and a quiet female voice launched into the Latin name, its uses, where it grew, why it was aromatic, and some of the ways it had been utilized by the original cultures who lived in the area.

"This is wonderful." My mind was already leaping ahead to what I wanted to ask when I was alone.

We finished our dessert and spent the evening on the deck, listening to the horses nickering and watching stars pop out as they did so brilliantly here during the new moon phase.

"See the Big Dipper?" Maya pointed.

I nodded, then, since it was dark and she might not see it, I said, "Yes."

"Follow the handle out and down."

"To Arcturus?"

"Ah, I should have anticipated that you would know the night sky as well as any astronomer."

I blushed at the compliment. I hadn't known of Arcturus until Robert Louis pointed it out.

"Look to the right of Arcturus. We call that constellation the Lovers. Do you know it?"

"I don't remember that one in my star mapping books."

"It was named not so long ago as most," Maya said softly. "See her arm, reaching out to her mate? I watch it wheel across the night sky, sometimes all night. It comforts me."

"It looks like he's reaching out to her, too," I said. "The stars are beautiful here. They were beautiful where I grew up."

"Plato said that every star has a companion. The Lovers is a perfect example of that. They stand beside each other, reaching out, ready to hold onto each other if needed." She paused before adding, her voice full of emotion, "It is an epic love story."

She brought out her pyramid—hers was swirled in white and pale pink—and showed me images of her daughters, Xanthe and Alecto. She told me they lived a few hours to the north.

"Near the Redwoods," Nash said. Gravely, he added, "You would like those, Zoë."

My voice came out in a whisper. "I would." I told them about the mountains around the Schloss, and how the mountain with three peaks was named after the Erinyes: Alecto, Megaera, and Tisiphone, maybe because of the wind they often generated.

We fell silent, we three, thinking our own thoughts, as night deepened. As soon as I thought I could without seeming rude, I told them goodnight and retreated to my bedroom.

After making sure the window screen was closed, I set the pyramid on the bed.

"Show Odenwylde."

"There are eight Odenwyldes in the historical annals," I was told.

His ancestors, perhaps. "Bastien Günther Jäger-Abelard," I said, adding, "general in the German military, around 2080."

The gold swirls expanded. A younger Odenwylde than I had known paced before a formation of men at attention. His hair was shorter, probably regulation, and he wore a peaked visored cap. Braiding, colored bars, and medals completed his uniform. The men he was apparently inspecting were dressed in the same grey service uniforms with red berets as those who guarded me during my time in the city.

The cap was pulled so low over his forehead, I could hardly make out his face. "Are there more images?" I asked.

The scene dissipated and another formed. This one depicted him at his trial, thin, ill, bruised. I couldn't bear it, and told the pyramid to stop the display. "Can you show me Odenwylde's daughter, Louisa?"

There was only one image of her, walking into a building, holding Robert Louis's hand. Phaedre walked on her other side. Louisa was smiling up at her father. He was smiling down at her.

This had to be after she agreed to be tested, shortly before she was murdered.

She resembled him.

Again, too grievously sad. "Show me Fauna." It brought up the same image of her beneath the oak. Who was she? Whose hand was she holding? When I turned my head, hoping the male would come into clarity, he didn't, though that trick did work on other images.

From what Maya had said when I eavesdropped, it seemed Fauna might be connected to me in some way. Why hadn't they told me, if so?

It wasn't until I came out of the bathroom, donned in a nightgown, my teeth brushed, that I noticed the leather-bound book on the bedside table. Had it been there before? Maybe. I'd been so engrossed in wanting to experiment with the pyramid that I'd paid no attention to anything else.

I picked it up. The leather was old and distressed, like it had accompanied a sea captain across the world and suffered its share of salt water and rough weather. A long leather strap, wrapped around the middle, ended in a stylistic tree formed of silver, the trunk of which was tucked into a leather loop on the cover. I slipped the tree from its loop, unwound the strap, and opened the book. The scent of old leather and old paper drifted to my nose. The paper was deckle-edged, discolored around the margins. The pages were filled with graceless writing in pencil, like that of a child who hasn't quite mastered the art.

I turned to the first page.

Chapter 8

Book Ten, September 17th:

My tenth workbook. Ever since Adam saved me, I have been learning how to read and write, and what things are called. I'm better, but English is hard! Sometimes I want to throw these diaries on the ground and sit by a stream, listen to the birds, and forget. No matter how much I learn, I feel I have barely begun, and sometimes, even though he tries to hide it, I catch Adam smiling at some word I've used. I know it must be wrong, or silly. And math. It is worse. How I hate it!

But now everything is changed. I cannot wait to practice writing.

Adam has told me I am pregnant! I asked how he knew. He said he could tell by my eyes, by my smile, and by the thing he calls an "aura" surrounding me. It is color, he says. He says we are all surrounded in colors, but not everyone can see them. I cannot.

Every moment of the night you were conceived is burned into my memory. Every incredible moment. Every kiss. Every touch.

Adam gives me that smile that moves from his lips to his eyes. I think he is remembering that night, too.

From now on, I am not simply practicing my writing. From now on, I write to you, to my unborn daughter.

Never in my life until now have I been with a man of my own free will. Adam knew that. He seemed content to wait. He waited four and a half years and I believe he would have waited four and a half more, or ten and a half, or forever, but I asked for a change. I was surprised to learn that my asking was what he had waited for. No man has ever cared about my wishes when it comes to such things.

When he is with me, I feel confident and brave, but when we are not together the old fear returns. What sort of protection can I offer you, I, who lived nearly all my life in a cage? What if those days return? I think they could. Adam says we will fight, but he doesn't say it can't happen, or it won't, and that frightens me.

Do you wonder why I call you my daughter? Adam told me you're a girl. He knows these unknowable things because a Goddess speaks to him. Goddess Athene.

He knows because he has seen everything this world has done, good and bad. Now he lives with me in this place and time. He loves me. I love him. You are coming from that love, and we will be three. Then, if Athene grants us a miracle, everything will be perfect.

September 30th:

We are in Germany, in a little mountain village. I was tired today, so Adam took Vita out for a run without me. When they returned, he gave me flowers that smell of rain and soil and sunlight, and flaky cream-filled pastries.

I hated to waste a day inside. Soon I won't be able to go outside, rain or shine. When my pregnancy shows, we will have to be very careful. I will have to keep hidden. I don't let myself think too much about what they would do if they found out.

Sometimes I feel my old cage is chained to my legs, dragging behind me wherever I go. But then I remember that Adam loves me. It is me he loves!

How I wish I could stand in the village square and shout that I am pregnant, that there is hope for everyone, and it lives inside me. But he is right to insist I keep it a secret. There's more at stake than my life. There is your life, my daughter, to consider.

October 12th:

Sometimes I think it would be better if Homo ~~sapeins~~ died out. "Sapiens." I forgot about the rule. I before e, except after c. Why is there such a rule? Why is it not always i before e?

Athene could start over. Perhaps the next batch of humans would turn out better.

THERE IT WAS AGAIN. ATHENE. PART OF ME WANTED TO LAUGH, YET something…something inside sparked. This woman seemed comfortable speaking of a Greek goddess she considered formidable enough to create a second human race. It made me wonder if she was caught in the same fantasy world as my Schloss mother.

Athene was the goddess of wisdom and war. A daughter of Zeus, she sprang fully-armed from her father's forehead. She never took a lover. I easily recalled my tutor's disinterested glossing-over of the Olympians. Hera, Zeus's wife, was silly and vindictive. Aphrodite went about naked and toyed with people's emotions. Poseidon rode ocean waves in a chariot, causing storms and destruction.

It was clear the poor woman lived a troubled existence until her Adam came along and lifted her out of misery.

I glanced at the crystal pyramid on the nightstand. All I had so far was the name of a man—a rather common name—and the name of what I assumed was a dog. There were no years added to the dates; I flipped through multiple pages to be sure. The woman never named herself. There was simply not enough in this penciled account to pull up any information from the pyramid. She probably never thought a stranger would see her writing exercises.

It was late but I didn't feel tired. I climbed into bed, intending to read until I fell asleep.

November 24th:

I wish I could see into the future. Am I really the mother of the mother of the world? Will my child return life? Should we be given another chance?

You know what you might be? Franz said to me once. The mother of the future—of the next human race. How does that sound, little girl?

This record must have been written after the onset of sterility. The woman seemed both proud and afraid, as I could well imagine, if she was one of the last on earth to bear a child.

I turned onto my side and snuggled deeper in the blanket.

December 1st:

People fear and blame the dust. They have embraced the idea that chaste, contrite living and hard physical labor will clean the air, soothe the anger of their gods, and stimulate fertility. Adam tells me disasters always bring out this kind of thinking.
Leaders use religion, threats, and fear to force obedience. Adam says the word I want is "oppression," and he explained it to me. Almost everything becomes a sin, and almost anything can be used to punish and enslave those of us the rulers call different, those who are the lesser sex, or who have the wrong skin color, the wrong desires, the wrong personalities. Especially those who are defiant, who can think, and act on their thoughts.

I am angry at how quickly Mother Erin's efforts have been rejected. Everything is spiraling backward. They have convinced themselves that bad air and sin has made them sterile. How quickly they have forgotten the events leading to the death of the dictator Novikov and the release of women.

I have never had the courage to say out loud that she gave everything for nothing. I am afraid of the pain those words might cause Adam. But I do think it sometimes—that her sacrifice was a waste. Athene's promise is buried as deeply as ever. Men and women are becoming ~~vishus~~ vicious again. I suspect it was like this when women were caged the first time—before I was born. Many are calling for a return to that hell. Caged women were fertile, they shout, suggesting that releasing us caused an extinction event. (Adam had to explain that to me, too.) Mostly men, of course. They are not the ones who would lose their freedom, be starved and beaten, sold to whomever paid the most money, raped over and over again. But there are women who want it too. Some are my Cage sisters. In a way, I understand. The Cages were all we knew, and freedom has shown us very little kindness. I am lucky that I have Adam to keep me safe.

Since we came to this village, I have felt the ravens speaking to me, and though I said nothing about it, he knew. Last night, as we were falling asleep, he said, "Do you want to fly? Close your eyes."

I did, and Adam sent me flying inside a raven, in the moonlight. I flew over trees, over the village, over the countryside. It was a kind of freedom I never could have imagined on my own.

When I came out of the vision, he said simply, "Believe in miracles."

On the floor beside the bed, Vita sighed and thumped her tail against the floor.

My gaze returned to the name *Novikov*. My tutor covered him once or twice. He was a despot who overthrew many countries and killed many people. He'd died in a bombing. An assassination, was the general belief, though no one was ever arrested.

December 6th:

Adam moved us to a city. He says it is easier to hide when you are two among many. It's true we were drawing attention in the village—especially with a wolf as our pet. Adam passed Vita off as a wolf-dog hybrid, which satisfied most people, but there were a few—hunters, probably—who seemed to know better.

He sent Vita away. He knelt and put his forehead to hers. She whined. She brought up her foreleg and scraped his arm with her paw, but he would not relent. He stood, he pointed, and he said, "Go." It was a command. Vita turned and slunk away. It broke my heart. "Why?" I asked. He told me it was to protect her.

It was silly of me to let myself believe our trip to Germany was a romantic getaway. He thinks I don't know that there are those who would pay huge sums to have us, others who would murder us—those who hated Erin and her crusade. People stripped of power by what she did.

He is keeping something from me. I don't like it.

Even without knowing of my pregnancy, the owner of the hotel in the heart of the city would clearly like to send us away, but when Adam handed over the papers identifying him as a fertility scientist, he backed down. No one dares oppose the scientists. Whatever they want, they get.

I hardly blame the man. Foreigners—especially women—are regarded with suspicion. Letting us have a room could draw unwelcome attention. Some might harm him or his hotel. There are armed street patrols, criminals with authority. They constantly detain and terrify people, mostly women, sometimes hurting them. I am entering my fourth month now, and starting to show, though I can still hide it. We don't dare let them see us.

If it got out that I am pregnant, there would be riots. Adam would be imprisoned, maybe even killed. I would be kidnapped at the very least. Every country, including this one, would kill without hesitation to have me as their prisoner. Adam could probably intimidate them as he did the hotel owner, but I am still afraid.

His papers identify him as a high-ranking British fertility scientist named Cyril…something. He styled himself with the title of "vycount," and is routinely addressed as "Lord Silverthorne," a name he made up. He said he saw it on a road sign in America.

Everyone treats him with half-fear, half-sniveling flattery. He speaks German as if he grew up here, and when needed, he also speaks with what he's told me is an Oxford educated accent. It's some town in England. I wonder as I listen to his exchanges where in his long life he learned such things? There is so much I don't know about this man who was brought to me by a miracle of Athene.

I couldn't stop there, though it was becoming harder and harder to keep my eyes open. What was this woman's husband up to? What would it mean for her, and the baby?

If it got out that I am pregnant, there would be riots. Those words brought back the granite prison where I was studied and abused. Every day people thronged the street below my window. Many days it seemed uncomfortably close to riots. The majority had been women—frantic women, hour after hour, shouting, weeping, annoying my doctors.

December 11th:

I watched, terrified, from our room as soldiers surrounded
Adam on the street. The one in charge demanded his papers.
Herr Oberst von Bäumer, one of his men called him. Adam was
calm, as any fertility scientist would be. They let him go, but the
leader stared at our window as Adam walked away. He must
know which room is ours. I felt hatred and danger coming off
the man like smoke. I pray to Goddess Athene we do not have
to deal with him again.

DIZZINESS FLOODED. I CLOSED MY EYES. HERR VON BÄUMER. IT MUST BE
the same man, though the writer said nothing about scars. An odd
sensation, like a wisp of feathers, tickled the back of my neck. I saw
him in memory, leaning towards me.
You have the look of your mother.

December 17th:

You are kicking up a tidal wave, Chloe, or Zoë, or Io. I haven't
decided yet on your name, but it must be Greek in honor of the
place where this all began.

Those two dots. They're called an "umlaut," but not all the time.
Sometimes they're called something else I forget. But if I decide
to name you Zoë, I'm using them, because from what I understand, if I don't, some people will pronounce your name "Zo."
It's "Zo-ee!"

I long for the day I can hold you, yet I don't want to give up the
closeness that comes from having you safe inside.
Sometimes I wish I could go on being pregnant forever. Can you
hear me singing to you? Can you hear the poems I read?

Little Indian, Sioux or Crow,
Little frosty Eskimo,
Little Turk or Japanee,
O! don't you wish that you were me?

Wind rattled something outside. I heard a sound like a scatter of raindrops or leaves blowing across the deck. It was past midnight by now. The house was still, with a listening kind of stillness.

Herr von Bäumer…she might name her daughter Zoë…they lived in Germany…and she'd read what had once been my favorite poem to her unborn child.

My hands were shaking.

Perhaps I could solve these dawning suspicions by skipping to the end. I flipped through the diary, pausing on May tenth.

My birthday.

I cannot stop crying.

A star lingered, low and bright, over the city as you were born. It remained even after the sun rose, causing much comment among the doctors and nurses. The yellow dust, usually almost invisible, grew into a storm, piling upon the glass dome over the hospital.

Mother Erin sends it. She is watching.

I think Adam is with her. He watches too.

If only they could be with me. If only…but it does no good to wish for things that can never be. I live by the hour now, holding you close, my Zoë, knowing that at any moment, they may take you from me.

WHICH IS EXACTLY WHAT THEY MUST HAVE DONE.

Everything inside fell away, leaving hollow, cold ruins. Only gradually did I hear myself gasping.

You were two, and still with your mother, the doctor at my prison said while trying to convince me of Odenwylde's evil. They must have allowed her to keep me for two years. Then they took me from her.

This was my mother's diary. My real mother.

The unborn child this woman wrote to…was me.

Chapter 9

My heart raced ferociously. I leaped out of bed, pressing my hands to my cheeks, spilling a good deal of water as I poured a cup.

The book lay where I'd dropped it, open on the floor. *Come back, Zoë!* the lines called. *Don't stop now!*

When at last I could breathe, I picked it up, anxious, fearful, yet drawn inexorably. Under an erratic surface perception, a deeper layer ran, the ageless soul perhaps, that understood what reading these words meant. Though I was but thirteen when all this happened, I knew that the knowledge in these pages would never let me return to the girl I was comfortable with, the Zoë I knew. At the same time, I couldn't wait to absorb every phrase, implant every clumsily-penciled letter, into my brain.

My mother. My lost mother. Not the crazy drugged woman. My real mother.

I sat on the braided rug beside the bed, my spine against the frame, and propped the diary on my knees, flipping backward through the pages. If only one could flip one's mind to a point before they'd made some dreadful discovery…but was this dreadful? I couldn't tell. Logic and reason had "up and deserted me," as Maya would say.

I'd skipped from December 17th to May 10th. Nervously chewing my lower lip, I shuffled until I found the next December entry—the 22nd.

What was her name? I hoped she would say. I was glad she picked Zoë for me. And who was this *Adam* she spoke of so tenderly? My father. My real *father!* On this page she addressed the subject. Her handwriting acquired a smoother, prettier flow, lending the impression that writing about him gave her pleasure, and she wanted to do her best.

December 22nd:

I look forward to watching you with your father. You will love him. He is handsome and brave, oh, and older, not by a year or two, but over a thousand, though he only looks about ten years older than me. I cannot tell you my age, because I don't know, but I do know that I was put into Carnevale as soon as I reached maturity, so I am still young. Probably not yet twenty.

Yes, I wrote "over a thousand." That is not a mistake in my ability to add, though I admit I am no good at math. It sounds impossible of course, but you will see. So many things will become clear once you know him. He will make everything clear.

I, OF ALL PEOPLE, UNDERSTOOD. ROBERT LOUIS WAS TWENTY-EIGHT YEARS my senior, and it never concerned me. Never. But—a thousand? Nobody lived that long. Again, I wondered. Was I reading the fantasies of a madwoman?

A very small voice, in the deepest recesses of my mind, asked, *Am I mad, too?* I saw Teófilo, moving and speaking and giving me his love. But for others, he was lifeless stone.

Adam's eyes are blue. Not like any other blue-eyed person you will ever meet, though. His eyes glow in certain light, or when he feels something strongly. They lay you bare. Well, me, anyway. He has told me he was born around the year 503 or 504. He has forgotten exactly when. That is the era, I am told, some call "The Dark Ages." And his name isn't really Adam. It is Adamantinus, a Latin word—I looked it up. My English dictionary tells me it means "incorruptible." Something that is adamantine is like a diamond. Shining and unbreakable.

That is our Adam. Yours and mine!

The things he has seen and lived through—I can only imagine. He is the opposite of me, purely, completely opposite. Not only is he a man to my woman, which is the smallest part, he has lived a life of unconditional, endless freedom.

I should not write these things. What if someone found this book?

They would simply think me insane. I hope you do not.

Guilt ran through me, and I remembered that the Schloss woman had not been mad. She was drugged.

Adam gave me a ring today. I love it so much! I had told him a story about my time in the Cages, how one day during our daily exercise I saw a stone on the ground that glittered. I hid it in my hand and took it back to my cage, but in there, it didn't glitter. It was no longer pretty. I tossed it through the bars. It landed in the sunlight and glittered again. I wanted it back but couldn't reach it. He had a ring made for me out of something called "goldstone," that glitters even in the faintest light. Purple heart shaped stones. In the middle are blue-white stones he calls rainbow moonstones. They change color too! It is the most beautiful thing I have ever seen.

If not for what is going on in the world around us, I would burst from happiness.

I have come upon him, staring out the window at Mother Erin's constellation, yet I know his focus is inward. But on what? It is useless to ask. I see this same focus when he assumes the other face—the cruel scientist, or when he rattles off commands in German. I recognize it because this ability is one thing we have in common. To go somewhere else without leaving our bodies. When I was growing up and the men did what they wanted to my body, I left, in my mind, and they could not stop me.

Someday I will explain. But not here, not in writing. Your father and I will explain it together when you are old enough to understand.

I am reminded of something I can share with you, though. Something that shows his magic. It wasn't long after Mother Erin left us that I woke from a nightmare. Adam heard me crying and came into my room. He soothed me and I went back to sleep. I didn't want him to know about my nightmares. But when it happened again, he asked me to tell him, so I did. I used to see the faces of the men who used my body, starved me, and beat me, almost every night in dreams. Adam said, "I can take that from you." He placed his hand on my cheek and I fell asleep against his chest, and when I woke, I felt happy and free. Those faces were small and I could see through them, and then, they disappeared. Adam says I am strong like a stag's antlers. They shed and sometimes they break, but they always grow back.

The important thing for you to know right now is that he would leap into a bonfire for my sake and yours. His courage is never-ending. Watching it, day to day, has helped me improve mine.

He is tall, so much taller than me. His hair is the color of the shiny bowls and pitchers the village innkeeper displayed. She called them "heirlooms," and "copper." As old as he is, there is not a single grey strand. It is long for a man's hair, thick and smooth and whispering, with strange shadows. I cut it once, but the next morning, it was long again. I pray that when the time comes, many years from now, you will find someone like him for your own. If you do, and if you can be with him—both huge "if's" in this world, you will always be happy.

I REMOVED MY WEDDING RING AND TURNED IT, WATCHING THE ENDLESS sparkles in the goldstone, and the shimmering blue within the white of the moonstones.

Robert Louis gave me my mother's wedding ring. How had it come into his possession? I held the ring against my cheek and wept, experiencing the awe of it all over again.

My effort to picture them was incomplete and hazy. I saw Adam's smooth coppery hair, which must explain how I got mine, and his blue eyes, but the rest remained a void. I couldn't construct anything of my mother. When I tried, I saw only sparkles, reflecting like the goldstone ring she and I both loved.

Perhaps, if I read on, she would make herself clearer.

Chapter 10

Not wanting to wake anyone, I tiptoed to the kitchen and opened the coffee tin. The smell of fresh grounds tickled my nose and helped alleviate the sandy tiredness in my eyes. While I waited for the coffee to brew, I sat at the kitchen table and opened the diary, pulling my robe close about me, for it grew chilly at night on this high plateau, even in August.

January 1st:

A new year. With any luck, it will be our year of rebirth. Now comes the hard part, little Zoë or Io. (I'm narrowing it down.) I must tell you difficult, painful things that I wish you never had to hear, never had to think about.

Adam is helping me write this part. It is too hard for me. I don't have the words.

Nobody knows when I was taken from my mother and put into a cage. I can't remember my mother or father, or what my name was when I was born—or if I was given a name. In the Cages, I was called 84040og902. That didn't change, and I thought nothing of it, until Adam came. He gave me a name. A human name.

I stopped reading to think about that. In some ways, her history was similar to my own. I had no memory of her or of my father. All I knew were the Schloss couple who were hired to playact as my parents. But at least I was allowed to keep the name she gave me.

Nervous energy crackled through my arms and legs. My stomach growled, but I didn't want to get up, not even for a quick slice of bread.

Have I told you that Adam is Mother Erin's son? Together they set this world on its heels. Adam shared that phrase with me (and many others). "Set the world on its heels." It fits. Erin challenged every country that fell to Grigory Andreiovich Novikov, the dictator, and his accomplices: Redmond Warwick and Raphael Konstantinou, who was Erin's husband and Adam's biological father.

The odds were against her. She had to keep ahead of her enemies, which were many. Had any of them caught her, she would have vanished and life upon this planet would be very different. Someday I will tell you what those devils were plotting.

But she was not caught. She, Adam, Maya, and Erin's granddaughter, Brianne (I think she was your cousin, but I do not understand family relationships very well) confronted those evil men...and won.

My mind automatically set the pieces in place as I continued to read. If Adam was the son of this "Erin" my mother spoke of, and

Adam was my real father, then Erin was my grandmother. In that case, it would make sense that my mother sometimes called Erin "Mother Erin." And I had a cousin! I could not wait to learn more and read on swiftly.

The words Erin spoke, strengthened by Athene's magic, brought about the release of women, the razing of the Cages, and the final end to Novikov. She created a new path for all humanity, wide open and smooth, with signposts to guide us. All we had to do was set out and walk.

But the world floundered. The women freed so suddenly from the Cages had no idea how to care for themselves, how to protect themselves, how to survive. The ones like me, who had never lived outside of the Cages, had no education, and only simple words. It was like tossing small children into the streets to live or die.

Try to imagine hundreds of thousands of women, released all at once, and in the Northern Hemisphere this happened in winter. Left on their own, they were soon victimized. Many fell ill and died after eating rotted food from garbage heaps or drinking polluted water from fields and roadways. Across the world, wretched, terrified women could be seen shivering, starving, congregating in dark places like alleys and subpod concourses. Murdered women turned up in rivers and ditches. Women no longer lived in the relative "safety" of the Cages and they were preyed upon, much as they always had been, but on a larger, more vicious scale. The Cage guards had to keep us alive or they would be punished. Those who attacked us after we were released did not care about that.

There were many who were against releasing us at all. They claimed the cost of the aid would bankrupt every country on earth. There were violent protests from people enraged that even a fraction of their taxes might go to help the refugees. They said the world had been peaceful under Novikov and Warwick.

Men felt valued. They spoke this twisted truth again and again, trying to make it accepted fact and a worthy goal, leaving out the numbers of men who vanished or lost their minds, and females who were treated like stock animals.

Those people have never stopped blaming Erin and her followers for what happened during that first year. Many want those of her followers who still live to be executed, and many have been, in horrible ways. Sometimes the killers are arrested, but not always. How can Adam and I ever have a normal life, and how do they think infertility will ever be reversed if they go around killing women?

The women were sent to every country that would take them in an effort to spread the burden out equally. The Independent Territories (those are countries that never set up cages) took in the most, and enlisted their free, educated women to help train and counsel the newcomers. These were Germany, Norway—which was taken over by Germany—Greece, Scotland, Sweden, Mexico, and Greenland, and five states in America: California, Oregon, Connecticut, Illinois, and Vermont.

Germany invited five thousand women from the Cages to take part in their integration training, and Germany's free women were recruited to run the programs. They didn't have enough who were qualified, though. They had to reach out to other countries.

That is how I came in. Adam's official papers name him a fertility scientist, which gives him the freedom to go wherever he wishes, and mine list me as his wife, and a teacher. A teacher! Me! Only Adam could pull off such a lie.

Every country set up strict conditions that are still in effect, almost five years after Mother Erin destroyed Novikov's colosseum and we said goodbye on Amnisos Beach.

I won't go into all that here. Adam and I have her book—*The*

Erinys Archives, it's called. When you are old enough, having it will make her story easier for you to understand.

In order to receive the monthly stipend, job training, education assistance, and trauma therapy, the freed women have to appear once a month for testing at the Fertility Centers. The tattoos branded into the women's arms in the Cages were reworked into codes that can be read every month—providing proof to the various aid centers that the women have fulfilled their obligation. Only then do they receive aid. These conditions soothed the moderate objectors, because the women give something that might pay off if it results in pregnancies.

Germany had another condition, advanced by the new leader—a Chancellor, they call him. The fertility specialists wanted marriage partners to be chosen by blood and DNA, which they claimed would increase the possibility of pregnancy and live births.

The Chancellor won because of his promise to find a cure for infertility. He is a mild spoken man who inspires trust, but he advocated monthly testing on every female under sixty and marriage unions chosen by genetics. Adam says this man would have been tossed out of office for such attacks on liberty in times past, but not now. With his support, the initiatives were adopted.

"Profound necessity." That is what they call it. Most countries have followed Germany's lead.

Adam and I play their game, pretending we were chosen for marriage because of our DNA. It is safer that way, and we have papers certifying our state-sanctioned union if needed.

Chthonia sees how wrong all this is. I wish I could tell you about them, but they work in the shadows, trying to help women, and they all have bounties on their heads.

I closed my eyes and rubbed my tired lids. When I opened them there was Maya, standing in the doorway, anxiously observing me.

"Are you all right?" she asked.

I nodded. "I found a diary," I said unnecessarily. It was sitting, open, on the table. "My-my mother's diary." Then it struck me. "Did you put it in my room?"

"Yes. She was writing to you, so I felt you should see it."

"Please, will you sit?"

She came into the room, poured coffee, and fetched milk in a little pitcher. The sugar bowl was already on the table. "You've been up all night, haven't you?" she asked. "Would you like some mint tea, instead of coffee? I could sprinkle it with lavender or ginseng to help you fall asleep."

"No." I spooned sugar into the coffee, then a splash of milk. "I should sleep, but I don't want to, not yet." Remembering that I had seen her name in my mother's writing, I asked, "You knew her, didn't you? My mother."

"Yes, I did. Fauna."

"O-ooh." My stomach lurched and for an instant, my mind froze. Part of me must have known. Why else would Nash show me an image of her? Why else would Maya say, *It's like Fauna is alive again*?

I thought back to the scene created by the pyramid. "Nash said she was more deer than human."

Maya smiled slowly. Her eyes sparkled. "He is such a visionary, yet he never shows that side to anyone. Except, now, you. You have broken through his barriers."

"Will you tell me everything? The diary leaves such holes."

"Everything I know." She sat across from me. "The image Nash showed you was made in Scotland, not long after Adam—your father —rescued Fauna from the Cages."

I waited, biting my lip to stop myself from interrupting.

Chapter 11

By the time Maya wound down, the sun had risen. Both of us were surprised when Carmen entered the kitchen to prepare breakfast. We told her we weren't hungry and adjourned to the deck.

Maya left me briefly. When she returned, she was carrying a wooden box. She withdrew a leather frame as she sat down, and handed it to me. Gazing out from a rather grainy photograph was an older woman, dressed in a loose robe with draping sleeves. A small black snake coiled around one wrist. I couldn't tell if it was real or some kind of jewelry.

The only other accessory the woman wore was a chain around her neck with a circular ornament at the end.

"This is your grandmother, Erin," Maya said. "Not long before the end. I took this photo just before one of her last rallies, in Sequoia National Park."

"Where Nash and I went?"

"Yes, exactly. That rally was a turning point for our revolution, Zoë."

"My grandmother. My mother…my father. Are they all…dead?"

"Your father is," she said quietly. "We don't know what happened to your mother. She disappeared long ago, and no one has been able to find her. She is probably dead, Zoë. Your grandmother, while not exactly dead, is gone."

The face in the photo had lovely symmetry and showed few signs of aging, but the eyes…the eyes were incredible, fiercely blue and glistening. The color was like nothing I had ever seen.

"I'm sorry," Maya was saying. "I haven't looked at these things in a long time. The flannel slipped off the necklace and it tarnished. We can polish it, though."

She was holding out a silver charm attached to a chain. Two crescents, like horned moons facing each other, cupped a brilliant blue bead. It looked like the ornament from the photograph. Where the flannel had fallen away the tarnish was very bad.

"The diary and this necklace were smuggled out of Germany and to us after you were born," she said.

A curious sensation occurred when I touched it, like light running into my fingertips and through my arm. I shivered but the feeling wasn't painful—more like glorious intoxication that made me want to run, to dance, to laugh. Colors burst at the edges of my eyesight like fireworks and goose bumps washed across my skin.

"Erin entrusted it to your mother," Maya said.

She was holding two more things, waiting to give them to me. "Long ago, this was a complete knife."

All that was left was a handle and a slot where the blade had fitted. I ran my hand over the likeness of a woman with an owl on her shoulder. "Is it ivory?"

She nodded. "The blade was obsidian. Deadly sharp. It had to be destroyed. But I keep the haft, to remind myself of how far we have come."

The last item was another knife, made from an elephant tusk. "It is the sacred king-killer," she said. "Both of these knives are immensely old, from the Bronze Age."

I placed it on my lap with the other items. New treasures, each one making me feel closer to my mother's story.

"Erin was my heart-sister," Maya said. "That's a sister not of blood, but of the heart."

I lifted my gaze in time to see pain flash through her eyes. She missed her heart-sister.

"Franz told me it's her fault women are infertile. He said she cracked the moon and brought the yellow dust."

Maya smiled, which was strange. None of this was funny.

She leaned forward. "The decline in births started long before your grandmother. It was the brainchild of her husband—Raphael Konstan-tinou. He didn't like how many people there were in the world, and it is true, there were too many. But the way he, and the president, and the dictator who overthrew Russia chose to solve the problem? That was the true crime. Erin merely took them by their collars and forced them to face the conclusion of their hubris."

Maya explained how she, Erin, and my cousin Brianne lit the spark that culminated in the death of the dictator, Grigory Novikov, the fissure through the center of the blue moon, and the release of caged women after twenty-five years of captivity.

She told me how Novikov's scientists developed artificial humans so lifelike it was nearly impossible to tell they weren't real, and how, after Erin's revolutionary group exposed the plots being perfected by his government and America's, the android production was aban-doned. Human females became part of civilization again, although, Maya said quietly, it could never be said they were an equal part, not with the way they were cut loose from the Cages, nor with the manda-tory monthly exams and forced selection of marriage partners, not one of which had resulted in a successful pregnancy.

She added new details to what I had read. Those who supported the defeated regimes fought to revive them, even though they'd lost their three figureheads. Hard-liners lobbied to have women thrown back into the Cages. They believed, or said they did, that women were of the devil, and the cause of every problem the world had ever faced. Maya described how that argument had been used in the decades leading up to the original imprisonment, so they tried it again. They also demanded a restart of the android program, arguing that if there were no more babies, the androids could care for the human popula-tion as it aged and became infirm.

"I hate to admit it, but there were many among the freed women who wanted to go back," Maya said. "In a perverted way, the Cages meant home and safety. Freedom offered only a different kind of suffering."

My mother had written as much. I didn't know what these cages looked like, how roomy they were, what comforts they provided, or anything, but it seemed sad to me that any human being would choose them over freedom.

Maya told me that violent militias twice nearly succeeded in over-throwing newly established democratic governments—once in London and again in Moscow. They triumphed for a time in disorganized Colombia, Thailand, and Poland, and had to be defeated in bloody wars.

At first, Germany was considered one of the best places on earth for the women because it crushed the terrorists. The new Chancellor had clear goals, and no patience for malcontents who, he said, merely hated women and did not care about the future of the earth.

"We learned eventually that the German government had put on a democratic front to hide its true goals. The Chancellor was with the terrorists all along. He lied to get elected so he could clear the way for their objectives."

She asked me about my childhood and I told her everything except for Teófilo. "You were kept in a little chrysalis, like a pinned butterfly," she said. "While they waited for you to come of age."

Tucking my hand in hers, she said, "Zoë, you remind me so much of your mother. As you now know, she grew up very isolated. The things others take for granted were new to her. Learning of her life made me see everything differently." She turned her gaze outward to the landscape, where twisty breezes were forming dust devils. "I, too, spent years in a cage. It's why my arthritis is so bad. But Fauna had no memory of anything else. I was a doctor before they took me. I knew what freedom felt like, and what it felt like when it was stolen. Fauna didn't. But she stood up before thousands and spoke in her natural voice of what she had lived. She was one of the main reasons Halcyon was so successful. Everyone loved her and wanted to be close to her."

"Halcyon?"

"That was what we called ourselves, after the kingfisher. I'll tell you more about it after you finish reading the diary."

"What about my…father?"

A groove slashed between her eyes. "We thought Adam took Fauna to Germany because he believed she would be safer there. But after everything happened, and after I read Fauna's diary, it was clear he had a different purpose. I can't tell you why Adam did what he did, or why he allowed himself to be killed. Make no mistake, Zoë. It was his choice." She paused. "He could have changed the world in a split second, but he didn't. There was purpose behind that, too. I think it was because we humans had to take up the fight for ourselves. We have to fight for our lives, Zoë, and for our future. I thought we'd won the night Erin and Rafe and Will left us. I thought the fight was over." She sighed deeply. "Now I wonder if it ever will be."

"Do you know how my father died?"

"It's in the diary." Her grip tightened. "I would rather you read about it in Fauna's words."

"All right."

"After Adam died, she was taken to Berlin. Shortly after you were born, the two of you were relocated and kept under heavy guard. When you were two, they took you to the Schloss, and she was moved again, so clandestinely that no one was ever able to find her. She was simply gone. Vanished. Rumors came to us that she died of pneumonia, but it was never confirmed. They certainly wouldn't have let her go, as the last woman to carry a child to term. They would have gone on and on testing her. But no other child has been born since you, at least not that anyone knows of. I gave up hope years ago that she could still be alive. In fact, my hope is that she died quickly after they took you from her. I can't bear the thought that she had to suffer being an experimental subject, all alone, while grieving for you and Adam."

I wondered if Robert Louis knew where she was taken. "Can I see my father in the pyramid?"

"No, sweetheart. There are no images of him." She frowned. "I'm not sure why."

I drank the final sips of my now-cold coffee and thought about all I had learned. "Would you mind if I finish reading now? There isn't much left."

"What about lunch? You've been up all night. You're still in your nightgown."

"I want to finish. I—I think I'll get dressed and go for a walk, if that is acceptable to you."

"Of course." She squeezed my hand and rose. "I'm here, Zoë. If you need me, if you want to talk. I'm here." She started to leave.

"What are the Erinys Archives?" I asked.

"Erin's book. An account of her life and the revolution. It was necessary to keep a true record, so it could never be forgotten, lied about, or distorted. I added a chapter or two from my perspective. Unfortunately, the book is gone. Adam took it to Germany, but it did not come to us with Fauna's diary and the necklace. We've searched for years, but nobody has been able to find it."

I nodded, trying to hide my disappointment, and she left me.

Chapter 12

MY MOTHER'S WRITING AND MAYA'S REMINISCENCES MADE VIVID PICTURES in my mind, the kind I shied away from. I didn't want to believe that my species could be so casually cruel to others of their own kind, even though Robert Louis had given me warning, the day he entered the brick building with the chimney. He understood human nature, but that didn't save him. In the end, he was destroyed by men much more ignorant than he.

I shivered, not for the first time since opening the diary, and closed my eyes, resting the back of my head against the chair Maya had called an "Adirondack." I thought about throwing the book into the sagebrush, or better yet, off a cliff. I would live the rest of my life unenlightened, always wondering, but that might be the safer choice.

What was the use of knowledge, anyway? Governments would go on doing whatever they pleased. People would continue to disagree, fight, and kill each other. There was certainly nothing I could do to alter human nature.

Finishing my mother's account would change my life. Of that I had no doubt. Before reading the rest, I had to decide. Did I want to know the details of my father's death? Did I want to see my mother's last words?

Leave the past buried…or dig it up and endure the consequences?

DONNING TROUSERS, A TEE SHIRT, AND SNEAKERS, I WENT FOR A walkabout, taking the diary with me. At the last moment I grabbed the silver necklace, too. Carmen, wooden pins sticking out of her mouth, waved as she draped a wet sheet over the clothesline. Come night, my bed would hold the intoxicating scents of sunlight, sagebrush, and cactus.

I was happy here, in this unsullied place of solitude and beauty, but for the continued ache of missing Robert Louis.

Bastien. *Call him by his real name, Zoë.*

Spelled slightly differently, a *bastion* became a *stronghold*, a *bulwark*, a *citadel*. He'd tried to be those things to me, but the ruthlessness of his enemies overcame him, much like the cannonball crushed the battlement at the Schloss and killed my only friend.

My mother's diary would add more sorrow to that pain. It would strip away the surface peace born from ignorance. It might make hopelessness the chief emotion within me. That's what I feared.

I climbed to a place I called the Painted Cliffs, since the rocks changed colors depending on the time of day and weather conditions. Sometimes the quartz glittered like billions of minute stars and the granite blazed. On grey days the cliffs were blanketed in a purple bluish tinge and at times, rarely, I was offered many colors at once. It was always windy. Eagles and hawks loved to catch thermals, and I often heard the distant clatter of mountain goat hooves. Once I'd listened to the trailing echoes of an avalanche—like distant thunder that went on, and on, and on.

Scrambling onto a rocky perch, I was soothed by the silent play of light and shadow in the canyon below.

The book lay on the ground beside me. The pages fluttered, pausing on a section I had read before that described the German Chancellor's election and the new laws he initiated. Genetic testing. Marriage based on DNA. Profound Necessity.

I picked up the diary, placed it gently on my lap, and smoothed the paper.

A rather odd phenomenon had occurred now and then since I landed in this place. I would suddenly feel like I was a stranger to myself. I would recall my experiences and believe, for an instant, that the memories were aberrations. Sometimes, when doing some mundane thing like brushing my teeth, I would not recognize the face in the mirror.

Had I known a man—a duke—named Bastien Jäger-Abelard? Had I performed *Romeo and Juliet* for him beneath colored lights? Had he been put to death for trying to protect me?

At these times I felt like an alien in my own skin. It itched. I wanted to scrape and scrape until all thought was expunged and I was nothing but flowing blood.

Maybe the only true realities are the voices I hear inside trees.

Chapter 13

February 16th:

The soldiers came in the night.

Adam put his arms around me. I woke and sleepily pressed against his throat—my favorite place to be. I kissed the pulse beating there, and felt it quicken. His arms tightened. Very softly, he said, "My task is finished, Fauna. Another is coming forward now. Be strong for our daughter."

"What?" I asked, confused, but that was all the time we had. Armed men broke through the door and flooded into our room. Adam was torn from my arms. They held a gun to his head and forced him into a chair.

Once the soldiers had us both restrained and searched, another man entered, clearly the one in charge. He wore a uniform with high black boots, both of which had knife sheaths, and knives. Medals covered his jacket. A strap ran over one shoulder, supporting a pistol in a holster under his left arm, and a sheath hung from his belt, holding a third knife. He kept his hands folded behind his back, his fingers idly weaving the handle of a whip between them.

His stance terrified me. His many weapons terrified me. Most of all, his expression terrified me.

If only Adam had not sent Vita away. She would have warned us. She would have ripped out their throats. But they would have shot her as soon as they came in. She would not have had a chance against bullets. He truly had protected her by sending her away. I understood then that he knew this day was coming. Perhaps he had known it all his life.

Two men stood on either side of me, holding my arms and keeping me on my knees on the bed. I learned hard lessons growing up in the Cages. One of them was to make no sound in times of danger. I was crying now, but silently.

The commander approached Adam and stared at him. Adam gazed back, perfectly calm. A horn blared outside, and someone laughed. The soldier to my right coughed.

Another soldier came in. I recognized the man who had detained Adam in the street. His pistol was drawn. He asked the leader a question, calling him the German word for "General," and "Odenwylde."

THE DIARY FELL FROM MY HANDS. "NO," I WHISPERED. "NO."

I sat there, my face against my knees, dumbfounded betrayal sweeping like acid through my body.

Sunlight and August heat pounded the back of my head. A raven croaked. Out over the canyon, a red-tailed hawk gave a screeling cry.

After moments, or hours, or days, I gathered myself and picked up the book.

I had to know the truth.

The commander made no response. He seemed unaware of any of us, and unable to look away from Adam. I watched a drop of sweat track down his temple.

Adam finally turned away from him and looked at me. His face softened. I saw no fear. No anger. Only sadness.

"I love you," I said, without making a sound.

He never took his gaze from me—not even when the man who had threatened him in the street raised his pistol and shot him in the forehead.

His body jerked a little. But he still watched me. His eyes still said, *Be strong*.

At first, Odenwylde seemed horrified. He stared at Adam. Then he turned on von Bäumer, who backed away, lifting his hands, speaking rapidly. He sounded defensive and he looked frightened.

I hadn't learned very much German at that point. I was having enough trouble with English. I think the commander was accusing von Bäumer of disobeying an order. He gestured at Adam, shouting the same few words, over and over again. Something like "Befiya."

The men on either side of Adam backed away. I felt like they were afraid, very afraid, of this Odenwylde.

Von Bäumer spoke harshly, pointing at the door. The soldiers left, including the ones holding me, leaving only von Bäumer and Odenwylde.

There was more shouting. Von Bäumer was trying to defend himself, I think. He put his pistol into its holster and held up both hands.

Odenwylde drew his pistol. Von Bäumer fumbled for his again, his hands shaking.

I smelled death in the lingering scent from von Bäumer's gun. I saw it in their faces.

Then Odenwylde lowered his weapon and rubbed his eyes. He turned back to Adam. Von Bäumer lowered his pistol, but kept it in his hand.

While they were shouting, a seam formed by the window. It wavered then split like a torn curtain, and within the split there was darkness but for pinpoints of swirling colorful light.

I saw this before, in Sequoia National Forest, at one of Erin's last rallies, when Adam, Will, Nash, and many, many others, came through what Erin called a "rift." The rift is a way to travel between places very quickly. This opening was the same.

For one second, against all reason, even though my husband lay dead in front of me, I hoped he would step through, alive and smiling, like he had that other time. But it was not to be. Four sparkling, ghostly people, two women and two men, entered the room. They paid no attention to the German soldiers, who were now utterly motionless, like statues. They did not even blink.

The men gathered Adam in their arms. The women bent and kissed his face, weeping. The men carried Adam back into the rift, and the younger woman followed. The older woman turned to me. "Don't be afraid, Fauna."

Courage rushed through me like a fire. I didn't know where it came from. The woman, maybe? I needed it, and was grateful. "I am not," I said.

She stepped into the rift and it vanished. My Adam was gone.

The general and von Bäumer woke from their frozen state. They stared at each other. At the empty chair. At me. Von Bäumer, especially, seemed to think I had played a trick on them. He came right up in my face and shouted at me. I tried my best to show nothing but contempt.

He slapped me repeatedly and spoke what I am sure were threats.

The general seized von Bäumer and pulled him from me. He was shouting too. Everything happened very quickly then. The general drew one of his knives. He brutally slashed von Bäumer in the face. Blood spurted. Von Bäumer screamed and tried to both hold off the general and reach for his pistol.

The other men ran in and separated the two. They took von Bäumer's gun and the general's knife. Through it all they tried to show respect and deference.

The general straightened his coat and ran a hand through his hair. He said something, gave an order, maybe. Three men carried a moaning, nearly unconscious von Bäumer out of the room, leaving two behind, at attention.

The general spoke to them. They shook their heads and replied, assuring him, no doubt, that Adam had not risen from the dead and passed them in the corridor. He nodded towards me. I was pulled off the bed and they took me away in my nightgown.

The last I saw of him, he was standing next to the chair, frowning.

The part of my life that I will remember with joy for however much longer I live, is over. All I have left is our child. Adam's child.

Chapter 14

Odenwylde was in the room when my father was killed. He was in charge. He gave the orders.

Odenwylde killed my father and imprisoned my mother.

The man I gave my whole heart to.

I threw the diary. It landed at the edge of the cliff. If there was any justice in this world, wind would blow the damn thing off.

From now on, I write to you, to my unborn daughter.

That line wavered before my eyes, filled with wonder and joy.

Could I take what my mother wrote—to me—and let it fall into oblivion? Would she chronicle things she thought would destroy me?

She didn't realize I would come to know and trust Odenwylde. To love him. She didn't know how fragile I would be when I received her diary.

The wind blew playfully. The hawk shrieked.

"I know just how you feel," a voice said right behind me.

I leaped to my feet, heart pounding, and faced a woman—the woman, I realized instantly, whose picture I'd seen earlier. Erin. My grandmother. She looked younger in person, her skin youthful, her lips full. But her eyes were the same, like fiery blue stars.

She tilted her head a bit. The hem of her white gown fluttered—it was as gauzy as the wings of a dragonfly—and I saw that her feet were bare. Her hair hung in loose waves to her waist. Something moved at the back of her neck and I glimpsed the smooth head and unblinking eyes of a serpent. Its body trailed down over her right breast and its tail flicked.

"H-how can you be here?" I asked. I started to say, *You're dead*, before I remembered. Maya didn't say she was dead, only that she was "gone."

She waved a hand. "That's not important. I came to tell you something. It's no use. Believe me. You might as well do what's asked of you. She won't leave you alone. I know. I've been in your shoes. I got so damn tired of the harping."

"Harping?"

She bent, picked up the necklace, and watched it swing, the blue bead—almost as blue as my grandmother's eyes—glimmering within the curves of the horned moons.

"This thing is stuffed with spells and magic." She held it out. "It wants you."

I took it. It was hot. I distinctly felt it pulse like a beating heart.

"It will share things if you listen," she said.

Flecks of gold and fragile white seams intersected the bead, like tiny rivers flowing across a blue planet. "Did you crack the moon and bring the poison?"

"I brought the world to this place. Now I give it to you."

I gaped, then realized what I was doing and closed my mouth. "Why me?"

"Because at the end of oblivion lies hope, and only you can find it."

The words rang in my ears with weight and color.

"Read your mother's book, Zoë. It won't destroy you." She cupped my cheeks in her hands, smiling a bit wistfully. "Look at you. Adam never did anything by halves." She paused, and for me, time stopped. "Everything has to happen as it is meant to happen," she said quietly. "I learned that the hard way." Meeting my gaze, she asked, "May I kiss you?"

I nodded wordlessly.

She leaned forward and I closed my eyes. I felt her lips, warm and tangible, on my eyelids. One kiss on each lid.

Do you believe we are born again? That we live more than one life?

When I opened my eyes, she was gone.

Chapter 15

THERE WAS NO SIGN OF ANY HUMAN—JUST A PAIR OF GOLDEN EAGLES, lazily drifting. I must have been dreaming. To make sure, I pinched my forearm. It hurt.

Laughter echoed on a gust of wind.

"All right." I returned to my perch. "I'll read it. I'll read the damn thing."

Sudden calm came over me.

I thought of the words she spoke just before she vanished. *Do you believe we are born again? That we live more than one life?*

If such a thing were real, then my husband could be reborn. Of course, I'd be old by the time he grew up. If such a thing were real—if it were real…Odenwylde might actually have been the reincarnation of Robert Louis Stevenson. I might not have been unbalanced every time I felt my idol's presence so strongly.

I watched the eagles and relived my happiest moments with Teófilo on the battlements.

Teófilo loved me unconditionally, even when I acted in an unlovable, selfish manner, which I admit I did.

There were only a few more pages. I picked up the diary and turned to the next entry.

My grandmother promised it wouldn't destroy me. But at this moment, I could not imagine feeling more destroyed.

April 7th:

The ancient ways live on, as potent as ever, but once again they have gone into hiding. Maya, Adam, and I were given prophecy that one is still to come—Mother Erin's inheritor.

The sign will be a star that hangs over the place of her birth. It will show everyone that divine forgiveness is within their reach, if they want. If they choose. Naturally, it reminds me of the Christian birth story, and I marvel at the way religions lace together, even when all their supporters do is attack each other in real life. There are grains of truth in all of them.

The one prophesied is you. You will live. You are its fulfillment.

I stood on the beach at Amnisos. Athene lifted her hand and pulled the dust from the moon. She called it "glamour." I know what it brings, because Adam told me. It is not illness or infertility, death or destruction. It is life. It is corn pollen, a magical substance. It floats all around us and through us as we walk the pollen path.

The dust is not a death sentence. It is choice and wisdom, if we open our eyes, our minds, and our hearts.

Erin opened *L'ombre Moon* to save us. Everything must open, to allow light in and let it shine out. We who stood on Amnisos Beach were witnesses to the hope and the doom.

Hope that you will open the world and bring the light.

Doom because you might choose not to.

I GLANCED BEHIND ME, HALF-FEARING MY GRANDMOTHER WOULD BE THERE watching with that cynical yet sparkling smile. *Adam never did anything*

by halves, she said fondly—that is, if I hadn't lost my mind, which seemed the likeliest possibility.

There was only a small beetle scurrying over pebbles. I turned back to the book, tightening my grip on the necklace.

No more children. No more love. Not until they all lie dead. Then we will begin again.

Had I read those words? No, they weren't there on the page. I heard them. They seeped into my skin from the necklace.

Awed and breathless, I closed my eyes, feeling the weight of the sorcery flow into my blood and begin its journey through my body, sharing its very long history with me.

Then we will begin again. Did that mean that somehow, we could come back from extinction?

With my eyes closed, concentrating, I heard more.

Some say it comes from a lake of silver on the moon.

I shivered, not from cold but from the sense that I was in the night sky, surrounded by starlight.

The necklace was crafted in a legendary pool, a secret cavern where the moon went into hiding when it disappeared from the skies. Though the queen is long dead, her great civilization lost, the necklace goes on casting her spell, century after century, for within it is forged the amaranthine light of the moon.

I sat like that for some time, eyes shut, feeling, sensing, and hearing the magic of the necklace. When I opened my eyes, I felt stronger, ready to continue reading.

You must wonder why I write to you like this, like I won't be there to explain things. Athene's handmaid came to me in a dream. It turns out you will be taken from me. There is no one now who can ease the pain, so I keep it inside. I wish the world were different. I wish I could be simply your mother, and you my child, and we could be together.

Athene leaves nothing to chance. You will find the way, or the way will be shown to you. When you are ready, you will be given understanding. Nevertheless, I have a wish. I want you to know about me, and about your exceptional father. I want you to know that I hated losing you and hated missing out on your life. I want you to know that I love you.

My sweet, sweet girl, if you are reading this, my wish was granted.

Study the old religions. The oldest, especially from Crete. You will have to learn how to tell truth from myths invented by the Hellenes and modernized into the kind of trickery that keeps half of us in bondage. Whenever you see something that says Athene was born from Zeus's forehead, you are reading lies. I will tell you the meaning of Athene's name. It is and always will be, "I have come from myself."

Dig deeper. Learn the mystery of corn pollen, for it is all around you. It is in every cell of your body. Do you understand, little Zoë?

Zoë. Yes. I like how it flows from my pencil onto the paper. And I like the meaning. Life.

If we cannot find our lost divinity, human civilization will perish. And it should. Woman is humankind's connection to the sublime. It is hard to remember that in these terrible times, when women have been scorned and dishonored. We have traveled deep into the dragon's lair, and have lost the stars.

Find the truth. Learn what happened. And then, my darling, it is up to you. You will know what to do.

Chapter 16

I turned the page and inhaled slowly, for there was Odenwylde's name again.

Date unknown:

After Adam died, Odenwylde and his men took me from the hotel. I have not been mistreated. In fact, I live in luxury. They even left me my diary. I'm sure they intend to take it from me at some point. I am spoken to respectfully. Nobody wants me getting upset. It could harm the baby.

I haven't felt like writing in this book since they killed my Adam, but I must record what happened today, for it concerns you, Zoë.

The general, Odenwylde, came to see me. He sent the guards away. When they were gone, he placed a silver disk on my throat and his. He said they would scramble our voices to any who eavesdropped. I didn't trust him, so I said nothing.

In excellent English, he claimed that Adam spoke to him in the hotel room. I knew he was lying. I was there. Adam said not one word to Odenwylde.

He tapped his forehead. "He spoke into my mind. I cannot explain it, but it happened, and I am…changed."

I knew Adam could do things other people couldn't. Did he not heal the deepest of wounds within me? He healed them so thoroughly they didn't even leave a scar. I waited to hear what the general would say next.

"Your husband knew things no one else knows, things I have kept secret." Odenwylde frowned. "He knew I have a daughter."

I moved away cautiously as he clenched his hands. He didn't seem to notice. "It's true, Fauna," he said. "I do have a daughter, but no one knows about her. How did Adam know?"

He stared at me as though he wanted me to explain. I shrugged.

"Adam said to me, as clearly as I speak to you now, 'I have a daughter too. You are the only one I trust to protect her.'"

Adam trusted this man? The man who was responsible for his death? It could not be. He was lying.

"That was when I learned you were pregnant," Odenwylde said. "We had no idea. We were told Adam was a dangerous revolutionary. But now I know we were sent there to capture you. We were ordered to kill him but not to harm you or let you be harmed."

I gritted my teeth and waited for him to get to his point.

"Your Adam put a spell on me," Odenwylde said. "Something…his eyes…his thoughts…his face. He did something to me and I cannot get free of it."

Still, I waited. He may have earned Adam's trust somehow, but he had not yet earned mine.

"I have told my superiors that I will attempt to trick you or frighten you into revealing where the other insurgents are hiding, what their plans are, and most of all, where their leader, Erin Aragon, is hiding. They want her very badly. We know you knew her. That is why I have been sent to talk to you."

I tried to appear unafraid. I would tell him nothing. They could kill me if they wished. They could torture me. But I knew they wouldn't. I had the upper hand.

He shook his head. "I am not going to ask you about any of that. I only want to know one thing. How did your husband find out about my daughter? Her mother and I have gone to great lengths to keep her existence a secret."

"He knew things," I said. "It was a power he had. He knew you were going to kill him before you broke down the door. He told me goodbye just before you came in. But he didn't tell me the reason he was allowing it to happen."

"I don't understand why he said he trusted me, especially if he knew we were coming, and what our orders were. I should be the last person your husband would trust."

"Maybe he knew more about you than you know about yourself."

Odenwylde stared at the floor, then he said, "I am going to do everything I can to protect you and give you back your freedom."

I wanted to trust him, because Adam did. But I didn't dare. He seemed to understand. He said, "Adam washed your feet. In a grove, as a doe and stag stood watch."

I am not sure I managed to hide my shock. This happened, Zoë, the night I met your father.

"Vengeance," Odenwylde said. "That was his vow to you, to the girl he named Fauna."

"He kept his vows," I said sharply, unable to stop the tears. I knew then that Adam had spoken to him, and that Odenwylde was somehow transformed. What that meant, I could not guess.

"I don't care about my freedom," I said. "But my daughter…"

"I will give my life to protect her."

"Will you?"

"You have my word."

"If you give your life, who will protect her then?"

He was quiet for a bit, then he said, "You are right. Dying for her is not the way to protect her."

He ran a hand through his hair. He looked tired.

"Would you like some tea?" I asked.

He nodded, and I went away to the little kitchen. When it was ready, I brought the cups and teapot on a tray. He poured, and we drank without speaking for a few minutes.

Then he told me about himself.

His daughter's name is Louisa. She is five years old, and this government does not know about her. No government does. The fact that he told me…well, my trust increased, both in him and the disks on our throats.

He and his wife, Phaedre, were married on a Greek island. She refused to live with him in Berlin. At first this angered him, but after a few years he accepted her wisdom. He told me that he has not trusted his government for a long time, and his loyalty now is tarnished beyond repair. He said the new Chancellor is "rotted to the core" and has sold himself to the terrorists and fertility scientists—who are, he says, terrorists in disguise. He came to be glad that Phaedre was hidden and no one knew about his marriage. When she became pregnant with Louisa, they understood what would happen if people found out. The scientists would take her. She would become a curiosity, a test subject.

I wasn't sure why he was telling me these things. Maybe to make me feel closer to him. It gave me an idea. "I want my daughter to live a life as free as any man," I said. "Can you make that happen?"

He did not answer right away. It boosted my confidence that he was considering. I could see that he knew this would not be easy.

I was moved by his eyes. They are expressive. Everything fell into place and I knew the promise I wanted from him. "As far as the world knows," I said, "you are a single man. Become my daughter's guardian. I want you to bind her to you in every legal way. Let it be known that I have betrothed her to you. When the time comes, you will marry her. Can you arrange that?"

After a moment, he said, "My position carries considerable privilege. If you declare your wish and sign papers to that effect, it will be accepted. They won't care, not while she is a child. I will tell them that you have come to trust me, which is what they want, and I agreed to this because it is what you want. Germany holds guardianships sacrosanct. None will oppose your will and testament—until she is mature. When that time comes, they will declare your wishes void so they can take control of her. But until she is old enough, they will go along with it, to keep you happy if nothing else. Creating a life of freedom for her will be harder. Most of the doctors want her right here, under the dome, both to control the air she breathes and her diet, and especially so they can study her. If I can convince them that her mental and emotional health is as important as her body, I think I can sway them into something else. I will do my best to give your daughter a free childhood and an education. Yes, Fauna. I will make it happen."

"And you will be ready for them."

"I will preserve their trust. When the time is right, when they plot to seize her, I will step in. I am not sure how, but I will find a way, and I will make arrangements so that if anything happens to me, someone will take my place."

"You will not presume on the betrothal."

He was offended, I saw, shocked, but I did not apologize. He shook his head. "Never." I was more reassured by his physical reaction than his pledge.

"I have lost faith in my government," he said, "but I have not known what to do, how to fight, not until Adam changed me. He said something else, just before von Bäumer shot him. He said I would soon have a choice to make. This is it. This is my choice. This is my turning point."

His eyes filled with tears.

I explained what I have told you—that you have a greater purpose. That you were prophesied.

He listened. He said nothing. I think he believed me.

He waited, drinking tea, while I wrote all this in my diary. He is taking it with him, along with my wedding ring and the neck-lace Mother Erin gave me. He promises to place them in your hands when the time is right.

I see now why Adam brought me to Germany. It was to meet Odenwylde. Adam brought me here so Odenwylde could take his place.

Zoë, Adam chose this man for you.

He has earned my trust. I hope you will trust him, too.

THE WORDS BLURRED. MY TEARS FELL, SMEARING HER WRITING.

I missed them so much. I missed my mother, though I never met her. I missed my father, the magical Adam who lived over a thousand years before falling to the people of my age.

Odenwylde was the force protecting me all those years. He, not the Schloss father, had arranged for my tutoring, which molded the girl I now was. He had done so very much, and I never knew.

I missed Odenwylde.

"Why couldn't you tell me more, Mother?" I whispered. "Why couldn't you be clearer? Why did Odenwylde not tell me what I am to do?"

I lowered my head and closed my eyes, feeling wholly inadequate and alone.

This time, no spectre appeared to comfort me.

Chapter 17

I have always loved learning. I set out, wanting to fulfill the wishes of those who meant the most to me. I studied nearly every day, but this time around, much of what I needed to learn had been suppressed or completely erased. I kept at it. I read between the lines and dug into the nooks and corners of history.

Maya was extraordinarily helpful. She talked so knowledgeably about the past that I began to wonder if she had lived in other eras. She produced rare books and manuscripts she had collected over the years, which gave insight I could find nowhere else.

Nash knew all about corn pollen, as it was used extensively in his tribe. He did his best to explain its magic, though it is not so easily explained to an outsider. He had long suspected what the yellow dust was, having grown up with pollen ceremonies, so was not surprised when he read what my mother wrote in her diary. Still, I noticed when we talked about it, his eyes sparked in a way I hadn't seen before.

He told me how the Diné used corn pollen in every ceremony but one—the ceremony of death. Pollen had power to restore good things…love and hózhó, and was all about life. He gave a faraway smile when I asked what hózhó was, and said it brought to his mind my grandmother asking the same question.

Had the Greek goddess Athene brought pollen pouring out of the

second moon? If my mother and Nash were correct about the proper-
ties of pollen, that meant it was the opposite of evil, death, or infertility. When Nash called corn pollen "prayer dust," I shivered and gazed
into the heavens at the fractured moon. Had our earth been inundated
with prayer? With love? With hózhó?

Chapter 18

Four years I've spent studying. Four long years. I began with the Eleusinian Mysteries—most of that never written down—and the matriarchies of Crete—what little hadn't been destroyed—and methodically, I inched my way to the most recent fall of civilization, which began in 2046, when *L'ombre Moon* entered orbit.

I feel the weight of my obligation. Those women who were born before me are getting older every day. At some point they will be too old to bear children.

Nash helps relight the waning spark of my enthusiasm by flying me to the sequoias or other enchanted green places, but the charge I have been given hangs over me, waiting for me to make a decision.

He talks about the changes he sees around us. The trees spreading into huge forests, the horses increasing their herds, the deer multiplying. None of this could have happened but for diminishing numbers of humans.

His gaze upon me is perceptive. He says, "I see by the gleam in your eye that you might choose trees over humans."

I cannot deny it.

WHEN I WAS YOUNG, I WOULD WASH AN APPLE AND EAT IT WITHOUT MUCH thought, but after studying the revelations of the past, I couldn't wash an apple without feeling it, smelling it, digging my nails into the veined white meat below the crisp outer skin and wondering if apples felt pain when eaten.

I became high-strung, twitchy. Several times I heard tree voices, even inside the house. Once, the wind brought the call of the Redwoods from eight hundred kilometers away. I tried to decipher what they were saying. I ran outside and listened, but I couldn't. It was too faint.

What I have learned makes me angry. Humans deserve to die. Blood and death shrouds every one of us. If I am forced into the role of "mother of the world," then I say, "let us die." If given another chance, what would stop us from degenerating into cruelty again, destroying each other with new perversions and degradations?

Many years ago, in one of humankind's countless wars, millions were tortured and murdered. I see that ruin, the one that nearly brought Robert Louis to his knees. The barbed wire…the watchtowers…the brick chimney…and his agony after spending a solitary half-hour beside what I now know was a gas chamber. That atrocity should have been enough to teach us, to change us, yet a hundred years later, almost every woman in the world was thrown into a cage, and less than fifty years after that, I was imprisoned for being born—my body invaded, cut open, robbed.

Humans are incapable of learning, of changing, even when history stares them in the face with cloudy, ghoulish eyes, and the fetid exhalations of death.

My first night here, Maya said she hoped humans would accept their demise and adopt kindness and respect towards each other, but the doubt was clear, in her face, in her voice. She didn't believe we were capable of learning or changing either.

Sometimes anger becomes a raging cyclone inside me.

Inevitably, I will then see in my mind Maya and Nash, Clotilda and Beata and Dagmar, Elena, Demetri, Phaedre, and Franz. I see all the ferrymen who aided in our journey, the innkeepers and their wives. I see Blackbeard. They all gave themselves to me—some gave their lives.

No matter how much cynicism washes over me, when my mind recreates Robert Louis's face, everything comes to a standstill.

Though I may end up witnessing humanity's last breath—I

suppose it is possible I could be the last living person—I can't help but consider myself charmed, blessed beyond measure, because Robert Louis—Bastien Günther Jäger-Abelard—showed me what can be.

Möglichkeit. The possibility.

If there is one human being left on this earth who believes in possibilities, does she…or he…deserve another chance?

A frail, thin, ill man was my Hercules, my Perceval. My champion and my hero. As I step outside to greet the sunrise, I take a deep breath and vow to honor his sacrifice the only way I can.

By following my own choices.

Chapter 19

I REST MY CHEEK AGAINST BREATHING BARK.

Take heart, Zoë.

"If he were here, I would."

But he isn't. He is dead and the world is arid and colorless without him.

"What should I do?"

The bristlecone's voice is deep and gnarled, yet its rumbly cadence soothes. *We will miss you if you go. You are interesting and we like watching you. But the world will survive, and maybe, someday, humans will evolve again. In the meantime, animals can flourish, and so will we.*

I imagine the world without people. Cities slowly crumbling, roadways vanishing beneath weeds. The only enemy of trees an occasional fire. I like that image.

Silence but for birdsong, wind, and thunderstorms. I like those images too.

There is a catch—the beauty would flourish, yes, the moons would glow and the stars twinkle, but who would write sonnets about it? Who would sing the songs to glorify it?

Why did he never tell me what he desired for humanity, for Earth?

He didn't want to influence me. But I wish I knew what he thought, or hoped. I wish we could sit beside a fire roasting a hare and talk. "Hash it all out," as Maya would say.

One night, his voice came to me so clearly in a dream that I woke with a gasp. I sat up, staring into darkness, sure he was in the room, or had been a mere second ago.

History is more important than we sometimes realize. Understanding our history can help us avoid making the same mistakes as our ancestors. You see, Zoë, the key to our future is found actually, in our past.

I returned to my pillow, closing my eyes, and saw my mother's writing.

Her name is and always will be, "I have come from myself."
Go farther, dig deeper.
I brought the world to this place. Now I am giving it to you.
At the end of oblivion lies hope, and only you can find it.
Learn the mystery of corn pollen. It is in every cell of your body.
I promise you, Zoë. I promise another knight will come.
I had my signposts. All I had to do was follow them.
"Thank you," I whispered.

Chapter 20

A painting hung over the fireplace in the living room. I'd never paid much attention to it, other than to note the skill of the artist. One afternoon when I was out of sorts—I was suffering through one of my painful menstrual periods and could not be satisfied with anything—I threw myself, with a book, into an easy chair in that room. I didn't feel like reading though, nor did I feel like riding. It was the hottest part of the day and I had cramps. I heard Carmen puttering in the kitchen and, more distantly, Marco and Nash talking about the horses.

I stared for a long time into the neatly swept fireplace before my gaze rose to the painting. It depicted a beach, a sea, and our two moons in the heavens, the furthest cracked as it was now. Just off shore a curved white boat floated and nearby, on the sand, a woman dressed in white gazed over her shoulder directly at me.

Faint rays of light came off her, shooting in every direction.

All at once, like a thunderclap, I relived my Schloss mother at the dinner table, kneading her pearl necklace and querulously asking my Schloss father if he had found the painting…the white boat taking the star to the castle in the sea. *It's a secret, you know,* she'd insisted peevishly.

He merely chuckled and shoved mashed potatoes into his mouth.

Had she really said that, or was my mind playing tricks, trying to make more of the past than it was?

When I was a lab rat at the domed hospital in the city, I sometimes wished I could return to those lost days. They were simple and honest, for me anyway, though most around me were lying.

I lived in contented ignorance.

As I stared at the painting, I mentally traveled backward and tried to make sense of that child and her life. Were there clues in Teófilo's pleas to carry me into a rainbow? Something that would help me plot a wise course here and now?

I went to the fireplace and gripped the edge of the mantel. The woman's eyes were breathtakingly blue, her hair, black.

It was my grandmother, no doubt there. A glow spiraled down from the heavens, into her and through her fingers and eyes, like she was drawing in the light, focusing it, and sending it out.

"Do you like it?"

I turned and there was Maya.

"I think...I think this painting is important," I said slowly.

"The artist was a friend of mine. His name was Jean-Michel. Would you like to hear the story behind the inspiration for it? It is a good one, but quite long."

"Please."

"Come and sit. We'll have a chat."

———————————————

Chapter 21

———————————————

AT MY REQUEST, NASH FLEW ME TO THE BRISTLECONES. I HEARD THEM calling before we landed. They knew I was coming. They might have even known what I would end up saying, though I wasn't yet sure. It wouldn't surprise me.

He let me go in alone.

I put my hands on the trunk of the oldest one. "Methuselah," it was called. It was believed to be the oldest living thing on earth.

If humans died out, it could live with no fear of some small-minded person cutting it down to make a table.

I looked up as the tree bonded with me through my palms. The colors that teased at the very edges of my sight intensified, and there was the yellow dust, swirling almost invisibly between me and fathomless space.

I felt the bristlecone twine around my heart.

Robert Louis and Chthonia saved me, not because they thought I could in turn save the human race by having babies. Not because, like the rural people, they thought I had the power to rid the earth of the dust, or bring Erin back. In their minds, I deserved respect for no particular reason outside of common humanity.

Thanks to Maya, I now knew most, if not all, of my grandmother's story. Stories, I should say, since there were seven of them.

For several moments I simply stood, my hands on the bristlecone. It waited patiently.

At last, I whispered, "Let's try again." My voice shook. I was afraid, but I couldn't let my grandmother's stories be lost. Hers, Maya's, and the others. They never gave up. I could do no less.

The message swirled down through the bark, into the roots. Fierce wind lifted around me, capturing my words and carrying them to every corner of the earth.

Almost too softly to comprehend, the wind spoke.

You are our dance of love, Zoë.

Chapter 22

THE MAN FOUND ME ON MY FAVORITE RIDGE.

I heard a sound. It took a moment to realize it was not goat hooves but the grate of boots. Stabbed with sudden instinctive fright, I stood.

He worked his way up the scree, sliding now and then, head bent, concentrating on his efforts. I looked down on him and wondered whether to run.

But I didn't.

When he reached the top he paused, huffing. He untied a handkerchief from around his neck and scrubbed away the sweat on his face.

That's when he spotted me standing beside the trunk of a *Pinus balfouriana*, a foxtail pine, cousin to the bristlecone.

He wore a baseball cap and sunglasses so black I couldn't discern any hint of his eyes. He was clean-shaven. Young.

"*Guten Tag,*" he said.

My heart stumbled then started racing.

He came closer. "I've been looking for you for hours. I was afraid I would have to give up."

Eons had passed since I'd heard so many words in German. I'd forgotten what I was supposed to do or say.

"Sorry," he said, switching to English. "You're wondering who I am. My name is Stefan. We met once...in not so pleasant circumstances."

He removed his sunglasses, and I knew him.

I saw again that cruel, arrogant sneer, the eyes flicking over me then away in dismissal. I saw the squared shoulders beneath jaunty epaulets, and the medals, proof of his loyalty and military talent. The proud ramrod soldier who removed me from the city prison and dumped me on a train that never reached its appointed destination.

Chapter 23

Kaleidoscopes erupted before my eyes. I started to pass out.

He moved quickly, putting one arm around my waist, grasping my shoulder with the other. I inhaled hints of tobacco and sweat. His eyes, just above mine, were a keen, azure blue. They reminded me of someone's...but I couldn't put my finger on whose.

"Sit." He ushered me to the trunk and knelt beside me, alert, ready to intercede if needed.

After a moment he said, "It's hot. Let me get you some water." He rose and crossed to the nearby stream.

It was my chance. I must flee. I knew this country and could hide. Yet an odd lethargy held my muscles in a vise. It was as though they understood the gig was up and no matter how much I might wish for it, escape was beyond reach. Using the tree trunk for support, I forced myself to stand and managed to take a few steps. My head started to clear and I broke into a stumbling run.

I heard him, slipping on loose rocks, cursing.

He caught my arm. He swung me around.

"You must listen," he said, panting. "Listen to me."

I struggled to free my arm.

"I am Stefan. Stefan Metaneira, but I know that means nothing to you. My mother sent me, Zoë."

"Let me go. Let me go—"

He shook me. "Who do you think got you off that train and to this place?"

I stilled.

"Me. I did that."

"Who are you?"

His grip relaxed. "Don't you know?"

I pressed the palm of my hand over my mouth, trying to contain my emotion. Then, transfixed, I reached out and touched the curved outer rim of his ear, the dark brown hair cropped short above it, his severe, straight nose, the nostrils slightly flared. I brushed one finger over long, dark lashes.

Somewhere in my studies I had seen a photo of Alexander the Great depicted as the sun god, Helios. Stefan shared that royal bearing, yet his lips looked as though they could be bruised by kissing. I traced them, awed out of shyness by their resemblance to another's.

"Don't," Stefan said. "Don't cry, Zoë." He took me in his arms.

I closed my eyes and felt his father come back to me.

Chapter 24

As we hiked to the ranch, Stefan described himself, with an embarrassed shrug, as Phaedre and Bastien's love child. Four years older than Louisa, he'd come as a shock to his parents, who hadn't known each other very long, and who were very young themselves, Bastien only nineteen, Phaedre seventeen.

Phaedre reared their son on the island, but his father coached him in our language and customs so well that he could pass for a native. After I was taken from my mother, after she vanished and Louisa was murdered, Stefan had, along with his father, joined the subversive group Chthonia, who refused to accept that an individual's rights must be lost due to the criminal evil of governments. He was just eleven years old, but he knew what he wanted. Using his mother's surname, he enlisted in our country's military the moment he was old enough. He streaked through the various ranks, becoming the youngest Brigadegeneral in all our long history…with Odenwylde's discreet assistance.

"My father pretended to believe the lies about Louisa's death, though I know it was the hardest thing he ever did. They spun a tale about a sudden onset of meningitis. He did that for you, so he could continue to protect you."

"He gave up so much. Because of me."

"Don't think that," he ordered. I would become familiar in time with his tendency to order rather than ask; it helped me learn how to stand up for myself.

"Being your guardian healed him. Odenwylde—" Stefan often referred to his father this way, as *Odenwylde* rather than *Father*, perhaps because of the heavy secrets they shared— "told me that your father had true magic. He felt his mind, his body, and his soul transforming as Adam communicated with him."

Stefan clasped my elbow as we maneuvered over some slippery rocks. "Odenwylde told me he woke from what he called Adam's spell when the pistol discharged, and only then realized what had happened. He said he would have put himself between the bullet and Adam, had Adam released him. At the inquiry, von Bäumer insisted he was following orders when he killed Adam. He claimed Odenwylde attacked him for no reason."

The adobe house was in sight. I slowed my pace. I wanted to keep Stefan to myself a little longer. "Did he tell you what he said to von Bäumer?" I asked, remembering how my mother struggled to understand the German as they shouted at each other.

"It was brought up at the inquiry. *Er war unser Befreier.*"

"He was our savior."

"Colonel von Bäumer wanted that put into the record. He wanted Odenwylde executed for treason, but many soldiers came forward and testified to Odenwylde's loyalty. Not one person stood up for von Bäumer. My father was acquitted, and from that moment, he and von Bäumer were bitter enemies. When my father took you from the Schloss, von Bäumer was vindicated. He was promoted and put in charge of capturing you, as an official apology."

I pictured it as we walked. In her diary, my mother wrote that Odenwylde promised to make arrangements for another to step in if anything happened to him. Robert Louis's secret son, trusted by the government, was influential enough to banish the red tape and spirit me out of the hospital prison.

"But—" I said haltingly. "When you...the way you looked. I thought you hated me."

His gaze flicked away. "I was grieving. I loved my father. But you did not ask him to do what he did. He died as he lived, serving a higher cause."

Stefan held me and stroked my hair as I succumbed to more tears. While he had me there, he bent close to my ear and said, "The man who brought your meals in the hospital documented everything. He spread it far and wide. Our government is deposed. The Chancellor is in prison. So are the others who colluded with the scientists. Odenwylde has been declared a hero. It's over, Zoë. The experiments, confinements, tests. The arranged marriages, everything. Not just in Germany. Everywhere. Something happened that I don't understand. Chthonia has a theory, though. They call it 'collective perception,' a syncing of minds. Some believe it came out of the moon-dust, because that has changed, too. But that is only part of their theory. The other part is you. You and my father."

I stepped away so I could study his solemn face. I had believed the scientists, the military, and the corrupt government defeated Robert Louis when they hanged him. Yet at this moment, half-drowning in his son's steady gaze, I realized with a shivering thrill that it was the other way around.

We were free. The terrible sacrifice had not been in vain.

"People are using Athene as their symbol," he said. "Chthonia reveres her. Her messenger is a woman. Erin—"

"My grandmother."

He smiled. It was a beautiful thing, eradicating the warrior and introducing me to a champion. I knew that smile would remain clear in my memories for as long as I might live, even if I lived to be a thousand. I will never forget the moment when Stefan first smiled at me.

"You read your mother's diary," he said.

I considered telling him of my encounter on the cliffs with the white-gowned barefoot lady, but decided that ought to wait for another time, and simply nodded.

He grabbed my hand and pulled me into the house. A leather satchel I'd never seen before sat on the floor in the entryway.

"My mother asked me to give you some things." Stefan dug through the satchel and brought out my old velvet bag, handing it to me with a quick smile.

Almost all of the granite shards were gone. I tried not to let my unhappiness show. Maybe Phaedre had emptied it out, thinking the pieces meant nothing.

Next, he brought out the biography, which Phaedre had kept safe all this time. Shadow and light caressed Robert Louis's face on a spotless new book-jacket. A sheet of paper protruded from the middle of the book. I drew it out and read the lovely scrawl that matched its owner.

Dear Zoë,

Here is my son. Please take good care of him.

"She also sent the dress she made for Louisa," Stefan said. "You wore it once? The housekeeper took it to iron out the wrinkles."

Glimmering gold writing in the satchel drew my eye. "What—what is that?" I asked, pointing.

"It was found on the shore at Amnisos, on Crete, after a storm. Luckily, or perhaps by design, it made its way to us." He brought out a book and fanned the pages. "Maya says there are new chapters, written by Erin's husband and her lover. She says it is now complete and ready to take its place in history—after you read it, of course."

He gave it to me.

The book was thick and quite heavy. A myth with meat.

The Erinys Archives.

I itched to drop to the floor right there and begin, but Stefan gently took it from me and set it on top of the satchel. "Later," he said.

He hauled me through the house and onto the deck. "I have a gift for you, too," he said. "Well, really, it is from my father."

Bastien Günther Jäger-Abelard. The name zipped round and round in my head.

I am Odenwylde.

Yet…the last words he spoke to me were Robert Louis Stevenson's.

Maya and Nash were there, standing in a riot of sagebrush, yarrow, wild mustard, and lupine. Between them was something quite large covered in a voluminous cloth.

"My father asked me to get you away from the doctors, and to do this."

Stefan crossed to the object and plucked off the cloth with a flourish.

Teófilo.

My Teófilo.

I took a deep breath. My throat hurt.

"He said you were fond of the gargoyle at the Schloss. He described and sketched it, and asked me to have it recast for you."

I had never…never told…never mentioned Teófilo. I was too fearful of the expression that might come over his face if I tried to explain my inexplicable friendship with carved stone.

"He told me to work in those pieces from your bag, so that's what we did, in case you were wondering what happened to them."

I smiled weakly as he returned to my side and tucked my hands in his. "That's not all. He ordered me to learn this, word for word, and recite it to you."

Let Beauty awake in the morn from beautiful dreams,
Beauty awake from rest...
Let Beauty awake
For Beauty's sake
In the hour when the birds awake in the brake
And the stars are bright in the west...
Let Beauty awake in the eve from the slumber of day,
Awake in the crimson eve...
In the day's dusk end
When the shades ascend,
Let her wake to the kiss of a tender friend
To render again and receive.

He watched my eyes fill with tears then he leaned forward and kissed me. Not a dutiful peck, either. This was a slow kiss that offered too many unfamiliar messages and emotions for a sheltered girl like me to decipher. It was fierce and whisper-soft at the same time.

My first kiss.

Presumptuous, I told myself, trying to tamp down a flood of sensations.

Lifting his face oh-so-slightly, he said, "Do you know how I have dreamed of this? Of meeting you face to face, as I truly am?"

Deciphering could wait. Right now, all I wanted was to melt like a stick of butter in the heat of those cerulean eyes.

I wasn't the purest, Odenwylde told me in his cell. *Not the worthiest. But I promise you, Zoë. I promise another knight will come.*

Teófilo, Odenwylde, and Stefan. My three knights, each drawing strength from the one before. Each reaching higher from the heart of the diamond. From my father, Adamantinus.

On the day of his death, my father knew Odenwylde was standing outside the door, getting ready to bash it in and end the life he'd had with Fauna. But he also knew what Odenwylde was capable of. At that moment, before the door opened, Adam handed off his knighthood to Odenwylde. Later, Odenwylde handed off his to Stefan.

The dragon was defeated. The princess was free. The knight was victorious.

Woman is humankind's connection to the sublime, my mother wrote in her diary. Maybe, but the moral of the princess story, it seemed to me, was that the connection required both, woman and man. Without the other, the magic failed.

Each must choose to see and hear, to open themselves to magic.

Everything must open, to allow light in and let it shine out.

The veils of dust exploded like fireworks, filling the sky with rainbows. We all gasped as we saw it happen. Gradually, the rainbows subsided, but they remained around the edge of everything, a glittery luster like the goldstone hearts in my ring. Æythral, I would later learn was the name of this phenomenon. The sky deepened to the most vivid blue I had ever seen. I breathed, and felt Stefan breathing beside me. There was something about the air. Each breath renewed my body with light, joy, serenity, and color. Purple like grapes, brown like earth, white like salt, blue like twilight. An endless ocean of color bursting on my tongue.

I was wrong to think Robert Louis hadn't shared his hopes for humanity with me. He had. And he never left me alone.

Behind Stefan, Teófilo's eye twinkled.

Chapter 25

Teófilo swore that if I would blow the bubbles and climb onto his back, he would fly me into a rainbow.

Later, he vowed that as long as I wore my mother's wedding ring, we would never be separated.

He kept his promises.

Chapter 26

"Zoë?"

I turned. Truthfully, I needed a moment to catch my breath. A moment of grounding, before diving into living color for the rest of my life.

Two women stood in the doorway. One was my grandmother, Erin. She rested her arm across the shoulders of an unfamiliar-yet-familiar lady garbed in a loose, sleeveless dress, a slim, ageless lady with light brown hair that fell almost to her knees. She was exactly what I had always imagined a willow dryad would look like. An animal stood between them. A dog maybe, though it seemed different from a dog. More than a dog.

Something about the way the lady held herself...something about the dog...

It whined, and she placed her hand upon its head.

She was more deer than human. In certain light, I could see her antlers.

"Mother," I whispered.

Stefan's grip tightened and he smiled, well satisfied.

My children ask me to tell this story all the time, even my oldest, who is twenty. They never tire of it, and weep with me at the sad parts.

They also love hearing about Aridela, and Selene, and Themiste, about Chrysaleon and Menoetius, whose stories Maya shared with me that day in the living room while my grandmother looked on from the painting above the fireplace.

Let me tell it from the beginning, she said. *It is a long story, but it has brought you to this place; it has brought the whole earth to this place. Everything that led you here began long ago, when your grandmother and I first met, on Crete.*

I will say "once upon a time," but understand—this is no fairy tale, even though you will hear about magic, foul deeds, trickery, and of course, love. Memorable love.

THE END

Epilogue

The Dominion of the Thirteenth Age

What did it mean when I lost the soft hills?
Time melts into mine, jewels and ancient forgiveness.

"Aurelia, wake up. Wake up, donnah!"

Aurelia opened bleary eyes to find her wife, Rislinn, staring anxiously down at her.

She looked from side to side. Deep, deliberate breathing helped her heart return to a normal pace and her olfactory system helped further as she breathed in soothing scents of vanilla and forest moss.

She was in her own bedroom, open around the perimeter so the heavenly summer breezes could freely enter. The draperies puffed and floated like gossamer.

How could one have such sinister nightmares when one's life was so consistently pleasant? It made no sense yet she did, too often to be dismissed as happenstance or caffeine.

Surreptitiously, hidden by the bedsheet, she captured a pinch of skin between her thumb and forefinger and squeezed, digging in her nails for good measure. It hurt, thank the ever-benevolent Infinite Mother. The dream retreated.

"You had another one," Rislinn said unnecessarily.

"Did I speak?" Aurelia resisted the urge to respond with sarcasm.

"'Palantina,' like always."

"I'm sorry I woke you, ethle. Go back to sleep."

"Every year at the approach of Lughnasadh, this happens. Will you be able to sleep, or are you getting up?"

"I'll be fast asleep before you can say *Alba of Dawn*. This dream wasn't so bad as some have been." She kissed Rislinn's cheek. "Promise."

Rislinn accepted the assurance and rolled away. She plumped her pillow and was breathing heavily within a few moments. Aurelia envied her wife's ability to fall asleep quickly. It was the sign of an untroubled spirit.

She hated lying. The dream had been one of the worst she could remember, sickeningly violent in fact. But there was no need to burden others with the gory details. Shortly after sunrise, Rislinn was leading a pilgrimage to the sanctified island of Inis Tearmann. Submerged for many centuries, it miraculously rose to the surface when Zoë, the Dryad Goddess, transmuted the pollen into Æythral and chose life for humanity.

The children and old people would require extra care and attention. Even using the nimble Pinwheel, which could fly so fast and change direction so suddenly one could see its movements no better than the blur of a hummingbird's wings, the day would be long and tiring. Aurelia couldn't imagine the time it took to get anywhere in the days of automobiles, ships, and airplanes, much less horses and wagons.

She rose and filled a shallow bowl with water and fresh lotus flowers, then set out in the dark for Alma Mater, force of habit never allowing her to attend the Goddess without a gift. At the last minute, she strapped a small hamper of minnows to her back. The central courtyard of the O-shaped temple was home to a hundred kingfishers, all of which were endlessly hungry. They would swarm and fill the air with their squeaky chattering, and magically, her mood would be revived. The dream would be expunged.

It wasn't.

After feeding the birds and placing the lotus flowers on the chancel in the sanctuary, she sat on a prayer rug, listening to soothing fountains and soft night breezes and gazing up at the Aridela star, the blazing apex of the hallowed constellation.

She was still meditating when the door chime sounded.

Someone was up and about bright and early.

Getting to her feet after sitting so long with her legs crossed was tricky. Glad there was no one around to witness, she managed, ungracefully, and went off to the little south door where petitioners often rang, even though the temple was open on every other side. The screens were only pulled into place when the weather was cold or wet.

Donning her welcome smile, she opened the door, expecting to see one of the village women, who probably had spotted candlelight and knew she was there. They liked to help clean the temple or ask for private tours. But it was not a village woman on the step.

"Forgive me, Aurelia," the woman said. "I have startled you."

"Oh…no, Palantina." A chill ran through her. For an instant, Palantina's heart-shaped face vanished in a stream of sparkly Æythral. "It's only that I haven't seen you in so long. How are you? How are the children, and your beautiful little seaside cottage?"

"All is well, including the cottage, though it bursts at the seams. There has been talk of moving."

"And this one?" Aurelia glanced at Palantina's rounded stomach. "How is the newest of your flock?"

"The midwife predicts she will join us in a fortnight. I can't wait to see her little face!"

Aurelia stepped back, opening the door wider. Only as Palantina entered did she see that the woman's second youngest daughter was holding her hand.

"Lilibet." Aurelia bent to kiss the child's fragile cheeks. "My, how you have grown since I last saw you!"

The child beamed and curtseyed. "Tante," she said in her diaphanous, fairy-wing voice.

"She is why we are here," Palantina said. "She insisted on seeing you, though it means she will not be able to join the pilgrimage. She won't tell me why. Just that you are the only one who understands."

Aurelia glimpsed the hurt in Palantina's eyes and heard it in her voice. "I am the story keeper, the guardian of the sanctuary, and one of only three Time Shapers. Perhaps she has a question I am best suited to answer. If it is not complicated, she might still reach the landing pad in time."

"It was to be her first sojourn without us." Palantina frowned at her daughter. "She has been talking about the pilgrimage since Rislinn came up with the idea, but now she won't listen to reason."

The three crossed into the spacious hallway that circled the open courtyard and led to the sanctuary on the east side, also built in a circle. The entire complex was one circle after another, some spread out and others fitting snugly inside bigger ones.

Aurelia spoke directly to Lilibet. "Has something frightened you?"

The child shook her head.

"What is it you want, darkling?"

"I want to go to the gallery, through the via dolorosa, with you." Lilibet grasped Aurelia's hand.

Aurelia smiled. "I would be happy to take you." She turned to Palantina. "Will you wait in the shell-chapel?"

Palantina's frown did not diminish. Aurelia gave her friend's arm a reassuring squeeze. "You will find fresh coffee and tea, newly baked bread, and ripe blackberries. I can vouch for how sweet they are. Sit, Palantina, put up your feet. Enjoy the quiet. I'm sure you don't get enough of that. We won't be long."

Still reluctant, Palantina nodded. She was such a protective mother. Every one of her ducklings was equally important to her.

Aurelia led Lilibet into the via dolorosa, artfully designed to create shadows offset with pools of gentle illumination. As they walked, Aurelia noticed something she had never seen before—an aura surrounding Lilibet's head and shoulders. There was something about it. Something about the colors…

She barely restrained an audible gasp. They were the colors that surrounded Erinys the Fury in every one of her lives. Lavender and gold.

They approached a set of dark velvet drapes punctuated by a single glass case inset in the wall. Within, beneath a diffused glow, a knife rested upon a purple cushion. The blade was obsidian, with an ivory hilt carved into the likeness of a robed woman, an owl perched upon her shoulder.

Lilibet stood on tiptoe so she could touch the glass. "This scares me."

Aurelia lifted her. The child was nearly as light as down feathers, thank the benevolent Lady. "It has no power. No evil. It is a fabrication…a copy of the knife that caused so much harm. There is no need to be afraid, little ethle."

"The part you hold is real," Lilibet whispered.

"True. The haft was carved in the likeness of the Infinite Mother and her wise owl. It has come to us through the mists of time and is a symbol of her love. We used to let people touch it for good luck, until we felt it needed protection from the oils in our skin."

The child's scent reminded Aurelia of the days her mother hung freshly washed laundry outside to absorb light, wind, and the essences of grass, flowers, and trees.

Placing Lilibet carefully on her own two feet, she pulled back the drape and they entered the circular art gallery. The silence was heavy, the air scented of old books, beeswax, and lavender. The walls were covered with paintings, and throughout the room were sculptures, artifacts, and documents, preserved and protected behind special gas-permeated glass that kept the old paper from degenerating. The far side, opposite the curtain, was dominated by a single enormous portrait that molded to the wall's curvature and stretched from ceiling to floor.

Lilibet crossed to it swiftly. "Read the 'scription, Tante."

Aurelia knelt before the marker post and read the white scrolled lettering. "'Together we bring forth a new world, and nothing can ever part us.'"

"I had a dream last night."

Aurelia smoothed black unruly curls from the child's small white forehead. *A dream. An important one, apparently. Could it be linked to mine?*

"Come, let's back up." They retreated to the center of the gallery so the painting could be viewed in its entirety. "Athene's Prince made that vow to his love, our Queen of Moons and Stars, when Lady Earth was just beginning her long descent into darkness and despair."

"And he knew…he knew, even then. Even without knowing what was going to happen."

Aurelia let that confusing statement pass without challenge. "Areia Athene blessed him especially, for he was her beloved son."

Lilibet stared at the painting. "Tell me about her."

Following the child's gaze and knowing her mind as she did, Aurelia did not need to ask who. She pointed to the central figure in the portrait, a woman dressed in white, standing very straight, though not very tall. The figures surrounding her made that clear.

"Erinys, the Queen of Moons and Stars, the sentinel of *L'ombre Moon*."

The child had the most amazing eyes. Direct and perceptive. What lay behind them? What had happened to bring her here this morning?

"The ancient lore tells us that Erinys is Athene's spiritual daughter, and that she lived seven human lives, in seven different eras, under seven different names and in seven different bodies, in order to learn the secrets and mysteries that would return us in joy and reverence to our sacred Mother, to health and wellbeing. Can you tell me some of her names and what they mean, young shelshone?"

Lilibet blushed at the complimentary title, which meant "Radiance." Solemnly and proudly, she recited, "Aridela, *Utterly Clear*. Eamhair, *swift water*. Caparina, *Spanish Butterfly*. Shashi, *moonlight*. Lilith, *of the Night*. Morrigan, *phantom queen*."

"*Très bien*, child." Aurelia suppressed a smile. "There are different meanings to Aridela's name. Utterly Clear is perhaps the best known, because it hearkens to the Aridela star. And Erinys?"

"Vengeance."

Aurelia pointed again at the painting, at the woman who stood to the left of Erinys. "Here is Maya. You are her direct descendant, little one. She had two daughters. They had twelve children between them, and those children had many more, which, in due course, brought you into your mother's life, and mine."

"Mama says I have her eyes."

"That is so, darkling. I can verify it. You have her curly hair, too. Maya was our Queen's truest friend. She faithfully followed Erinys from the beginning, and was the bravest of warriors. Maya gave everything she had, including her life, in loyal assistance to she who led us home, and she remained even after Erinys left us, so she could help guide the Dryad Goddess. Can you tell me a few of her names?"

"Selene, Rhalanse, and…and…oh, I don't want to."

Aurelia realized she was making a lesson out of the story and spoiling the magic Lilibet wanted to experience. She pointed to the man who stood on the other side of Erinys. His hand rested on her shoulder.

"The Prince." The image of Athene's Prince, depicted as William Konstantinou, was painted long, long ago—centuries past—by Jean-

Michel, who lived in the same historical period as the heroes in their last incarnation, and was close to Dame Maya. The Prince's grave gaze followed no matter where the viewer stood in the great round room. He seemed so real that at times, in the quiet of night, with the lighting extinguished but for a single candle, Aurelia's heart would falter, her breath catch. Her flesh would prickle as she fancied him stepping out of the frame and speaking to her. Oh, how she wished that could happen. In her excursions through time, she was confined to guiding Erin and Maya, and only in dreams, so they would never suspect they were being manipulated by anything other than their own imaginations or Lady Athene. It was a cardinal rule that she never appear corporeally to any of Athene's great paladins. She knew why that was, and agreed that the law was imperative, but sometimes, in her own dreams, she interacted with them. She could even touch them, and they, her.

"And Raa-Raphael?"

Aurelia's thoughts jarred and returned to the little girl waiting for her to continue.

"Ah, yes. Raphael."

Aurelia studied the figure who knelt on one knee next to his brother. He lacked the vivid reality of the others. Jean-Michel had painted him as illusion, the same way Aurelia fancied she might have appeared to the heroes on the rare occasions when they glimpsed her as they woke from their dreams and she slipped away.

Unlike the Prince, Raphael did not look out upon the world. His eyes, the only part Jean-Michel had painted in clear, defined color, remained forever focused upon his Queen.

"He who began his long journey as Chrysaleon, the gold lion of Mycenae."

"Erinys loved him."

Aurelia nodded. "She forgave him. Though his crimes can never be excused or diminished, she deemed him worthy of redemption, for at the end, he knew what he had done, and felt true remorse."

A moonlit sea, a beach, and a white boat made up the backdrop behind the central group. Two figures, both very tall, one a male, the other female, held hands at the water's edge. A wolf leaned against the male's legs. Though they were behind the more prominent cast of Erinys, Will, Raphael, and Maya, Jean-Michel had painted them in great detail, in a style similar to the Pre-Raphaelites of the Victorian

Age. All the characters in the portrait but for Raphael seemed extraordinarily lifelike, as if they would leave the frame at any moment and walk past the observers in the room. There was the slightest hint of a glow around the male, and a suggestion of antlers floating in a nimbus above the female—so slight that most never saw it, and only studied historians knew the significance.

"Why was there a boat, Tante?" Lilibet tugged on Aurelia's forearm. "Why could they not fly away like birds?"

"It was the fulfillment of a promise. Lady Athene wanted her daughter to know that there would be peace and paradise at the end. The boat was there to take the Queen and her Prince wherever they wanted to go." She added, dreamily, "Some say they sail the world still, exploring the farthest reaches of the oceans."

"And those two in front of the boat. I—I can't say his name. It's too hard."

"Adamantinus. You can call him Adam, my love. He was the male force, the indelible origin to the power Erinys wielded. He stands near Fauna, his true love, she who wrote the melancholy Song of Dawn, which you and your classmates sing every morning. Our legends promise that Adam was reunited with his mother and father after he was taken from this world, and when Alba Fauna died, long after, she too was reunited with Adam, and Erinys, and Will. They are all together again and forevermore. Isn't that nice, ethle?"

"Tell me from the beginning, when Erinys lived her first life on Kaphtor."

"Oh, my goddess, Lilibet. We do not have that much time. My voice would give out. We would die of hunger." She smiled.

"How long ago was it, Tante?" Lilibet didn't return the smile. She really was being very serious.

"In the old methods of calculating, and as best as we can tell, she was born for the very first time in the year sixteen-hundred and forty-four, or thereabouts, in the timeline they called BCE—Before the Common Era."

Lilibet made a face. "Their dates weren't pretty like ours. Numbers and more numbers. It's so confusing."

"Why is it confusing?"

"They had those big numbers that went backwards, like a wheel turning, and then the wheel slowed up and stopped, and they had to strike it with a hammer, and when it started up again, the same numbers went forwards." She wrinkled her nose. "They always had to add that end thing. 'BCE' or 'AD.' I liked their other names better. 'The Dark Ages.' 'The Age of Discovery.' 'The Industrial Age.' That one always makes me think of smelly smoke."

"We did something similar, with the Dominion of the First through the Seventh Ages. Now here we are, so very far from that time, in the Thirteenth Age."

"Please, Tante, I don't like dates. Tell me the story of Erinys."

"Come, let us sit and be comfortable. My old bones don't appreciate all this standing, even for a short while, much less the time it will take to please you, ethle." Aurelia led the child to a cushioned loveseat and they settled in. Lilibet crossed her legs underneath her and waited expectantly.

"You will definitely miss the pilgrimage if I tell this story."

"There will be another one," she said carelessly.

"It is your choice." Aurelia closed her eyes and gave herself a moment to gather her thoughts. She began the story as it always began, as it had begun for as long as humans had calculated time after the Dominion of the Seventh Age—five hundred years in the old style, which the storykeepers and Time Shapers were compelled to thoroughly learn before ever taking a single step through time. "Listen to the story, *enfant de la lune*, from the beginning. It is long, but we all must understand, young and old, for it brought us to this place; it brought the entire world to this moment. We tell the story of our history often, as we have been allowed to see it, through the eyes of the Queen of Moons and Stars. I, Aurelia, the twelfth Time Shaper, am the most recent repository of the stories. I follow Diana, my mother, who received the story from Io, her mother, who learned it from Elena, her mother, and on straight back to the first repository, Fauna, she who served our Queen faithfully in her final incarnation, and who gave birth to—"

"Zoë!" Lilibet grabbed Aurelia's arm. "The Dryad Goddess!"

Aurelia opened her eyes. Ah, the heart of the matter. The reason Lilibet was willing to forego the pilgrimage had something to do with Zoë.

"You may not like reciting facts, Lili," she said, "but you have learned them well."

Lilibet grinned. "I like her best. I dream of her. She is my friend!"

"Zoë was given the heavy burden of choosing whether we would live or succumb to our end. Her diary is preserved and protected right here in this special reinforced room, along with her mother's, the Fauna Diaries, and her grandmother's, the Erinys Archives." She gestured to the priceless historical records, written so very long ago and kept under glass. Students worked with copies. "Zoë recorded her own wisdom and thoughts over her long life. Her work has helped us understand those distant eras, and learn the importance of record-keeping. In her diary she talks about how difficult it was to study the history that came before her, because so much had been destroyed. She has written that if she had not been able to read her mother's diary and the Erinys Archives, she would have floundered, and she might have made different choices, choices that might have stopped humanity altogether. She was tempted. We know this. We can thank her for our family tradition of recording life histories, which are passed along to the children, who then take up the custom. This keeps our family stories, our lineages, and our ancestries alive and fresh."

"She was thirteen!"

"Yes, she learned of the task when she was thirteen. Not much older than you. She kept writing in her diary even when she was over a hundred, after she had her own children, grandchildren, and great grandchildren, after her beloved mother died of old, old age in her arms." Clearing her throat, Aurelia gazed upon the portrait and re-centered her thoughts. "Our Lady Athene gave us heroes. They fought with courage so we could be here today, right now. Everything that we know and are began when Erinys ruled her vast and wondrous society as Queen Aridela, forty-two hundred years ago, using the ancients' way of calculating."

Caught by Lilibet's transfixed gaze, Aurelia paused. "You have heard this story countless times, yet you want to hear it again, now, today. Why, Lilibet? What is really going on with you?"

The child turned to look at the statue of Zoë, whose arm was wrapped around a living aspen tree. Her love, Stefan, father to the present evolution of humans, stood to her right, his hand on her shoulder, much like Athene's Prince touched Erinys in the portrait, and on her left stood Odenwylde, the hero who died for her.

"I have a dream. I walk on top of the ocean, and then I float up to the white boat. Lady McKenna and Lady Brianne hold out their hands to me."

Intrigued, Aurelia asked, "Do you take their hands?"

"Zoë comes as I reach for them. She asks me if I want to play moon games. We are the best of friends. We go back down and swim with dolphins and starfish in the moonlight."

"That sounds delightful."

Lilibet's smile faded. "Are you a spey-wife, Tante?"

Aurelia pondered how to reply so this intelligent, inquisitive child could understand. She was trained to sidestep questions that probed too deeply, but she realized she didn't want to do that with Lilibet.

A warm glow of understanding ignited, followed by palpable relief. Time Shapers weren't like other people. They had to plan ahead and make arrangements for their legacy. She needed to choose an apprentice, and she wasn't getting any younger. That's what had been weighing on her, and her attempts to ignore the obligation had manifested in bad dreams.

She would not evade Lilibet's questions. Not evading meant she was committing to a path.

"A spey-wife foretells the future," she said, patting Lilibet's hand gently. "I cannot see or manipulate the future. But I can travel into the past, and sometimes, I can influence it…slightly. If I am very careful, I can shape temporal events through dreams. That is why women like me are called Time Shapers. We attempt to form an alternate outlook based on what we know from the future."

"Did you make me dream playing with Zoë?"

"No," Aurelia said firmly. "I cannot enter the dreams of those now living. Your dreams are entirely your own, Lilibet."

"Is it hard…shaping the temp—temp thing?"

"It is a learned skill, like anything else. Like learning how to write, or how to speak another language."

"Mommy told me it is secret."

"I'm not sure why, but that's true. It always has been. Time Shapers belong to an order, and in my experience, orders usually want to be secret. Perhaps it's no more than custom."

The child fell silent. Aurelia could see her mind working things out.

"Everything is intertwined, el anoshla, the past, the present, and the future, in circles, big and small. It is a symphony, which needs many instruments to make beautiful music. It is the same with our minds and souls. Long ago, the symphony was nearly destroyed. The music was stripped away, but Erinys found it and brought it back. That is why we revere her and her followers."

"You told her how to find the music in a dream?"

"I made it possible for her to see different outcomes. She retained her own free will, her own determination. I simply showed her where each choice might take her."

"You saw her, Tante. You saw Erinys."

"I did."

"I want to do that."

"You can never see our champions. They are gone, and traveling back to see them now might change our present."

"Even Zoë?"

"Even Zoë. Hopefully, there will never come another time when creatures like me will have to travel and influence events in order to save the future. That is why we carefully teach history to our young ones."

The child still wore a confused expression, but there was no more time to explain.

"Here you are!"

A pack of children raced into the gallery, their chatter and laughter echoing.

Palantina, accompanied by her husband, followed them in. "Hush, hush, children," Palantina cried. "This is a holy place. Not for your rude screeching." Obediently, her brood circled her and grew quiet.

"I am stuffed with bread, cheese, blackberries, and tea," the young mother said. "And I am tired of waiting, Lilibet. You were so looking forward to the pilgrimage, and now the opportunity has passed. I saw the Pinwheel take off. Come now. We will go picnicking. The day is lovely. You will play with your brothers and sisters." She held out her hand.

The child left Aurelia and crossed to her parents. Aurelia glanced at Isander, handsome and cheery in a soft felt hat, loose dark trousers, and a billowy striped shirt. He put a sheltering arm around Lilibet. "I will take the children and go ahead." With a courteous nod to Aurelia, he added, "You two take your time, Tina. You know where to find us."

Palantina nodded and they exchanged an intimate smile.

He rounded up their chicks and led them away.

Rearranging her fringed shawl, she turned to Aurelia. "Is she all right?"

"I think so. She only wanted to hear the story." *She has been singled out. Our heroes have marked her. She came to me this morning at their direction, so I would see and recognize their wishes and my own.*

Palantina glanced at the painting, touching first her chest then her forehead and giving a quick curtsey. "Of all my children, Lilibet is the most spiritual."

"I feel such a connection with her. Lilibet makes me see these artifacts in new ways, as though it's the first time."

"Life is what it is. Do you need to hear it, my friend? Our children are safe and happy. We live in a world of abundance."

"Leave it to you to see through darkness to the sheen of truth."

"Children have a way of clearing the brain and keeping us centered on what's important. Why not come to the seashore with us? Isander tells me he has packed a basket with goat cheese, grapes, and a Pinot Gris from your own French hills. I will throw your own directive back at you. Come and sit in the salty breezes. Eat and get some sun. You spend too much time alone, in the dark, with serpents and old paintings."

"I would love to. Thank you for asking me."

"You're always welcome to join us." Palantina kissed Aurelia's cheek. "Tante, will you tell me what my baby is feeling right now?"

"It would be my pleasure." Aurelia placed both hands on Palantina's stomach and closed her eyes. She possessed the rare, ancient art of *subliquara,* and could sense many things from touch. "Light and peace," she whispered. "Your womb shimmers with Æythral, Palantina, and she is swimming in rainbows. Even now, she laughs."

Palantina's eyes filled with tears. "Oh, that makes me happy. I love children so much."

"That, my dear, is patently obvious."

Palantina giggled, and for an instant looked very much like Lilibet. "Let's go by way of the park, shall we?"

"Let me fetch my shawl."

The two women descended the thirteen shallow steps that surrounded Alma Mater, and followed the path, the soles of their sandals crunching on crisp white gravel.

"I confess it is strange, or perhaps serendipitous, that you appeared at the sanctuary door this morning," Aurelia said. "I was startled, you were right about that. I dreamed the old dream last night. The one where I was not human and you suffered at the hands of brutal men."

Palantina knew no more than the rudiments of the dream, and not how Aurelia had used it when she traveled backward in time, planting it in the minds of Erinys and Maya, hoping it would nudge them onto the path that made this walk through a pristine park possible, five hundred years on. At the time, Aurelia feared it wouldn't work, and she would have no future to return to.

"I am sorry to hear that. I know the dream is somehow devastating. I was under the impression that you managed to expel it. I thought it would never haunt you again."

"Unfortunately, it does return now and then. 'Haunt.' That is exactly what it feels like. A haunting. Whenever I have the dream, I am left despairing and crushed. Almost to the point of wishing I could die."

"Oh, Aurelia! I had no idea."

"Only because it showed so clearly where humans were headed. It could have come true, Palantina. It very nearly did."

They approached a platform swing hanging by ropes from the massive branch of a shady oak tree, and paused to gently rock back and forth. Above them, a squirrel chittered its annoyance and soon after, a pair of mourning doves hidden amongst the leaves cooed.

"But," Aurelia said thoughtfully, "since I spent After Dawn with that magical creature who is your daughter, my outlook has changed. My eyes are now opened, and I am reminded to rejoice, to celebrate, to appreciate all we have accomplished."

Aurelia rose from the swing and walked into the adjacent clearing of close-cropped grass. The center was dominated by a marble statue of a woman in a flowing robe, standing upon the lower curve of a crescent moon that extended over her head. The woman gazed downward and her hands were open as though to offer blessings to those who strolled past. Around the base lay many gifts. Aurelia spotted conch shells, dishes of fruit, linen-covered jars of honey, woven baskets stuffed with fragrant flowers, and many imaginative containers filled with Æythral-infused corn pollen.

Palantina joined her, easing herself onto the grass with a pained grimace.

Aurelia knelt in front of the bare marble toes that peeked beneath folds in the robe. She put her fingers into the deeply carved name at the base and slowly traced each letter.

E R I N Y S

So many others had done the same that the slots forming the letters were noticeably darker than the rest of the base.

Below the name was an inscription.

FROM BETRAYAL CAME SALVATION

Aurelia looked up at the face, distinctive with its fall of marble hair and the eyes that mimicked the shape of Erin Konstantinou's. "Just after I woke, I feared it came as a warning that some half-forgotten flaw in us was reemerging. One that might draw us back into discord, wars, or worse."

"Reemerging?" Palantina pulled a lone dandelion and twirled it against her nose, leaving behind a comical round patch of yellow dust. "I have never believed our flaws eradicated. They are there, inside us. Mistress Athene is not called 'Lady of the Wild Things' for no reason." She struck her chest with her balled fist. "We are the wildest of Her things. But we have learned. Our world is fragile, and we understand our most important task is to remember what we came from, and how far we've traveled. We are pledged, as a species, to never falling back into the mercenary eras that caused misery and unnecessary death. As Lady Brianne so wisely said, *The effort and journey of the goal, not the achievement, is what's important.*"

"She also said to do whatever we could each day." Aurelia hugged her knees to her chest and rocked.

"Tell me what happens in this dream of yours. We will break it down and find the good. Together we will blast it into tiny pieces that can never bother you again."

Aurelia traced the edge of the silver pin on her bodice, a circle containing two crescent moons, a star, and a kingfisher. "No, Palantina. Never. Especially not now."

"Why?"

"Babies listen, even before they join us. They make sense of their world while still safe in the womb. I would never inflict that dream upon her, or upon you. Never."

"This dream is much worse than you've let on."

"Yes."

"Mama! Mama! There you are." Shrill voices disrupted the stillness of the park. A crush of bodies half-buried poor Palantina.

"What are you doing—?"

"Why are you taking so long? We had to come back and look for you!"

"We're hungry! Papa won't let us eat until you come. We want our picnic. And we missed you. Papa missed you."

"He did?" Palantina struggled to her feet, holding the grubby hands of two children. Three more circled, pulling at her gown.

Isander came along more slowly, leaning on a knobbed walking stick. Crooked over his elbow was a basket covered with scalloped linen. Aurelia caught the scent of fresh rosemary bread.

Palantina watched him critically. "Isander? Are you well?"

"Yes, yes." He waved the cane valiantly. "My arthritis is acting up, and my bones say a storm is coming."

Aurelia turned her gaze to the sky. It was blue and cloudless, but her own arthritis agreed. A storm was coming.

Palantina wrapped her arms around his neck and gave him a kiss on each cheek. The children tumbled, noisy, laughing, smacking each other's faces with exaggerated kisses, grabbing handfuls of fruit from the basket and eating messily.

All but one. Lilibet came to Aurelia's side and slipped her hand into the older woman's.

"Lilibet, don't you want to play?"

"Only if you come with us, Tante."

"I am coming with you, anoshla. Now fetch me a piece of bread, would you, please? Otherwise, I think the food will be gone."

Lilibet shouted at the other children. "Leave some for Tante!"

They ignored her.

"It's all right," Aurelia said.

Lilibet would be her acolyte. She would teach the child the alchemic art of voyaging through time and fill her brain with stories. The world would remain in capable hands when she was too old to do anything but sit and swing and picnic by the sea with her wife, Goddess willing.

"I want to do what you do," Lilibet said softly, "but I don't understand the big words you use."

"You don't have to understand right now," Aurelia said, also quietly. "You will learn. I will teach you, sweet child."

Her eyes were big and shining with eagerness. She knew she was receiving a singular honor.

"You are ready for this," Aurelia whispered.

Palantina returned to Aurelia's side. "You know we all love you, don't you?" she asked.

"And I you. Palantina, there is something we need to discuss."

"Oh?"

"Don't be anxious. It is a good thing, isn't it, Lili?"

"Yes, Tante."

"From over the cobalt sea," Aurelia said, "Athene did bring Chrysaleon the Gold Lion and Menoetius the Black Bull, fulfilling ancient prophecy and setting in motion the odyssey that brought us to this day, this moment, where children laugh and Lilibet can ponder the magnificence and intricacies of life."

"I am glad you're here to keep the music in perfect tune," Palantina said.

Aurelia smiled, enjoying a newfound sense of peace. Tomorrow she would begin Lilibet's training. But for today…

A picnic.

Author's Notes

While *Swimming in the Rainbow* can be read as a standalone story, it also provides closure to the *The Child of the Erinyes* series. Thank you to those who have stuck with me over the many years it took to get all the books published!

This story is not only an homage to Robert Louis Stevenson, it is also an homage to Victoria Holt's *On the Night of the Seventh Moon*, and an homage to "The Gargoyle," a visionary work of art created by Michael Parkes.

Many years ago, I fell in thrall to Robert Louis Stevenson, the Renaissance Man, mostly because of his poetry.

When it came time to write the last book in *The Child of the Erinyes* series, I had difficulty getting started. I would sit at my desk staring, coming up with one idea then another, and discarding each one. My gaze kept returning to "The Gargoyle," holding pride of place on my wall. One day, I began to write in a fluid stream of consciousness, not knowing where I was going or where I would end up, just creating/continuing a story around a gargoyle leaping after bubbles. The result is *Swimming in the Rainbow*. While the book formed organically, love for RLS and The Gargoyle influenced every word.

The poems in this book, composed by Robert Louis Stevenson, 1850 – 1894, are in the public domain…

Except for the excerpts from Romeo and Juliet, which are of course Shakespeare's, and the quote from William Ernest Henley: 1849 – 1903:

Lean, large-boned, curved of beak, and touched with race,
Broad-lipped, rich-tinted, mutable as the sea,
The brown eyes radiant with vivacity…

W.E. Henley, "Apparition," in *Poems* London: David Nutt, 1889, p. 39

"In Hospital," Poems. 2nd Edition.

http://robert-louis-stevenson.org/friends/

https://www.public-domain-poetry.com/william-ernest-henley

In the words of Michael Parkes:

"As she begins to leave childhood, innocence mixes with knowledge to create magic. She is a magician's daughter, raised with ancient wisdom that she begins to play with for the first time."

~~copyright Michael Parkes

Used by permission

From his website: theworldofmichaelparkes.com

I didn't see this quote until years after I finished *Swimming in the Rainbow,* but it seems to me that Zoë WAS a magician's daughter, and ancient wisdom did follow her on her journey.

Reviews help readers decide what to invest their time and money on. Please consider leaving one.

- Sign up for my newsletter if you'd like to hear about my writing news.
- The full link is: http://eepurl.com/hSrs6P
- Follow me on BookBub. You'll be informed whenever there's a special deal.
- Full link: bookbub.com/authors/rebecca-lochlann
- Connect with me and read lots of extras at my website. I have bibliographies, maps, histories, character details, epilogues, author's notes, and links. Someday I might even have stories there. You can find me at rebeccalochlann.com, or simply scan this handy QR code:

Titles in The Child of the Erinyes Series

BOOK ONE: *THE YEAR-GOD'S DAUGHTER*
BOOK TWO: *THE THINARA KING*
BOOK THREE: *IN THE MOON OF ASTERION*
BOOK FOUR: *THE MOON CASTS A SPELL* (A NOVELLA)
BOOK FIVE: *THE SIXTH LABYRINTH*
BOOK SIX: *FALCON BLUE*
BOOK SEVEN: *WHEN THE MOON WHISPERS, FIRST CHRONICLE*
BOOK EIGHT: *WHEN THE MOON WHISPERS, SECOND CHRONICLE*
BOOK NINE: *SWIMMING IN THE RAINBOW*

Attributions

Girl in a dress stands in the clouds over the mountains
Shutterstock
Artist: Aleshyn_Andrei

Fantastic landscape with rainbow
Depositphotos
Camilabo

Woman Face. Hand painted
Shutterstock
Artist: Anna Ismagilova

Medieval Castle Carcassonne, France
Depositphotos
Artist: Maugli

Labrys Axe graphic © "Labrys-symbol" Licensed under Public domain via Wikimedia Commons http://commons.wikimedia.org/wiki/File: Labrys-symbol.svg#mediaviewer/File:Labrys-symbol.svg

Crescent moon, necklace, & Erinyes Press logo: Lance Ganey freelance ganey.com/

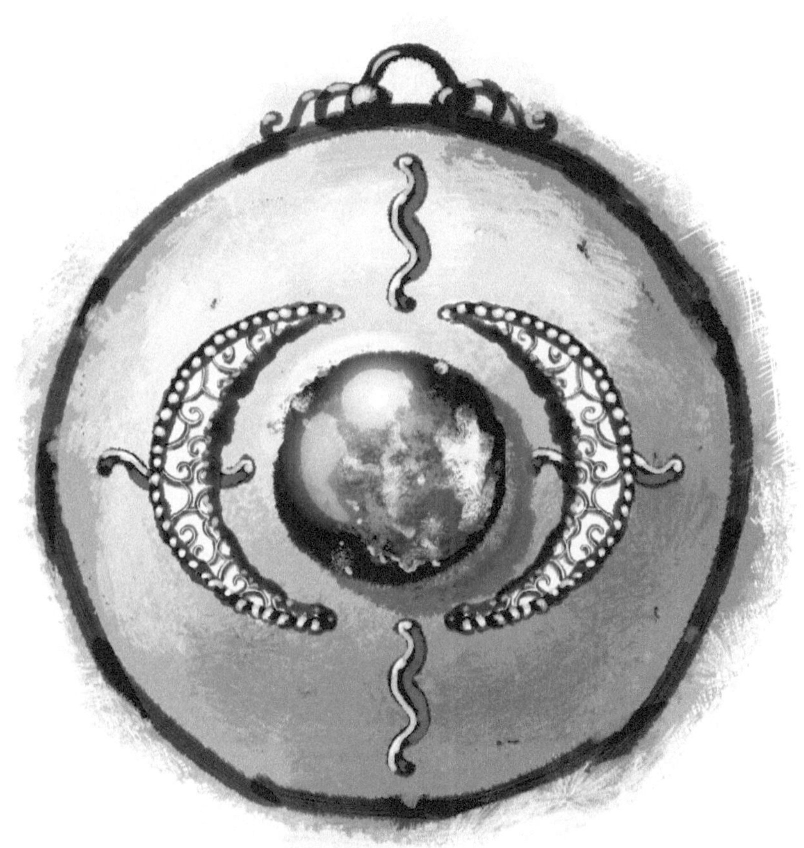

9 780999 826786